SEN

A SOUTHERN CRIME FAMILY NOVEL

CARLA SWAFFORD

Ebook ISBN 978-1-956518-23-8

Paperback ISBN 978-1-956518-24-5

Dear Readers,

During my research—possibly flawed—I found American Sign Language (ASL) has its own way of conveying a full sentence, and much of it is tied to facial expressions with hand/body movements. As a way to communicate quickly, a person signs only key words or/and descriptions. But I felt it best to include every word, along with prepositions, during the ASL dialogue. *They will be in italics and without quote marks to make it a smoother read.*

I also understand people who read lips cannot catch every word, despite what Hollywood and social media would like you to believe. *"But to make those scenes clearer whenever Tessa is reading lips (only in her point of view), I'll show every word in italics with the usual dialogue quote marks."*

So suspend disbelief in those instances, if you would please.

Thank you.

Carla

Tropes & Triggers

Book for adults only.

Bad Boy/Good Girl

Car Chases

Childhood Trauma

Cursing

Drug Use

Fighting (MMA & Self-Defense)

Forbidden Love

Gunplay

Kidnapping

Love Triangle

Morally Gray Heroes and Heroine

Romeo & Juliet-type romance, but with happily-ever-after ending

Torture

Violence

Why-Choose scene and conversations

CHAPTER 1

*L*ife had taught Townsend Whitfield—Sen to his family and friends—to keep a mask of indifference on his face whenever possible. After years of being teased or criticized about his heritage, he'd learned the best way to handle assholes was to stoically stand with shoulders back and chin up.

A mixture of satisfaction and finality enveloped him as he stared down his nose at the old man's casket. Calling the bastard "father" would be an insult to fathers everywhere. He crooked an eyebrow when the massive box disappeared into the cement vault.

Lifting his gaze—no need to watch the old bastard being covered with the red clay of Alabama—he clasped his hands at his back and scanned the crowd. Whispered aspersions swirled in the air around him and his brothers, and the gravesite from the sporadic huddles of mourners. No one stood around crying or sniffling, not even the beautiful woman who had lived with his old man for a few years.

She'd been nice to him when he was a kid. Even at five years old, he'd felt sorry for her. If someone had killed the bastard all of those years ago, she'd have been spared—hell, everyone would've been spared—a world of hurt.

He fought the morbid thoughts flooding his brain. Even his brothers who stood nearby had no idea of his opinion about the whole farce. Not that he understood it himself. It wasn't as if Dick Whitfield's death was a sad event. Like the so-called mourners, he sure as hell wasn't grief-stricken. Quite the opposite. When he heard the news, relief had seeped through his body.

He inhaled sharply and closed his eyes for a few seconds, trying to regain his equilibrium.

Wrong, wrong, wrong.

If his mother had still been alive and seen the euphoria shining in his eyes at that moment, he'd be at church for days reciting dozens of Our Fathers and Hail Marys.

"I hope you rot in hell, old man," Jake, Sen's eldest brother, said with a heated vehemence and then spat on the casket.

His brother obviously held no guilt in expressing his feelings about the old bastard.

The small crowd gasped and mumbled about disrespect and sin. The screech of the crank and the mutterings of the cemetery employee filled the air.

Sen searched the crowd once more. He refused to join in with his brother's blatant bitterness. It served no purpose and he needed to keep an eye on the old man's cronies and enemies. Speaking of enemy, Walter Finny stood off to the side. He was old Mac Tally's right-hand man until Mac died in the same fire with Dick Whitfield. What was he doing here? Sen would have to find out later. He doubted if any of them were there to show support for the Whitfields. Chances were they hoped the brothers would fight and put on a show at the cemetery. Infighting would weaken the Whitfield organization, especially between brothers.

His gaze landed on Lucius Quinn, the owner and funeral director of Quinn Funeral Home. One of Dick Whitfield's long-time associates and almost a bigger asshole.

Considering Sen's old man betrayed anyone who got close enough, he never had true friends. For sure, Dick had no problem using a person until they were no longer beneficial. In Quinn's case, he remained in his old man's inner circle only because his sons and employees needed the mortician to sew up knife and gunshot wounds without reporting the treatments to the authorities. In turn, his old man had made sure no other funeral home opened shop in the area.

"Do you see her?" Ethan, his younger brother, elbowed him in the side.

Sen's gaze traveled over the people standing around Quinn. The movement of a curvy-figured woman walking toward a silver SUV caught his attention.

"Yeah," he said beneath his breath.

He liked how her auburn hair, pulled back in a ponytail, flowed behind her in the hot June wind. Tessa Quinn. Just seeing her from a distance took his breath away. Fuck, she was gorgeous. He'd dared to hope she would be there. She was rarely seen out and about Marystown. Her father kept her busy in the funeral home and away from Dick Whitfield's sons.

Sen soaked in how Tessa picked her way between the headstones, her hips swaying with each step. He lost sight of her when Jake strode across his line of sight and nodded toward the waiting limo. A moment passed as he absorbed the view of Tessa once again until Ethan followed their older brother, then he pulled his attention away and headed in the same direction.

His whole life had involved watching his brothers' backs. Even days like this, he was still on alert, despite letting his scrutiny wander for a few seconds. An antsy sensation had grown since he received the news of the old man's death by fire. They suspected it was more than that, but they had to wait for the autopsy report.

The wind kicked up again, blowing dead flowers across the trimmed grass and causing small whirlwinds in flat areas. Cemeteries were creepy, but it was more than that. He sensed something out of place. For the hundredth time, he shook off the feeling of being watched. Of course, the so-called mourners—he really needed to stop calling them that—stared their way. Who knew what to expect from those wild Whitfield boys?

In the next second, the cherubic face of an angel disintegrated near Jake's head, pieces of marble spraying everywhere. Sen and his brothers ducked and darted to the opposite side of the old man's ancient, bulletproof limo. Several more pops of gunfire echoed around them.

What the fuck?

Sen's gaze searched the surrounding area. Relief filled him when he saw that Tessa was already in her SUV, pulling away. He remained crouched beside the limo's rear fender, hoping to spot the shooter. Ethan stooped near the headlights as Jake peered through the front seat's windows out the other side.

People screamed and shouted, scrambling behind stone crypts, lying stretched out along headstones, or running toward their automobiles.

"Damn! Who do you think it is? Some asshole out to get Jake for sleeping with his girlfriend?" Ethan teased. Everything was a joke to him.

Sen shook his head and checked the magazine of his Beretta. "Probably the girlfriend," he cracked back.

What could he say? He couldn't resist picking on his older brother too. Jake made it easy at times. The women he dated were more often crazy than not. A couple of years ago, one of them had sliced the tires and seats of his at-the-time new Corvette and then tried to enter the garage to do the same to their other cars.

"Most likely someone who's wanting to take over the old man's businesses," Jake said in his usual no-nonsense tone. "Or possibly the person who set the club on fire."

The man needed a sense of humor and a sane girlfriend. Truth be known, they all did. Though Sen had to admit, Jake was probably right. Whoever had killed the old man most likely wanted to take over. Why they thought he and his brothers would let that happen was beyond him. How had someone managed to take out his old man as he sat in the club before burning it down? Considering Mac Tally had died with his primary enemy, Dick Whitfield, at the same time proved foul play was afoot, and it'd been unlikely the Tallys. Maybe Finny had been hanging around, trying to figure out who in the Whitfield organization had murdered his boss. If that was the case, he was barking up the wrong tree.

The pop, pop, pop of a rifle firing had Sen and his brothers crouching closer to the pavement. Golf-ball-size holes appeared in the asphalt, sending debris flying.

Speaking of trees—considering the angle of the holes in the asphalt and the crack sounds of the gun firing—Sen stared off into the foliage several yards away.

"I think the shots are coming from that direction. See the old, rusted-out black van?" He nodded to where the road wound through the cemetery near the interstate fence and large oak trees.

"Yeah." Ethan peered over the hood.

"The sliding door is cracked opened. You think he's still in there?" Jake squinted his eyes at the van. "The smart thing for a shooter to do is leave with the crowd."

As the shooting slowed, people began cranking their automobiles and racing away.

"I'll go around and come up on the opposite side," Sen said. Time to stop the idiot.

Keeping a low profile, Sen ran alongside the cars whose owners were either stuck behind other cars leaving or too scared to move. Swerving between headstones, not wanting to make himself an easy target, he occasionally stopped behind large tree trunks before darting closer to the van.

Damn it. A figure dressed in black scooted behind the steering wheel. They were trying to get away.

Before the man had a chance to crank the van, the family limo sped by with a loud roar and T-boned it with a metal-crunching crash, bringing everything to a stop. Jake swung open the driver-side door of the limo as two people jumped out of the wrecked van and headed toward a thick copse of pines near the fence. Jake ran after the tallest of the two while Sen headed for the smaller one.

It was easier than he imagined. The shorter guy was merely a teenager wearing black leather pants and a black T-shirt with the words "Suck This" written in red ink dripping like blood. Sen grabbed the brat by his upper arm, jerking him to his tiptoes. He ignored the cursing as he held onto the kid and headed back to the van and limo. Along the way, he picked up a Remington rifle from the ground. Probably the kid dropped it as he ran.

"Asshole!"

"Shut up. I don't want to hurt you," Sen said, trying to hold onto his temper.

"I'm not afraid of you. You can't do anything to me." The teenager sneered.

"That only proves how stupid you are." Sen slammed the butt of the rifle stock into the teenager's stomach. Not too hard, mostly to knock the breath out of him and shut up the kid. "Hey, Jake, look at what I got!"

Jake's gaze assessed the boy and then the rifle Sen held up. His brother's attention returned to the woman who looked familiar. She, too, wore black leather with a matching ankle-length coat. Considering how hot it was, Sen shook his head in disbelief. Takes all kinds to live in this world.

"Kind of young for a boyfriend," Jake said to the woman with a lift of his chin toward the kid.

"You're sick. He's my brother. Leave him alone." She yanked at Jake's hold. "You're hurting me." She spat out each word.

Sen watched closely in case he needed to interfere. It was unlike Jake to hurt a woman, even crazy ones.

"I thought your granddaddy taught you better than that. Didn't he ever tell you Whitfields were mean sons of bitch-es?" Jake's eyes narrowed.

"Oh, I already knew that," she shot back.

His brother pulled her against his chest and stared down at her with interest.

Sen chuckled. Tension eased in his shoulders. So it was like that. Looking away for a second to regain his composure —wouldn't be good to laugh—he returned his attention to the drama being played out. His big brother was handling the situation fine without outside help. Sen waited off to the side, keeping a firm hand on the boy.

Jake dipped down and whispered something into her ear. She rolled her eyes. Whatever he'd said hadn't scared her.

"Anyone else in the van?" Jake straightened, retaining his hold on the woman, and glanced at Ethan.

Ethan leaned into the van and looked back at Jake, shaking his head.

"You better tell me, why did your brother try to kill us?" Jake glared at the woman.

"Maybe you deserved it for killing my granddaddy." She lifted her chin. The girl made her feelings plain about Jake. "Anyway, who says *he* shot at you? It could easily be me."

Sen already liked the girl. She had spunk. Jake needed someone who could stand up to him. She did look familiar.

"There's a possibility I deserve to be shot for many things, but I had nothing to do with your grandfather dying in that fire. Did you forget my old man died in it too? That has to tell you we weren't involved," Jake said.

Considering how much of an asshole the old man was, that wouldn't hold water. They all wanted him dead.

Then her identity came to him. Sally? Old man Mac Tally's granddaughter? No way. He eyed her. Well-stacked and curves all in the right places. Yep, she'd grown up. Nice.

"He's lying! What did I tell you?" The teenager reached for the rifle, but Sen quickly twisted his arm, lifting it up behind his back. The boy squealed like a stuck pig as he tiptoed to take pressure off Sen's hold.

"Quit hurting him!" She kicked at Jake. Yep, Sally Tally. No one else in Marystown but a Tally would have the guts to attack Jake.

Sen tossed the rifle to Ethan and eased his hold on the teenager's arm. He didn't like hurting kids, though the way the little asshole fought him, Sen might have to make an exception once more.

"Look at me." Jake shook the woman until her gaze met his. "You and your brother are in enough trouble. I don't have time to turn you over my knee again."

Whoa!

Sen knew that Jake loved a little domestic discipline in his sex play. Not that they shared women, but they were brothers and around each other a lot. Things come up and spill out while drinking or overheard during certain times.

The memory came back. Jake had been suspended in high

school because he'd spanked a girl. Must have been Sally. Interesting.

"Another reason you should be dead," Sally said in a low, deadly tone with an eat-shit glare.

Sen swallowed his laugh. The girl had guts for sure, probably more than what was healthy.

"Kill him, Angel!" her brother shouted.

Sally was no angel from what Sen had heard. He worked at holding back a smile. These two were cracking him up.

Her brother continued, "One less Whitfield we have to put up with. You know how," the brat taunted.

Sen elbowed him in the gut. The kid gasped and coughed. No air. No talking. Considering the kid was almost as tall as his sister and too mouthy for his own good, he changed his mind about feeling bad for hurting the kid.

Angel was probably the kid's nickname for his sister, though from the way she was dressed, she looked more like the angel of death. The kid's sister needed to teach him some manners, though hers could use some tweaking.

"You two have lost your minds." Jake's lips thinned with disgust. Then sirens echoed in the distance. Sand County's finest was on their way. Someone had finally called in the shooting. "Tick!"

Jake glanced over his shoulder at their driver. Tick Richards rolled down the window, peeking out, hazel eyes round and bald head shining.

Sen headed toward the limo, pulling the teenager behind him, while Jake asked Tick whether or not it was drivable. Just as Tick knew, Sen knew, too, the old man had the car made to take a beating and keep on ticking. Sen chuckled to himself as the pun was taken from an old watch commercial and the driver's name.

"Then let's get the hell out of here." Jake held onto Sally, pulling her to the open passenger door.

The teenager dug his heels into the dirt at the same time Sen heard a grunt from Jake. Whatever happened, Sally looked at her brother and the teenager stopped struggling. Grateful for the cooperation, Sen hung back while the teenager scooted across the bench seat facing the rear. Then Sen slipped in beside him. He crossed his arms and waited to see what would happen next. Maybe he should curtail the pleasure he received in watching a woman not fall all over his older brother.

Nah. It was too much fun.

"Check this and make sure there aren't any weapons." Jake tossed a backpack to Ethan.

In seconds, Jake had Sally by the hair and one arm twisted up to her shoulder blades, shoving her into the back seat across from Sen and the teenager. Damn, Jake meant business. First time to see his brother treating a woman so rough. Maybe the angry red spot on Jake's chin had something to do with it. The girl likely showed his brother what-for.

Sen eyed Sally's black hair with red tips, white makeup, and heavily lined eyes. Yeah. She looked as if she could protect herself, physically or with witchcraft. He ran his hand down his face, wiping off the smirk before Jake could see.

The limo rocked when Ethan and Tick slammed the front doors shut. In no time, they were barreling down a dirt service road out of the cemetery.

Over Sen's shoulder came Ethan's open palm holding a gun, showing what he'd found in the backpack. Raising his eyebrows at Jake, Sen kept quiet. His older brother frowned. The girl had been carrying. Ethan pulled back and a metallic snap came from the front as he stored it in the console, out of reach.

"Everyone buckle up," Jake said in his usual no-nonsense

tone after he jabbed Sally's seatbelt into the latch and then his.

Clicking seatbelts echoed in the limo. Tick's driving could be quite hairy at times. So no one wanted to take a chance of going headfirst through a window.

As the miles passed, he watched the subtle power play going on between Jake and Sally. Obviously the teenager didn't appreciate it, as he mumbled obscenities and wiggled as if he prepared for an attack.

"Be still." Damn teenagers.

Sally glared at Sen. So what if she had a problem with his tone?

Grabbing her attention, Jake asked, "So tell me, what made you believe I had something to do with your grandfather's death?"

"We don't have to tell you shit, you lying motherfucker!" Her brother leaned forward, spit spraying in his anger.

Frustration flooded Sen from head to toe. The kid needed to learn how to control his temper. Without a word, he slapped an arm across the teenager's chest and shoved him back into the seat.

"Damien," Sally said in a school teacher tone. "Shh!"

That was the boy's name? He could've sworn it was Buddy. Surely his memory wasn't going at twenty-nine. Hell, he would've changed it too. He had. Sort of. He fucking hated Townsend.

"Watch your mouth and shut up," Jake said at the same time as Sally. Then he pointed a finger. "Show some respect in how you talk in front of your sister."

If they weren't in the limo, Sen would've stood and clapped. Snot-nosed brat. Relieved, Sen basked in the peace and quiet. The kid had no idea of the danger he was in.

"Sally." Jake waited for her to turn his way. Frustration crossed his brother's face. "Angel."

Her gaze shifted to Jake.

All righty then, not just her brother called her that. And it wasn't an endearment from the tone Jake used. So Sally was now Angel. He rolled his eyes. Whatever.

"I don't have a lot of time to waste on this." Jake glared at her. "I can turn this limo around and take you and your brother to the police."

The woman snorted at his brother's warning. She sure had guts. Yeah. Sen liked her.

Jake's glare heated as he continued, "Tell me everything. Don't make me do anything you'll regret. There are messy ways for me to find out the truth."

No way would Jake follow through, but he didn't blame his brother for the threat.

Without looking Sen's way, Jake said, "Throw him out of the limo."

Sen knew exactly what to do.

He unlatched his and the kid's seatbelts, opened the door, and grabbed the back of the teenager's shirt.

"Let me go, you slant-eyed bastard!"

Dumb little prick. Sen sighed.

Angel's rebuke came quickly. "Damien!"

She stared at Sen with pure horror on her face. She really expected him to actually throw out the boy, and doubly so, for simply saying something stupid. Not like he hadn't heard it a million times. Mostly by the old man. The asshole loved calling him that and so many more racial slurs. He'd learned to pick his battles.

"Oh, I'm so sorry," Angel said. "He's upset or he'd never say that." She reached out her hands in entreaty to save her brother. "Please close the door. Don't hurt him." Once she realized he'd only listen to Jake's orders, she unbuckled and dove for the kid.

What she didn't know was the teenaged punk wasn't in

any true danger. Besides, Sen's mom had taught him to ignore what crackbrain people called him. He understood there was ignorance everywhere. But the kid needed to learn a lesson, to recognize danger when he was sitting in a car full of bastards.

Sen held tight to the teenager's waistband and the back of his shirt and stuck his head out the fast-moving car's door. "That's no way to talk to your elders, especially one holding your life in his hands."

With amazing strength, Damien screamed and grabbed for the side of the door as he kicked, almost landing a blow to Sen's groin. The kid was agile for a little shit.

"I'm sorry, sorry! I swear," the teenager shouted. "I don't know why that came out of my mouth. I never even wanted to say that before." Red-faced with snot glistening on his upper lip, he looked to be no more than a toddler.

"Okay! Okay! He apologized. I'll talk. Please don't." The boy's sister wiggled her fingers as if asking Sen to hand over the teenager.

Sen glanced toward Jake.

If his brother had been anything like the old bastard, Jake's next order to Sen would be to throw the kid, and not necessarily into a grassy area near the road. The old man had been mean. He and his brothers had learned not to show fear. Actually, to not show much emotion at all. That was why they had so many scars, physical and mental.

Good thing for the kid Sen had a tight hold. If not Jake, Sen could have been a total dirtwad like his old man. But no way would he throw him out, even if his brother went loony and really wanted him to let go. Roughing him up was one thing, he had the size to handle it, but not killing him. He was still a kid.

Enough of those sad thoughts.

"Leave him alone," she pleaded. "I'll tell you whatever you

want. I don't understand why you're pretending not to know, unless it's all to prove you're just as big of an asshole as your dad."

Jake nodded toward the interior of the limo.

As if the teenager weighed no more than an old duffle bag, Sen tossed him into the seat next to him.

Sen decided these two were not guilty of anything but being in the wrong place at the wrong time. In a way, he felt sorry for Sal…Angel. Her brother was her weakness. She'd never stand up to Jake, if he was determined to hold the kid hostage. Living with a father who found many reasons to beat and punish his sons, they'd learned to stand on their own two feet. Sure, people thought they didn't look after each other, but they misunderstood. The ones not being punished would circle around and find a way to divert the old man's attention without bringing hell down on their heads. By using their brains and not brawn, they learned to avoid direct conflict with the evil person who held all of the power over them.

As Jake and Angel argued, his mind drifted back to the moments before the shooting at the cemetery. Talk about holding all the power, Quinn kept a tight leash on his daughter. It never stopped Sen from soaking up the view of her luscious body, especially dressed in a tight, knee-length skirt like she wore at the funeral. He believed women called it a pencil skirt. Would she wear that on a date? The way it cupped her buttocks and how her hips swayed…ah hell, his hands itched to cup them. Fuck, it wasn't the time or place to have a cock-stand.

"Get your hands off my sister!" The teenager's voice shook.

The kid was a brave fuckwit, but as he remained seated, it showed he wasn't stupid enough to try to attack again. Sen relaxed.

Jake hovered over Angel, ignoring the kid's outburst.

"Stay out of it," his sister said as she signaled her brother to be quiet while warily eyeing Jake. His brother whispered something to her. If Sen had to guess, it was likely a warning.

When the kid opened his mouth, Sen covered it. He looked into the boy's frightened eyes and shook his head in warning. The little twerp really needed to learn to let his sister handle things. From the looks of things, she definitely knew how to handle Jake. No doubt about it, his gut cautioned that those two could boil over with some crazy drama in the next few minutes.

"We have to get married," she said, glowering at Jake.

CHAPTER 2

The interior of the limo shook with laughter from Tick, Ethan, and Jake. Sen merely grinned at the thought of Jake marrying a Tally. Was she high on crack? Did Angel really believe she could bring his big brother to heel?

Sen released his hold on the teenager and sat back, crossing his arms, waiting for Jake's response. What had his brother done? And how was he going to get out of it? Was that why she shot at them? Or had she? Hell, he was ready to see what happened next.

"Hon, I haven't seen you since high school. You'll have to find you another baby daddy." Jake smirked as he relaxed.

Angel shook her head. "No, no. I didn't say anything about a baby. You don't understand—"

"Hey, how old are you?" Ethan interrupted, the question directed toward the teenager as he hung over the front seat, arms and hands dangling..

Sen knew where his younger brother was coming from with that question. It had crossed his mind, too, but things didn't add up. "He's too tall. So he has to be too old." He looked hard at Damien.

"They grow 'em big nowadays," Ethan said before anyone could say more.

"True. Look at us," Sen interjected. His baby brother had a point. Of the three brothers, Sen was the shortest at six foot. Jake stood at six-two, same height as the old man, Ethan towered over everyone at six-four.

Sen opened his mouth to repeat Ethan's question when Damien said, "Fourteen." Contempt rang clearly in his tone.

"Thirteen," his sister said at the same time and then added, "He won't be fourteen until October. But that has nothing—"

With a firm grip on Damien's shoulder, Sen butted in, more so to tease his oldest brother. "The timing is about right."

"No way." Jake narrowed his gaze as he shook his head.

Palms out, silently asking them to stop, Angel shook her head.

"Hell no! Damien is my brother, remember? Just because I said we had to marry, you jump to the conclusion I'm preggers or he's our kid?"

She gritted her teeth as everyone started arguing and cussing.

Ethan grinned at Jake. "Considering how you can't keep your fucking dick in your pants—"

"You got shit for brains, asshole," Sen said, pushing Ethan back into the front seat.

Sen glanced over, checking on the driver. Tick, the only person in the limo not participating in the riot of profanity, continued to drive without flinching. The man was used to their bickering. Old man Whitfield had taught them every four-letter word and more that they tossed around.

"You all are a bunch of limp-dick assholes," the kid bellowed as he flipped off Jake.

Again, Sen brought his arm across the kid's chest and slammed him back into the seat.

"Damien!" Angel pointed a finger at her brother.

"We didn't ask for your motherf—" Ethan stopped in mid-sentence when a piercing whistle shut the shouting match down.

Jake stared hard at each person. "None of that matters," he said to Angel. "What the jackasses don't know is we never had sex." Jake pointedly made eye contact again with Ethan and then Sen. "So the kid isn't mine."

"You bet he's not. That's just scary." She wrinkled her nose, crossing her arms beneath her breasts.

Enough was enough. Sen was ready to get back home. So much needed to be seen to. The lawyer and the rest of the family waited for their return.

"They're just yanking my chain." Jake pulled out a cigarette, lit it, and then he cracked the window to blow out his first puff. "What's so scary about being with me?"

The question almost had Sen laughing. Everyone knew Jake was a scary son of a bitch, so much like their dad. Jake expected total obedience and his bare knuckles often meted out punishment. For Sen and Ethan, it was easy to follow their older brother. More than once, he kept them from being severely beaten by the old man. No. He didn't mourn his old man's death, but they needed to find out who killed him. He would shake the man's hand first, and then shoot him in the heart. No one got away with killing a Whitfield. Especially now that they were targets too.

"Scary?" Confusion flitted over her face then cleared. "Well, it's scary because I would've been a kid at the time I had him." Sarcasm obvious in her tone.

"The rumor was going around that you left to have a baby," Jake said in an even tone as he sucked in another lung full of nicotine.

Sen never understood the addiction. He rubbed his chest. It hurt just imagining having that killing smoke in his chest.

From the look on Angel's face, she found it fascinating. Whatever floats her boat. She was Jake's problem.

"Mom was sick after having Damien, and she needed me at home to help out. I know when the rumors started. It was after some of the kids from school saw me holding him at the grocery store, assuming he belonged to me. You know, trailer trash equals baby." Her pain flowed out with each word.

"I heard about your mom. That's rough," Sen said, understanding how rough it could be. His mom had died a year before Mrs. Tally's suicide.

"She'd been sick a long time." Her gaze drifted to Sen. "I was sorry to hear about your mom too."

He lifted his chin in acknowledgement of her understanding. Unable to take the pity in her gaze, he looked out the window again. If only he'd kept quiet. Memories flooded his thoughts for the next few miles. His mom beneath the thin hospital sheet, wasted away from the illness eating at her flesh. Cancer was a horrible way to go. She'd begged for the old man to come and say good-bye, but the asshole refused. Instead he sent flowers. Chrysanthemums. A flower his mom often sent to the funerals of friends. Sure, she was dying, but sending them to her while she lived was like wishing she was dead. The fucking asshole.

Silence reigned in the limo.

"Where are you taking us?" Her question hung in the air for a moment, drawing Sen's attention back into the limo's interior.

"We still have a lot to talk about. What with all the shooting and marrying involved..." Jake's amusement simmered on his face with each word as he flicked the cigarette out the window. "So tell me the truth."

"Maybe it's simply I don't want to be married to you," she stated barely above a whisper.

She hadn't explained why, and Jake appeared enthralled by her ultimatum. Arms crossed, Sen looked out the window again as he'd become bored with their constant back and forth.

Determined to indulge in better thoughts, he revisited the image of Tessa walking away at the cemetery. Nice skirt stretched tight across a prime ass. Damn, that skirt really stirred his blood. He needed to keep his mind out of the gutter. Tessa was a nice girl. Certainly not for the likes of him. But he had a surprise for her. He couldn't stop wanting her, and somehow he'd find a way to see Tessa alone again. Only how, without starting a war with her dad?

Tick turned down their drive and stopped at the side of the house near the garage. Several cars were already parked including their attorney's Cadillac SUV. The reading of the will would be in a few minutes. Probably the cousins and a handful of other family members were inside.

As Sen stepped onto the drive, he motioned for Tick to remain behind. Ethan stood on the sidewalk waiting for Sen and Jake to join him.

Tick was ordered to settle Angel and Damien in the big den downstairs and make them comfortable with plenty of food. What wasn't said, but Tick was aware, he was to guard them, make sure they didn't leave.

Staring up at the house in front of him, Sen started to sweat. The place always did that to him. It was a red-brick monster with more rooms than any one person needed. Hard to believe the huge presence of the old man would never fill the walls again. Sen had despised living there and as soon as he turned eighteen he'd moved out. His condominium in Marystown wasn't anything to brag about, but he soaked in the privacy.

As he walked into the foyer with his brothers, they were met by the old man's cousins, Teddy Bear and Rat Boy. He hated those two dickheads. They picked on Jake and Ethan, but saved their spleen for Sen. By looking a bit different from his brothers, it made him an easier target. Funny how their lack of imagination made their verbal attacks almost laughable. Besides, they were the ones stuck with the asinine nicknames.

"Jake boy, we need to talk," said Teddy Bear.

"This isn't a good time, Teddy." Jake continued to walk by the little freckle-faced leprechaun.

"I believe it'll be in your best interest to listen to me, boy." For sure, the little asshole was a Whitfield. But he was a dumb one for pressing Jake, and to call him boy.

When his brother nodded for Sen and Ethan to go on to the study, Sen was more than happy to let him handle the rednecks. They were never anything but trouble.

"We really need to cut those two sons of bitches out of Whitfield Industries. They've been nothing but trouble since the old man brought them onboard." Ethan looked at Sen and continued, "You and I know he did that because he believed in keeping his friends close and his enemies closer. I think that's bullshit. He didn't have any friends besides Quinn."

Sen nodded. Ethan wasn't saying anything new. "Jake can handle them."

As he strode down the hall, he heard murmurings. Jake's mom, Lydia, stood in the hallway next to Miss Jimmy Sue, the Whitfield housekeeper, along with Judd Richards, the lawyer, and several other cousins who were related to the old man, and from what Judd had told the brothers earlier, were mentioned in the will. Technically, they were related to Sen, but he wasn't close to them. Besides, if any of them borrowed money from the company and missed a payment, he would have to make a visit for payment with interest. When they didn't comply, he would be required to hurt them, maybe a broken leg or arm. Yeah. Collector was his position in the family. A job he detested but suited his skill set as his old man had told him since he was sixteen when he was forced to take martial art lessons. The racist asshole.

Each brother had a job. Jake was the natural leader being the oldest. The baby of the family, Ethan, known for his wild ways, handled the nightclubs and bars. As children of the biggest bastard in the county, they inherited many of the traits their old man had, but thankfully most were tempered by their mothers'. Yep. Mothers. Each brother, actually half brother, had a different mom. Old man Whitfield had never married their moms. A true asshole as the brothers were only months apart in age and all in the same year.

"Townsend honey, where's Jake? Big Judd said it's time for everyone to have a seat. Do you want something to drink?" Miss Jimmy Sue was one of those women who loved feeding and hydrating anyone in her vicinity, and she refused to call him Sen. She claimed it was a horrible nickname.

Sen respected her too much to complain. He'd tried explaining one time to her that, in Vietnamese, it meant old-fashionedly romantic, but she wouldn't have anything to do with it. No way would he tell her it could mean lotus, too, depending on how a person pronounced the "e."

"No. I'm fine. Jake should be here in a couple minutes," he answered.

Sen followed Ethan into the study. His brother started greeting everyone before sitting in the middle of the crowd. Unlike his gregarious younger brother, Sen pulled a chair over to the wall near the door. The position allowed him a view of the crowd while having an easy exit.

A few minutes later, Jake stomped in, and Judd Richards motioned for the last two cousins to enter.

"Gentlemen, if you would all have a seat, I'll read the section of Dick Whitfield's Last Will and Testament you've been waiting for in just a few minutes. For now, I've hit a snag. We're missing one more person." The big guy adjusted his small, dark-rimmed glasses and squinted at his cell phone. "It appears I've just located the last person named in the will, and she's in the last place I would've expected. She should be here any second." His bushy eyebrows lifted as he gave Jake a surprised look.

When Jake narrowed his eyes at Sen, he shrugged. Ethan did the same. There was a slight suspicion the missing *she* was Angel, but Sen wasn't about to stake his life on it by saying so. His older brother's temper was stretched thin enough.

After a couple of minutes went by, and before Sen could ask the lawyer what trick he was playing, in walked Angel. Without a word to anyone, she flopped onto a chair at the front. Tick must be with the teenager. There were a few murmurs and questions, but Jake ignored them while Big Judd told everyone to shut up. Took several false starts before the info from the will spilled out of the lawyer's mouth.

Sen leaned back against the wall and watched everyone's reactions to the news. The girl's eyes widened when she found out the old man had set up Jake to marry her, just as her granddad had. Well, that explained why she kept talking about marriage to Jake. That bit of news hadn't been included in the short version Judd had provided him earlier. There would be a discussion with the big guy later about what was important.

He was to receive the pawnshops and adult novelty shops, while maintaining their collection agency. The same businesses he routinely policed for the family. Nothing new. But the old man did include he would share Whitfield Industries with his brothers. The old man had never loosened the reins on that part of the family business. That would be interesting on how it would be handled between them.

To his frame of mind, all of this was for show. They needed to get back out into the streets and find the murderer. Then a shout drew his attention back to the goings-on.

"This reading is over. Everyone out! You two stay and you too." Jake motioned to him, Ethan, and Angel to not leave. "Where the hell are you going?" He pointed at Big Judd to stay put.

The man blinked, his face washed of all color, and remained behind the desk.

Jake spoke softly to his mom. Sen respected his brother for being good to the woman. She wasn't the brightest bulb in the pack, but no one could expect their mother to be perfect, especially if they'd fucked Dick Whitfield. A woman with any sense should have run for the hills.

Once the room emptied with the exception of the five of them, Jake turned to Angel.

"You! You have a lot to explain."

CHAPTER 3

In the time spent fighting, yeah, actual physical fighting and shouting, Sen found out Angel's grandfather had inserted the requirement of marrying a Whitfield heir, the oldest, in his will too. Who knew? The worst part was, if Jake didn't marry her, Sen would be next in line to walk down the aisle with Angel.

Fuck no.

Sure, she was sexy with her red-tipped black hair and deadly self-confidence, not counting she had a hell of a throwing arm. He was happy that it was Jake pissing her off. She had barely missed Jake with the knife she'd hidden in her clothing and then thrown, shattering the window above the desk. And moments later, she pulled another one and sliced Jake across his torso. Damn, he needed to remember to search her for weapons next time.

He had to remember she'd been the one who had shot at them. She appeared determined to take Jake out first.

Then again, big brother could take care of himself.

But Sen was ready to tie up the woman and put her in the

cell in the basement, perfectly designed for such troublemakers, if Jake didn't do it first.

Big Judd had been smart and scrambled out the door mumbling something about a phone call.

Without looking their way, Jake held up his hand, grabbing their attention.

"Sen. Ethan." He pointed to the hallway. "Guard the door and make sure I'm not interrupted. I believe Angel and I need to settle a few things." Jake glared at the woman standing defiantly in front of him.

Once the door was closed, the hum of voices on the other side of the wall continued.

The old man had built a solid house and ensured the walls muffled any conversations. Only the thick oak doors allowed sound to emerge near the keyhole. Sen refused to stoop, literally and figuratively, to listen to the conversation inside, but that didn't stop Ethan.

"He's threatening to spank her." His younger brother grinned up at him from where he knelt on the floor. "She gave him some sass back, and I think she wouldn't mind it. Fuck, big brother can pick them." Ethan chuckled and leaned his ear to the lock again.

"Get up. Shit, you should be ashamed of yourself. That's Jake's business. We need to talk about what to do next. Whoever set the club on fire and killed the old man needs to be put down. You know if he gets away with it, we'll have enemies swarming us left and right."

"How are you so sure it's not her? My money's on the freak inside. Her and the teenager were conveniently nearby." Ethan smirked.

"It looks that way. There's a small chance she shot at us, but I don't think she set the fire that killed the old man. She wouldn't jeopardize her grandfather's life. Remember, he died in the same blaze. She'll want to find the killer too."

"She probably believes we did the old men in." A cold look came over Ethan's face. The time in prison had changed him. He still tried to appear fun and free-hearted as he had as a kid, but a darkness came over him just as often.

"That's what I'm thinking too." Movement down the hall caught Sen's attention. Tick lifted his chin. Something happened. "Stay here and quit listening in, you pervert."

"Hey, I want to learn from a pro how to handle a woman," Ethan shot back.

Sen's stride lengthened as he ignored his brother and caught up with Tick.

"The boy giving you a problem?" Sen looked over Tick's shoulder. No one else stood in the hallway.

"Matt's keeping an eye on him. They're playing Grand Theft Auto right now. The kid has some mad skills."

"What's up then?"

Tick knew better than to leave his post without a good excuse.

"I was outside making sure the old man's cousins had left and saw Luc Quinn pull up at the end of the drive. He's there wanting to speak with the boss. He says it's important."

"And he won't tell you what it is," Sen said, more as a statement than a question. Quinn would never lower himself to talk to the help. And good thing Tick had checked on the cousins. He would not be surprised if they were sneaking around, trying to find something to steal.

"Nope. He's in a hurry and won't come in."

Sen returned to the office door and banged his fist on it.

"Hey! We got a problem!" Saying it was a *problem* would encourage Jake to come out. He heard whispering, but nothing clearly spoken to him.

The last thing he wanted to do was to interrupt his brother and whatever punishment he meted out to the woman, but he knew Jake needed to talk to Quinn. The man wouldn't stop by unless it was important.

He waited, trying to give Jake time to wrap up whatever he was doing. As the seconds ticked by, he shook his head and squeezed his eyes shut. Whatever was going on in there, he sure as hell didn't want to know, but knowing Luc rarely asked to see Jake, he'd better rush up his brother.

"What is it?" His brother finally answered through the door.

"You better quit what you're doing and get out here." Sen glared as if his brother could see him.

"If it isn't life or death, it can wait a little longer." Jake's voice was loud enough for Sen to make out the words and his impatience. Then a crash resounded from the other side.

Sen scowled at the ceiling in frustration. The magic word *problem* hadn't helped. So he turned to Tick.

"Go on back to the kid. I'll see if Quinn will talk with me. Jake's busy right now."

Tick nodded and turned toward the basement stairs. The steps creaked as he descended into the large entertainment room.

Sen gritted his teeth. He really dreaded facing Tessa's dad. Quinn hated his guts. He stared down the hallway to where Ethan listened in on their older brother's drama. No need to dwell on Quinn's hatred and Jake's woman issue. He needed the information Quinn probably had about the autopsy on the old men. Maybe there would be a clue as to who the murderer was. Presently, the authorities reported the deaths as fire related, but he and his brothers suspected more. Mac Tally and Dick Whitfield were mean sons of bitches and wouldn't lie down and die for anyone.

Quinn was sitting in his hearse, motor running, near the mail box. When Sen motioned for him to roll down the window, a cloud of smoke billowed out. The man smoked like a 1970 steel mill.

Once the smoke cleared, Sen rested an arm along the top of the hearse's driver-side window and leaned into the opening.

"Jake's busy. What did you find out?" No need for pleasantries. Sen would be lucky if the old man looked at him.

"Quit wasting my time." Quinn swiped his forehead and then over his shiny pate. He jerked his thumb toward the rear. "I have work to do. Get Jake out here."

Sen glanced in the back. A bagged body rested on a stretcher. They must be busy to use a hearse for pick up. Normally, it was a plain, white panel truck.

"If you told me, you could get back to your job." He kept his voice even in the hope Quinn would cooperate.

The man eyed him with distaste.

From what Sen had been told, Quinn had lost his dad in Vietnam; and in turn, he despised people of Asian descent. Considering Sen's mother had been Vietnamese, that meant Quinn hated his guts. Sen never understood the attitude of blanket prejudice. It was not like his mom started the war or even fought. She'd been a kid of five when she left her homeland and that was a couple of years after the U.S. military pulled out. His mom had lived in France and Canada before coming to the States. And besides, Sen was half Whitfield, and Quinn had been a good friend of his old man. It should count for something.

"I saw you staring at Tessa during the funeral. You think just because Dick gave you his last name means you're like everyone in Marystown. You're wrong." Quinn stared straight into Sen's face. "Now run along and get your better."

Sen was surprised the man hadn't flat out called him the racist names he normally did. Maybe he understood how things were changing and Sen had more power in their little county than ever before. Yeah. Quinn wasn't entirely stupid. A shame Tessa had grown up with a person like that. Next time he would send Ethan, but he had to admit he enjoyed ruffling the man's feathers. For now, he preferred not to get into an altercation with the ignorant man.

Pushing off the automobile's roof, Sen pursed his lips and nodded. "Whatever. Just don't expect Jake to be happy about the interruption." He'd given it a try.

Without another word, Sen strode down the drive toward the house. One day Quinn would regret his attitude.

Ethan smirked when Sen entered the hallway and reached the still closed door of the study.

"I knew the asshole wouldn't talk to you. Hell, I didn't volunteer because I know he loves to spread his hate to me too. Who would've guessed the man was funny about tattoos? Stupid, right? The old man is a prude. So fucking narrow-minded." Ethan laughed and crossed his arms, the ink covering the length of each and included the knuckles of one hand.

Sen shook his head. "How many times do I have to tell you, he hates you because you tattooed his daughter? I'm still a little pissed at you too."

"She wanted a simple, pretty little butterfly," Ethan said with a mischievous grin spreading across his face.

"It wasn't that little. It covered the small of her back, and she'd been only seventeen. Too young to do that without parental consent, you dumbass." Plus, Sen had to admit he hated the thought of his brother touching that sweet body, seeing even the top of her butt was too much. Some days he yearned to slam his fist into his brother's face, no matter how much he loved the guy.

He turned his back to Ethan and clasped the office door's frame and shouted, "I'm going to send Ethan in, if you don't hurry." His irritation dripped from each word.

Seconds ticked by to the point Sen reached for the door knob. At that moment, a loud *thunk* hit the door. He stepped away. Should he kick it in?

Then it opened. Jake strode into the hallway, blue eyes cold with anger. A letter opener vibrated in the door about eye level.

Damn. That took some talent, but now Sen knew what the *thunk* had been.

"What is so fucking important?" Jake asked.

Ignoring his brother's usual bad attitude, Sen relayed Quinn's request. Jake grunted and stomped off. Ethan motioned for Angel to follow, and the two headed off to the basement and Tick's care.

Sen exited out the front door onto the porch and made a private call to the one person who should know of any new rumors about the killers and certain info about the Tally family's organization.

"Hey, asshole, you got my text?" Sen asked.

"Yeah. You want to meet up with Tally's collector, right?" Digger Turner, all-round gossipmonger, chuckled.

In every county, there was one person who seemed to know about every shady deal in their area. Most people thought Sen was that person. Nope. In Sand County, it was Digger. The man was almost as dangerous as a Whitfield. Good thing he was Sen's best friend.

"Yep. So you can get me an introduction?" When his friend continued to laugh, Sen asked, "What's so funny?"

"First, there's nothing new about the old men's deaths. Everyone is talking about it, but rehashing what has already been said. You had asked about info on the collector. Now that's the interesting shit."

"Mm-hmm." Sen waited for his soon-to-be ex-friend to give him the answer.

"Their collector is a chick." Digger burst out laughing again.

"Fuck me." He'd never heard of a woman who was dangerous enough to do his job. Sure, there were one or two over the years who were over an organization's "collection agency" and sent out collectors, also called muscle, to collect what was due, but never the actual collector. "Who is it?"

"Mac Tally's granddaughter."

"That explains a lot." Frustration boiled up inside of Sen. Something had been so off about Angel and now he understood why.

"What?" Digger hated being left in the dark.

"Later." Sen would catch up Digger on the happenings later. So he ended the call. Hard to believe Angel was the Tally's collector, their muscle. At one time, it'd been Angel's father, but he'd been in prison since she was a kid.

Damn, he'd never guessed old man Mac Tally would be so progressive. So there was more to the woman than black leather and white makeup. Thank goodness she was Jake's problem.

Staring over the manicured front yard, he heard a whining engine. Then one of the UTVs they kept around for working on the large property came bouncing down the driveway. Ethan, behind the steering wheel, laughed like a mad man, and Jake, in the passenger seat with one foot braced on the dashboard, arms crossed, looked ready to shoot someone. Obviously, Quinn had no good news and Ethan's madcap driving didn't help their brother's mood.

His older brother jumped out of the UTV before it came to a complete stop and took the steps two at a time to where Sen stood.

"What happened?" Jake asked.

Sen was always surprised, though he tried not to show it, when his brother sensed his frame of mind.

"A couple years ago we heard the Tallys had a new collector." Sen hated piling on trouble, but it must be told.

"Yeah. Since he didn't mess with our people, I haven't heard much about the guy, and never met him."

Ethan joined them on the porch and shrugged in silent answer to Jake's questioning look.

Sen worked at hiding his smile. Jake's eyebrows lifted.

"I felt the same way, but today I decided to introduce myself," Sen said.

"Are you going to tell me or not?" Jake's pissed-off look was becoming darker by the second.

"It's Angel."

"You're shitting me!" Ethan's maniacal laughter nearly shook the roof of the porch.

"Angel? She's a good shot and crazy about knives, but there's no way she could intimidate anyone into paying their bills," Jake said, disbelief coloring each word.

"Strength isn't always needed to put fear in a person's heart." Sen leaned a shoulder on one of the large white columns.

"What's that? Some wise ancient Chinese saying?" Jake had caught on to Sen's teasing.

"How the fuck would I know?" Sen shrugged and held in his chuckle.

"That woman is—what's that riddle thing you always say?" Jake asked.

Sen sighed and shook his head. "It was Churchill. He said, 'A riddle wrapped in a mystery inside an enigma.'"

"Yeah. That's her." Jake stared off into the trees, rubbing his chin, in deep thought.

Ethan headed toward the front door. "You boys can stay out here, but I'm getting out of the heat."

The house was in turmoil. People shouted and ran every

which way as they entered the large foyer. Tick informed them that Angel and the boy had disappeared.

For over an hour, the house, garage, and grounds were searched. It was the missing Corvette that gave the biggest clue of why they couldn't find them. Jake acted calm, undisturbed by the news Angel had stolen his prized automobile. He simply pulled up the car's specialized GPS system on his laptop, and declared they were heading west. Sen couldn't help but think good riddance.

Before Jake left to chase after the crazy woman, he told Sen and Ethan what he'd learned from Quinn about the autopsy. It hadn't been the fire that killed them. They had massive shotgun wounds in their chests beforehand. The old men had been together, a secret meeting the brothers hadn't known anything about. No way could one person kill the two men in the same room without getting shot too. It had to be two shooters.

Sen agreed with his brothers. From what they'd seen from the local authorities, the law had no interest in solving the murders of two well-known criminals. They were happy to be rid of the scum. That left the brothers to hunt down the killers. Sen was okay with that.

After Jake's departure to chase down Angel and her brother, Sen and Ethan decided the first course of business was to check out the most obvious troublemakers. Top of the list was their two redneck cousins. Had they done the deed or hired it done?

"Hey, rock-paper-scissors on who gets stuck with which cousin," Ethan suggested as they sat in the rocking chairs on the front porch with the waning heat.

Sen cut his eyes away from Jake's departing SUV and narrowed them at his youngest brother. He was unsure which cousin was worse. But he had a better idea.

"I heard that Rat Boy has a place in Birmingham. You've

been wanting to get out of Marystown for a few days, how about you take him?"

Ethan eyed Sen suspiciously. "Where will Teddy Bear be?"

"Knowing the cousins, they'll be together."

"Then you need to come with me."

"No. I have another lead to check here in town. If you need me, call."

During the chaos of Angel and her brother disappearing, Sen had received a note from one of his shops. Someone had tried to pawn a rifle with serial numbers filed off. First, that was illegal, and second, his employee had said the guy acted weird. The man had worked at the Juicy Goose, the same night club where the old men had died.

Sen could tell Ethan, but decided to first check it out himself. It might be coincidence. Then again, he actually didn't believe in coincidences.

He needed to get there fast. The man could be one of the killers and preparing to disappear.

CHAPTER 4

*S*en ducked into the well-lit doorway beneath a brown cloth overhang with Quinn Funeral Home printed in white. He looked around, punched in the code, and then turned the knob with his right hand. His left remained in his hoodie pocket to keep blood from dripping on the cement and leaving a trail. Good thing he'd changed after the funeral. The hoodie could be thrown away, but the Tom Ford jacket would cost a ton to replace.

"Dammit, Quinn," he murmured as he tried to twist the door knob. "What's with bolting the backdoor?"

The owner had never done that before, knowing the Whitfields and their people often had injuries needing stitches or minor surgery without it being on public record.

Jogging around to the front, Sen slowed and checked the empty parking lot before strolling through the front doorway. Thankfully, the viewing rooms were empty of the living this late in the evening.

He checked the holster at his spine. His guns were stored in his motorcycle's saddlebags, with the smaller one in his belt holster. The Harley was hidden behind some bushes down the street.

He edged around a corner into a long hallway and passed the office where he heard the security guard talking on the phone. A few more steps and Sen reached the door marked EMPLOYEES ONLY that led to a small anteroom filled with extra folding chairs. On the other wall was another door marked KEEP OUT. He typed in the code—hopefully they hadn't changed it—and the door quietly opened onto a landing with steep stairs.

He released a sigh and then softly padded down the steps until he almost reached the prep room.

His skin crawled as the smell assaulted his nostrils. Not the smell of decay, but the sickening pickle odor of formaldehyde. The scent turned his stomach, and each time he entered the room, he'd hoped to never inhale it again. The same reason he hated pickles.

He peeked around a partial stairwell wall and cringed as he spotted the body of an elderly man laid out on a metal table. A cloth covered the male from the waist down. That stopped Sen.

Quinn never covered the bodies. Not that the old fart was a pervert or anything. As far as Sen knew, he just treated each body as if it was sexless. Nevertheless, his attitude didn't make a visitor comfortable around naked corpses.

After taking several more steps, he peeked over the banister to check the rest of the room. He spotted a woman standing near a sink, taking off a mask and gloves.

Tessa Quinn.

Fuck, fuck, fuck.

Sen leaned back against the wall, face toward the ceiling, and thumped his head on the cement blocks a few times in frustration. Closing his eyes, he waited for a moment as he tried to pull himself together. If he could go somewhere else to get stitched up, he would. But the way his pocket felt beyond soggy, he better make it sooner than later.

Not that he didn't want to see Tessa, just not now, not like this. Maybe in another month or so when all the shit that was going on in his life was over.

The manager at the pawn shop had pointed out the dumbass who wanted to sell a suspicious rifle. Sen had tried to play it cool by asking the stranger about buying the weapon, but before he knew it, the guy had lifted it and started shooting. Good thing Sen had been standing several feet away. He only received a graze to his arm before the asshole had run off.

Now he was at Quinn's Funeral Home needing to be patched up. It would be the second time she'd handled it. She would begin to think he was an idiot with weapons.

Exhaling without a sound. Time to quit wasting time. Nothing was being solved by standing there. Time to get his arm seen to and get the hell back on the road to find out what shadows the dickhead slinked into out there.

What a hell of a week it'd been. After the news of his old man dying and then being fired on at his funeral, topped off by the crazy man in the pawn shop, he felt as if the bull's eye normally painted on his back had widened.

Time to grow a pair and talk with the girl and get his arm stitched.

With a deep breath, he straightened and opened his eyes, staring directly into the most beautiful pair of expressive green eyes he'd ever known.

How had he not heard the wooden steps creak? The woman was sneaky quiet.

Tessa wiggled her fingers in a wave at Sen. Her eyes twinkled. She appeared happy to see him. His heart thudded. That was good and bad at the same time.

Without a word, he pointed to his left arm.

Her forehead wrinkled in concern, quickly followed by her face becoming pale.

Damn, he hated seeing her upset. He didn't have time to explain. All he needed was for her father to show up. Maybe one day, he'd find a way to see her without the threat of Quinn trying to kill him. Yeah. Like he needed another person trying to blow him away.

She waved him over to a beat-up, black leather chair positioned before a desk in the far corner. He knew the drill. Taking a seat, he dropped the hoodie easily enough. His next movements tested his pain tolerance. With one hand, he grabbed the end of his T-shirt and pulled it out as he tucked in his elbow. He jumped when he felt cool fingers slide over his heated back. Tessa lifted the shirt over his head before carefully pulling it over his wounded arm and off. Her help worked. No groans escaped his lips. Though really it didn't matter. Tessa was deaf. From what he'd learned, she'd been that way since the age of five from a bad bout of the mumps.

The first time she'd sewn him up was over two years earlier. He'd been sliced by a knife in the ribs during a barroom fight. He'd broken it up, but not without a memento of his interference. Maybe he was an idiot. When he'd shown up to get stitches, she'd been alone then too. The scoop around Marystown was she'd moved her apprenticeship to her dad's place. Her presence had proven the gossips right. That time, when she finished the last stitch, her dad had arrived. Considering how Quinn felt about him and how the old man had shouted and cussed, a person would assume he'd walked in to them being naked and getting it on.

If not for Jake, Tessa's dad probably would have shot him where he stood. As demonstrated earlier today, Quinn respected Jake, but had little patience with the other two Whitfield bastards. Since then, he'd avoided the funeral home and only ran into Tessa a few times at the grocery store or out and about Marystown. They'd nod at each other, but that was all.

Then a couple of months ago, a bullet had gone low and taken a chunk of meat off his thigh. At the time, chances were good Quinn would be working with his daughter. So Sen had taken care of the stitches himself. He was horrible at it. At this rate, he would look like Frankenstein's monster.

He loathed when Quinn patched him up. The man always claimed to be out of painkillers. Strangely enough, he had plenty whenever Jake came in, while Ethan preferred the pain and didn't care if Quinn used some or not. Crazy son of a bitch.

Tonight, he'd been desperate. If the furrow hadn't been in his shoulder and he could reach the spot, he would've tended to it himself. No matter what the asshole, Quinn, thought about him, Sen needed someone to do it who wouldn't report the wound to the police.

He jerked away when fire shot down his arm. She grabbed his wrist, holding on with a strong grip, to probe and squeeze the wound again.

"Watch it," he said between gritted teeth, his eyes meeting hers.

With a questioning look on her face, she waited for him to explain.

Tessa read lips fairly well, if people talked slowly and distinctly while facing her. Still, she couldn't catch every word as many were formed the same way by a person's lips, especially if the person gritted his teeth. Just as he was doing.

He tensed. Though he'd wanted to wait until he'd improved, he decided now was better than never. He carefully raised his bloody left hand to his right, pointing each index finger at the other, twisting his wrists as the fingers met as close to his left shoulder without screaming in agony.

It was one of the first signs he'd learned. He'd known he would be in pain the next time he saw her.

Her face lit up and her hands began to fly. The almost two years of classes he'd taken helped a little beyond the basics, but he missed a lot of what her hands told him. It wasn't like he had anyone to practice with at home and he had missed a few lessons.

"Whoa, whoa. You're going too fast." He signed as he spoke. The teachers had tried to break him of the habit of speaking while signing, but he lapsed whenever he became annoyed with his ability to keep up. He wanted her to understand everything he said, hell, signed. So maybe she could understand the gist between reading his lips and hands.

With a big grin still on her face, Tessa's hands moved a little slower.

You learned ASL, when?

Been going to classes, he signed and refrained from saying the words. *I'm not good at it. Slow.*

I think you are doing great.

He felt like a million bucks and made sure she could see it on his face. Most of his life, he hid his thoughts and feelings, but for Tessa he'd put them on full display to communicate with her. Otherwise, learning ASL, American Sign Language, would be for nothing. It was more than just hands.

They stared at each other for a long minute until the ache in his arm reminded him of why he was there. Unsure of how soon her father would be back, he needed her to do her magic before Quinn showed up or he bled to death.

Sen pointed at his wound.

Looking abashed, Tessa held up a finger, asking him to wait, and began arranging on a tray an assortment of sutures, alcohol wipes, tweezers, and other items he didn't want to think about. She directed him to sit farther back in the leather chair. Once his head settled on the padded headrest, she stuck a hypodermic needle near the wound. The intense pain steadily faded away. He doubted there was another funeral home that possessed anesthetic drugs, though he'd heard stupid shit about using embalming fluid to get high.

In no time, she'd sewed and cleaned him up. She was efficient and had a light touch.

She pointed to a glass on the desk next to him.

He leaned over and picked up the orange juice and downed it. It reminded him of when he'd donated blood. With careful movements, he slid the glass back onto the desk as he watched her toss the stainless steel instruments into a sterilizer and throw bloody gauze and other used pads into a bio hazard bin. Why would a funeral home need to sterilize anything? He really didn't want to know the answer.

Most men wouldn't call Tessa beautiful. Then again, most of the males he knew were dumbasses. With her long, curly reddish-brown hair tied in a ponytail and pale skin with freckles across a pert nose, she looked like a fire goddess. Those big green eyes had been the first feature to grab his attention, though he admitted her long legs and nicely rounded breasts and ass received equal shares of his scrutiny.

Unable to take his gaze from her, he soaked in the sight of her walking toward him. He moved his legs apart to allow his junk some room. His bare nipples pebbled. Maybe she wouldn't notice his reaction. It could easily be from the chilly room, though he couldn't say the same about his dick. Being the good girl that she was, she kept her attention above his waist, not noticing his hard-on.

She handed him his black hoodie and a clean, blue scrub shirt. Considering the size, most likely one of her father's.

Put this on or you will get cold and sick. Her delicate hands signed as she shifted her body.

With his right hand, he pressed his closed fingers to his lips and lowered them slightly toward her.

Thank you.

You are welcome. She dropped her hands to her waist. Biting her bottom lip as if holding back her laughter, she dipped her head and stared up at him from beneath her eyelashes.

Funny, what? He signed.

I'm happy you are signing. Nice to have a new person. No boring same-old, same-old.

He understood. Not many people in Marystown knew ALS. So he imagined just signing with her dad had become confining. For his lessons two or sometimes three times a week, he'd driven out to Sand City to learn and still hadn't mastered it.

As soon as he pulled on the loose shirt—her dad was a wide man—and his hoodie with her help, so as not to pull the stitches, his cell phone vibrated. He dug into his pants' pocket and pulled it out. He had a voicemail.

Ethan's concerned tone came across easily enough in the voicemail. "Call me when you can. Got some news."

His brother would have to wait for the return call. Being the youngest, Ethan was often the more excitable of the three brothers. Not like his old man was hunting him down to yell at him.

The old man was dead.

How many times must he tell himself that? Sen still had a hard time believing his old man had died with the Tally patriarch. His old man had treated him like a dog to be trained and set on the world with a long leash. So he wasn't necessarily broken up by his death, but he'd been surprised by the grief that had tightened his gut when he first heard the news.

Of course, the old asshole had gotten the last laugh on them, and Jake was the sacrificial lamb. Thank God, Sen was the second son. The bride-to-be was a bit more than he could handle, and that was before he found out she was the Tallys' collector. He wanted to wake up in the mornings with his nuts and cock still attached.

Just then, a cool hand took his left one and began wiping at it with a wet cloth. He jerked his attention back to the woman leaning over him.

Tessa concentrated on cleaning the blood from his hand. She carefully removed the dried and congealed mess between his fingers, even soaking the cloth a little more and seeing to his fingernails. Not since he was a child had a woman ever tended to him so congenially. The room blurred a little. He inhaled long and deep. Well, hell. He'd forgotten to breathe while watching her. She was just so damn fascinating.

She stepped away and quickly returned with a paper towel to dry his hands.

Once again, he signed, *Thank you.*

With a big grin on her face, she moved to the large red bin and tossed the bloody wadded paper inside.

Taking another deep breath, he forced his gaze away and stared at his cell phone, using it as an excuse to appear unfazed by her care.

Left-field thoughts crowded in. The Whitfields and Tallys had been feuding for decades. That was why none of the brothers believed what Angel had said about the will. The feud had started after Mac Tally stole his future wife from Dick Whitfield. Most of his life, Sen considered the reason for all of the fighting to be the most idiotic one he'd ever heard.

Then he met Tessa.

He understood. Despite her dad's feelings about him, Sen wanted her. He'd been working toward this moment for a long time. Though they met up tonight by happenstance, he didn't care. It was fate.

The longer he watched her move around in the preparation room, the more he became torn between taking her with him and keeping his distance. With bullets flying around the cemetery and pawn shop, it proved the people after him and his brothers cared little for who was caught in the crossfire. So the best place for her to be was away from him. Only, he was uncertain he could manage that.

Besides, the dumbnut in the pawn shop had shouted something Sen had found of interest. He closed his eyes and replayed the scene.

"Just as I hoped," the stringy haired psycho had said as he snatched the rifle off the counter and shot at Sen. The man had terrible aim.

Fuck. Why had it been loaded? All firearms and rifles were to be checked for ammo and the cartridges returned to the owner or locked away by his manager upon entrance into the store. The man would be looking for a new job tomorrow. Until then, the soon-to-be-fired employee had enough sense to duck behind the counter on the other side of the bullet-resistant glass.

Sen had hunched beside a display of musical instruments. He'd already pulled his gun from the shoulder rig beneath his hoodie.

"Put the gun down or I'll be dumping your dead ass in the trash," he shouted, aiming his weapon in the general direction of where the bastard had disappeared. Despite his threat, he only wanted to wound him. The asshole needed to be alive to answer questions.

"I'm not giving up that easy. I need the money. The contract on you Whitfield bastards is massive. You and your brothers are no more than the walking dead." The man slammed into a stand of bicycles and scrambled to his feet behind another group of shelves.

Sen shot a couple of times in the general area—good

thing the building's walls were made of cinderblock—hoping to frighten the man into giving up.

"Put the fucking rifle down," Sen repeated.

"I'll be back. When you least expect it and before someone else gets to you first." Another bang filled the air as the man crashed into the door, shattering the glass. He exited in a tumble and then jumped to his feet, running at a fast clip down the street. What was the guy high on?

Sen had felt the sharp pressure to his arm as he headed toward the door. One of the shots from earlier had hit him, more of a gouge. His brain was catching up. The stinging heat and wetness flowing down to his elbow would soon be topped by blessed numbness until the wound was cleaned. Then it would feel like burning hell.

He ignored the wound as he chased the man a block or more. When his vision became blurry, he realized the bleeding hadn't slowed, so he gave up catching the bastard.

That was when he decided to stop by Quinn's and have it stitched up.

If what the psycho said was true, anyone who hung around him would be vulnerable.

Sen opened his eyes and looked at Tessa. She glanced over her shoulder at him and smiled.

His gut clenched. He'd kill anyone who harmed a hair on her sweet head.

essa tried her best not to stare at the handsome, exotic man. Everything about Townsend Whitfield excited her. She loved how the corners of his lips lifted slowly into a smile, and his straight black hair fell over dark eyes so unlike her own. His whipcord lean body towered over her own five-four frame. Others called him Sen. She'd been told it was pronounced like sin, but she refused to think of him like that. Her mind often went into depraved areas she should be ashamed of, like did they call him that for a reason, besides being part of his name. She only knew he was different from any other man she'd ever met. So fascinating.

Still dressed in the powder blue scrub top that hung loosely on his broad shoulders, he stood slightly hunched while he stared at the cell phone screen.

It was so sweet of him to learn ASL. She never had anyone go out of their way to learn how to communicate with her, besides her dad. Nowadays, men were more apt to text as a means to talk with her, even when sitting across the table. She liked how Townsend looked into her eyes and the expressions he conveyed as he spoke with his hands. He made a couple of mistakes, but nothing too crazy, though she wasn't sure if she should tell him. She preferred to encourage him to continue his newfound method of communication.

While he drank the orange juice she'd poured for him from her private stash, she proceeded to clean up and place Mr. Johnson into the cooler unit. Moments before Townsend had shown up, she'd finished the older man's embalming. The prep work for the funeral would be handled in a few hours by her dad's assistant embalmer, and the morning staff. She enjoyed working the graveyard shift.

Well aware if Townsend could see her face, he would see the crooked grin brought on by her pun. Her dad's sick sense of humor matched hers and helped them to handle the work.

Time for her to go home.

As soon as she closed the steel door on the large cooling unit, Townsend stood. Apprehension darkened his face as he pocketed the phone.

Wanting to know what happened, her hands went flying. *What's wrong? Brothers okay?*

No worry. All okay.

Frustration boiled over her. She frowned, making sure he understood how she felt about his brushing off her concern.

His hands moved slowly as he concentrated on what he wanted to tell her. Ignoring a few errors, she understood his shooter was after him and he needed to get going. He pushed up from the chair and swayed.

Without thinking of how much taller and heavier he was, she quickly stepped up next to him and placed his good arm over her shoulders. She grabbed her purse and guided him toward the backdoor. With the vibration coming from his body against her, she guessed he was complaining about being too heavy or saying she would be safer staying inside the funeral home. Men. Especially southern men were so predictable.

Keeping a grip on his wrist dangling near one of her breasts, she flipped the lock and the door popped open.

She looked around. Other than the security guard's Volkswagen parked near the streetlight and her old Ford Explorer sitting in the dark only a few feet away, nothing. No motorcycle or extra car. Had he parked elsewhere? How far had he walked wounded?

The way Townsend's feet shuffled over the pavement as she led him to her automobile, it confirmed what she suspected. He'd lost a lot of blood before reaching the funeral home. His adrenaline from being shot must be dissipating.

Goodness, he was becoming heavier. She almost landed on her knees when he stumbled. Fortunately, he regained his balance, but what renewed energy he possessed dissolved fast after that.

Leaning him against her SUV, she opened the passenger door and deposited him into the seat with his weak help. She texted the guard that she had left for the long weekend she'd previously scheduled with her dad, technically her boss. Chewing on her bottom lip, she looked at the man in the car. His silhouette rested against the window. No way could she dump him off at his brothers' house. She didn't trust them to keep an eye on his wound. If someone was after Townsend, she had the perfect place for him to hide out. Oh, she was quite aware of what he did for a living. Everyone in Marystown knew. Tapping out another text, she sent a message to her dad so he wouldn't worry, neglecting to mention the wounded man.

Not expecting a reply from her dad until later, she touched Townsend's cheek. His gaze met hers.

In the dim light of the dashboard, she signed, *You are going with me.*

Does your father live with you?

My lake house, not his.

A few seconds eased by before he nodded and then closed his eyes.

She'd never done anything like this before. Sure, she'd patched up Townsend once before along with his brother, Jake, and a couple of other Whitfield employees over the years since she'd returned from school. Her dad had been taking care of the Whitfields and a few Tallys for many years. He'd explained the money he received for the simple patch jobs had helped pay for her education.

Tessa couldn't help but wonder if her mom had known about her dad's side job? She'd told Tessa being the wife to a funeral home director had been too difficult. Knowing what he handled everyday in the basement, and how people treated them differently because of it, used to drive her mom crazy. After Tessa graduated from high school at seventeen, her mom had moved to Arkansas to live with her older single sister, Tessa's aunt Lisa. Deserting not only her husband, but her daughter. When she was nineteen, her mom had died in a car accident, leaving her the lake house and a healthy bank account.

Though she had received emails from her mom a few times over the years, she'd wished she could have gone to visit. But even back then, the thought of driving hours alone on the unfamiliar interstate scared her, and never mind flying. What if something happened and she couldn't make someone understand her? She knew it was stupid to feel that way. She had several ways to communicate, like writing notes or using her cell phone or even the other way she hated, speaking.

Yeah. Basically, many of the Deaf could. But she'd been teased enough about how her voice sounded weird. She'd never forgotten the first time when she was twelve and finally tried it out on someone other than family and teachers. It had been a cute boy who lived down the street. She'd wanted to impress him. So she said a simple, hello and how are you? He'd laughed, pointed at her, making fun of her voice. Even though another boy had punched the boy in the nose, it had been one of the most mortifying times of her life. From then on, she stuck with family, teachers, and the boy who had championed her. He'd been her next door neighbor and first love. Nowadays, she couldn't care less what people thought, but still preferred signing,

Taking a deep breath, she shifted her car into gear and headed out of the parking lot just as a plain sedan slowed down and then sped by. She didn't think more about it until twenty minutes later when they drove through Birmingham's well-lit downtown area and beyond. Checking the rearview mirror, she worried her bottom lip. A car hung back but changed lanes whenever she did. What were the chances it was the same sedan? Coincidence?

She looked over at Townsend. His chest rose and fell in a steady rhythm, confirming he slept. Not wanting to bother him, she checked the rearview mirror again. Still there. In an effort to be cautious, she moved her foot off the gas and waited for the person to go around her. A mile later he eased over to the other lane and gradually moved on. Despite the street lights, she couldn't make out the driver.

Was she allowing her imagination to run wild?

Townsend had been shot by someone. Anyone could have followed and watched as he walked into the funeral home. She shook her head. Things like that only happened in the movies. But she was aware, with Townsend being the collector for the Whitfield family, many people would want to harm him. The businesses his family owned were in Sand County and mostly bars. The people he dealt with were dangerous and thought nothing of shooting at each other.

After wounding him, would whoever *they* were follow him?

Feeling a little silly, she continued traveling north. Her place by Smith Lake would be the perfect hideout. The house was big enough for a handful of friends and family to hang out. During the summertime with all the leaves on the trees, it was hidden from the road, providing privacy. Besides, she had planned to go there the next day to swim and relax. No problem arriving a few hours earlier.

Another glance over at Townsend confirmed she was doing the right thing. He needed the rest more than she did. She had plenty of clothes left there to use for a few days, and if she remembered correctly, her dad did too. Perfect for Sen to use until he was better. So no excuse not to go straight there.

After a few more miles, she exited the short stretch of interstate she was comfortable with and followed a long two-lane road. With a few twists and turns, she finally pulled into a long cement driveway. A motion-activated sensor turned on an outside light. She opened her console and clicked the remote control for her slot in the two-car garage. She pulled into a bay and pressed the button for the door to close. The large overhead light on the ceiling beamed through the SUV's sunroof into the dark interior.

When she killed the ignition, she turned to wake Townsend.

Head leaning against the headrest, his dark eyes watched her. Sluggishly, he lifted his hands.

Where are we?

You are safe. My house at Smith Lake.

He nodded and opened the passenger door. Positive he would do a face-plant, she scurried out and around to the other side. She reached him just in time and grabbed an arm. He slumped against the SUV and shook his head as he held onto the door handle. She helped him to stand up and place his arm over her shoulder. With one arm around his waist, she managed to reach the kitchen door without mishap.

Unlocking it, she shoved the door out of the way and stepped into the small hallway with the laundry room. Instead of walking through to the living room, she steered him toward another door that led into the bedroom she normally stayed in.

The queen-size mattress was barely long enough for his tall frame. Booted feet hanging off the spread, his head on the pillow, and wounded arm folded across his flat stomach, he looked pale, tired, and uncomfortable. She pulled off his boots and socks. He had beautiful, manly feet.

Rolling her eyes at the silly thought, she reached for his belt. Large hands covered hers.

She looked up. He shook his head. Face a little hot, she nodded.

Maybe she was getting a little carried away. Her mind had been on autopilot. How many male bodies had she undressed without letting her mind stray? No way could she do that with the lean, muscled, alpha male in front of her. The most obvious reasons were, one, he was alive, and two, her curiosity had gotten the better of her.

With a wary grin, she gave him her back and walked into the kitchen. When she returned, his eyes were closed and a fine layer of sweat covered his forehead. Holding the tin box to her body, she tiptoed to the bed and set the first aid kit on the nightstand. His wound needed checking and, with the seepage of blood on his sleeve, he'd probably broken a stitch or two. Sitting on the edge of the bed, she carefully lifted the scrub shirt off his good arm, over his head, and then down the injured arm, trying to prevent further injury. The adhesive pad was soaked with blood.

Goosebumps appeared on his arm. He was shivering. She pulled at the covers beneath him. He opened his eyes and waved her away as he tried rolling over some, but grimaced. The nights in early June still could be cool, but not enough to turn on the heat. She figured his blood loss didn't help.

She pressed on his chest and shook her head, indicating he should remain still. Running into the hallway that led to the other bedrooms, she opened a closet and pulled out a couple of thin blankets.

After spreading one over his bare feet—the most common area affected by the cold air—she gently peeled off the pad from his wound. One stitch had broken on the end. Using the tweezers, she picked it out, placed a dab of antibiotic ointment over the spot, and used a small butterfly closure from the kit. It should keep it from bleeding too much.

Picking up the shirt, she examined the sleeve. Only a small spot had soaked through where she'd noticed earlier. So the pad had contained most of the bleeding. His weakness confirmed he had lost a lot of blood before he'd reached the funeral home.

Remembering his hoodie was still in her car, she decided to check it out. It should give her an idea of what she was up against in taking care of him. She quickly covered the wound with a new adhesive pad, spread the other blanket over his chest and shoulders, and hurried into the garage.

Short minutes later, she returned, holding the hoodie away from her body, horrified. The left pocket was stiff, yet still damp, thick with blood. How far had he walked to the funeral home? His black jeans surely had blood running down the length of one leg. Only the color of his pants probably hid the gore. She refused to think about it any longer. If she concentrated on tending to him, she was less likely to panic.

She threw the hoodie into a tub full of cold water,

ignoring how the liquid swirled dark red from the cloth with strings of pink drifting along the edges.

With determined steps, she marched into the bedroom.

Townsend hadn't moved and appeared to be asleep. She needed to see for herself he wasn't hurt or bleeding anywhere else. No way was she going to let him sleep in bloody clothes.

Once more, she reached for his belt. And again his hands stopped her.

She narrowed her eyes and showed him her gritted teeth, hoping he understood what she meant. His dark eyes searched hers for a moment then resignation softened his stare. He released his hold. Before she reached for his pants again, he leaned over on one hip, reached toward his back, and pulled out a gun, tucking it underneath his pillow.

Eyebrows raised, she waited. On his nod, she unbuckled, unbuttoned, and unzipped before sliding down his pants. That was when she noticed the small holster attached to the back of his belt. No wonder the gun sat snug to the small of his back. Hadn't it hurt from lying on it? Her gaze drifted down. She'd planned to protect his modesty by leaving him his underwear. On seeing the formfitting black boxer briefs, she smirked. Nothing was left to her imagination. She sighed and then swallowed. Not sure if she did so to wet a dry mouth or to dispose of the drool threatening to come out.

With so much blood gone and as weak as he was—how could his cock be so thick and hard? She couldn't take her eyes from the hot-as-hell picture he made. Maybe she should be ashamed of herself, but she was no virgin, and she did enjoy the male form, particularly his. Slim physique, small hips, muscular thighs, broad chest and shoulders, and rippled abs leading to…oh, yes. Nice package.

Masculine fingers, palm down, wiggled near his hips to catch her attention.

Her head jerked up and she blinked at the wicked grin on his face.

My eyes are up here, he signed.

She rolled hers and wagged her head.

You have blood everywhere. She pointed to his left leg.

The deep pink tinge to his skin ran down his leg and confirmed what she thought. Without waiting for anymore wisecrack comments, she picked up his jeans and headed to the laundry room. Later, while the washer went through its cycle, she picked up a wash cloth and turned toward the bedroom with a pan of warm, soapy water. She grabbed a towel along the way.

His long legs sprawled over the sheets as if he'd fallen back to sleep, but she noticed the glint between his lashes. Ignoring his scrutiny, she allowed her gaze to drift over his lovely form.

His beautiful body didn't hide his violent past. Grotesque scars obviously created by knives and bullets marked his masculine torso. She worked at pretending faint interest in it all including his still hard penis. Goodness, he was sexy as all get out. Her fingers tingled with the need to touch every inch.

Instead, she began washing his leg. His underwear probably had blood on them, too, but she decided to not worry about anything else. A little modesty would be best. Her control was stretched thin.

CHAPTER 6

Sen bit back a groan. What was the woman trying to do? Make his penis explode? He'd never been so hard. Damn, it felt good having her take care of him, gliding the cloth down his ribs then his thighs and on down to his ankles. She followed each swipe with a pat of the towel to keep him from becoming chilled.

Only the pain returning to his wound prevented him from acting on instinct and scooping her up and kissing the hell out of her. He was undecided which hurt more, his wound or his cock.

Tessa pressed her palm to his cheek, turning it toward her. Her hands moved gracefully. Those expressive eyes pulled him in and a second or two flew away before he realized what she signed.

Sleep. I'll wake you in the morning.

He remembered nodding. Somehow, even with a hard-on, he drifted off to sleep.

It seemed only minutes passed before fingers smoothed his forehead and then a coolness touched his cheek again.

His eyes fluttered open. He smiled.

Tessa sat on the bed next to him, smiling back.

Are you hungry? Breakfast?

He almost said no but heard her stomach growl. Unable to hide his knowledge, he grinned as she blushed. He nodded. Something to eat would be good, to think of it.

As she walked toward the door and the hallway, he opened his mouth to draw her back and then snapped it shut. A habit he needed to work on. It was so easy to forget she couldn't hear. He might as well rest for a little while longer, eat, and then he'd find a way to leave. If anyone had followed, he'd know in the next hour or so.

Looking around he spotted a picture of Tessa with her father and a woman who he remembered was her mom. There were several photos spread throughout the room of more family shots and a couple of friends Sen guessed were from her school as he didn't recognize anyone. And he knew nearly everyone in Sand County.

To get a better view of the room, he pushed with one hand and both feet until he managed to scoot up to the headboard and rest his back against it. Though a little hazy, he remembered the lengthy driveway—perfect for privacy—they had driven on from the county road. He should be able to hear a car before anyone reached the house. No matter how much he wanted to stay, her safety was more important. Her transporting him out of Marystown worked to their advantage. No one would ever guess she brought the notorious Sen Whitfield to her place on Smith Lake.

He heard footsteps. The lightness of the stride told him it was likely Tessa returning.

She came in smiling, carrying clothes over one arm.

Carefully, she tossed a white T-shirt and blue jeans on a nearby chair. A little bigger in width, he suspected again he would be wearing her father's.

Dad is wider, but you can wear them until yours dries. Okay?
Then she walked out before he replied.

So that was what happened to his clothes. She'd washed them. It explained the hum near the direction of the kitchen. Nice. Except for Miss Jimmy Sue, it had been years since another woman had laundered his clothes. A warmth came over him and it had nothing to do with his wound.

Damn. He wished she'd been near enough for him to grab and kiss her in thanks. Those lips of hers needed to be sucked on and bitten.

Oh hell, until he left, his concentration should center on who wanted him and his brothers dead. Not on the things he wanted to do with her. People were depending on him to figure out what the hell was going on. Was it the same person who set the fire and killed his old man? Maybe he would call his brothers and find out what they'd learned so far.

He glanced across the room at his loaner pants draped over the chair next to a dresser. Tessa had placed his cell phone face down on the denim.

First, he'd call Digger. Though he trusted his brothers with his life, there always seemed to be an invisible barrier between them. When Jake enlisted with the U.S. Army and Ethan turned up in prison, Sen had been left alone to deal with the old man. The worst years ever. He never told a soul what he'd gone through until he and Digger became friends.

Their friendship started with a bar fight. An inebriated out-of-towner threw a punch at Sen during a college football watch party. Someone in the crowd had knocked the man's drink over. Sen had been the unlucky one walking by at the same time. Blows were exchanged and other partiers became involved. Before he knew it, Sen was facing a lanky, blond-headed stranger. The man's skill with his fists were ferocious, but give him a knife, he was almost unbeatable, except for Sen who matched his expertise. After coming to a stalemate, bloody and bruised, he and Digger sat together, sharing a couple of beers, and got to know each other.

Yeah. He needed to talk to him.

Taking it slow, he eased over to the edge of the bed, keeping the sheet across his lap. He wanted to avoid embarrassing Tessa if she returned before he grabbed his clothes. Though she had stared with a gleam in her eyes at his dick for several moments earlier, she was bright enough to know the difference between a dead body and a living, breathing horny male. Hell, she'd blushed while washing the blood off his leg. She didn't need to push her luck. There was a chance he might show her what it was used for. Not that he thought she was a virgin, but her staring was an invite, to his way of thinking.

Good thing the room was small enough he could reach his pants and cell phone by leaning over. He stretched out his good arm, and the tips of his fingers snagged the denim. His stitches pulled, shooting pain down his wounded arm as he gritted his teeth. The pants fell on the floor, his cell phone tumbling down with them. He bent over, grunting like an old man, and then sat up, victoriously holding up the phone.

With a tap on the name from his favorite list, he waited.

"Where the fuck have you been?" the raspy voice demanded.

"Keeping low. Did I wake you?"

"No problem. A friend needed my help in Birmingham last night and I got in early this morning." He yawned. "Shit. What time is it?"

Sen pulled the phone from his ear and looked at it. "Almost eight in the morning."

"Five hours. That's more than I usually get," Digger said and then yawned. Rustling of sheets came across the connection. "I know you're not checking on my sleeping habits, what do you need to know?"

The man knew him well. Sen checked the doorway to make sure Tessa wasn't near. "Have you heard any news yet on who killed the old men? I heard there may be a contract out for us. We've had several people shooting at me and my brothers."

"Since the funeral?"

"Yeah. But including the funeral. Got a nick on the arm from an idiot last night." His wound ached like a son of a bitch as if to say hello.

"Come over. My place is the safest in Sand County. No one'll dare shoot you here. Besides, the Brothers are coming by tomorrow…shit, this evening. They love to kick butt. The Barn games are happening tonight and tomorrow night, man."

The man was crazy if he thought he would show up with assholes like the Brothers of Mayhem partying at his place. The outlaw motorcycle club loved nothing more than to stir things up, and betting on fighting would only be the beginning. Last time Sen was at the Barn with the Brothers, they almost brought the roof down. Literally. Digger had bitched about the cost of repairs for weeks afterwards.

"I'm fine for now. Call if you hear anything, like who is wanting to eliminate the Whitfields." Sen leaned to the side in an effort to ease the pain in his upper arm.

"Sure. Just know, Grizzly told me he wanted a rematch. The prez said he'll sponsor you. I might even throw in a few grand to up the winnings. So if you change your mind, you know where I'll be." Digger ended their connection.

Sen then called Ethan. Like he figured would happen, it went straight to voicemail. Good thing, Ethan's voicemail wasn't full this time. He left a short message on where he was and for him to call if he still needed him.

Dropping the phone onto the bed, Sen sagged back,

resting his head on the pillows, his feet on the floor, going over the conversation with Digger.

Last thing he needed was to meet up with Grizzly. Fucking human bear. No relation to his cousin Teddy Bear, the evil version of Tom Sawyer. They were two different crazies. Grizzly, the six-foot-five man loved to hug his opponent until their ribs broke. Sen winced with the memory of his cracked ones from the last meet-up.

Digger was nuts if he thought he wanted to fight tonight. That was what happened when a person came into money and land and had too much time on their hands.

A few years ago, Digger had inherited around four hundred acres east of Marystown. In the middle of all that land sat an old barn, enough of a distance from his home to declare no knowledge of what went down there. The place had been part of the original homestead. The old house had caved in years ago, but the barn stood two stories and large enough to hold around one hundred people easily. Most fight nights, the place would be filled to the brim. People would hang off the rafters, in the empty hayloft, and watch from the main floor's wooden bleachers, pressed together like they were at a K-pop concert.

Usually, there were between ten and twenty fights in one night. But not just anyone could fight. They had to pay a hefty fee and present an endorser. The endorser was more like a second in a duel by helping the battered fighter out of the ring, and if needed, take him to the nearest emergency clinic. Their activities were never reported to the authorities as they were unsanctioned and flat-out illegal. Instead they reported they were mugged outside a bar or down a dark alley. Everyone understood no one talked about the Barn to outsiders, and for sure, no one filmed the fights on a camera or cell phone as they had to be left in their automobiles or at home. If caught with one, filming or not, the least that would happen was to have the phone or camera destroyed and their ass beaten by the crowd. The worst was to find themselves blocked from attending again and spending several weeks in a hospital with broken bones. The last thing anyone wanted was for law enforcement to show up and the fights shut down.

Sen had participated many times. When he was younger, his mom had taught him how to meditate, calming his mind and the temper he'd inherited from the old bastard. But as he'd aged, the stress of handling the dregs of the old man's business became too much. So the freedom of testing his skill against others more worthy of his expertise, actually kept him sane. At times, it helped to imagine his old man's face on his opponent.

No need to go into such dark thoughts for now.

Eyes closed, he replayed what he knew, which was much of nothing. No clues yet to who was behind the shooting and the nightclub fire. They could only guess, for there were a lot of people wanting the Whitfields dead, including an Atlanta syndicate wanting to takeover their part of Alabama.

Then again, Dick Whitfield had cheated, fucked over, and extorted so many people, any of those could have been involved in the old man's death. Hell, they were probably the same ones who wanted Sen and his brothers dead.

A bell chimed, drawing his attention.

Sounded like a metal one he'd heard in church during Christmas. Yeah. He'd been to church a lot as a young kid. The old man had gone through a spell where he decided his son's mom was right. The young heathen needed some churching. Yep, that same stretch of when Jake was in the service and Ethan in prison. Not long after that, his mom had died too.

The bell was still ringing. Could it be an alarm?

Easing up, he stepped into the pants she provided, not

worrying with a shirt. He grabbed his gun from beneath the pillow and cautiously creeped along, holding onto the wall. Along the hallway, he hesitated at each open doorway and peeked in before moving on. By the time he found the kitchen, it rung furiously again.

Wide green eyes stared into the barrel of his gun as he stepped into the room. She tilted her head and lifted the bell, holding it with two fingers as if showing it was harmless.

Damn, she was cute.

He smiled and locked the safety, placing it on the bar that divided the kitchen from a dining area. Nice to know she wouldn't try to pamper him by bringing breakfast to his bed.

Hands free, he signed, *Sorry. I'm glad to see all okay.*

Breakfast is ready.

She swept her hand out over the table. Bacon, sausage, scrambled eggs, milk gravy, and fluffy biscuits steamed from plates and bowls. He stood frozen, staring at the largest and most mouthwatering meal he'd seen in a long time. Maybe she was trying to fatten him up instead.

His stomach growled. He was hungrier than he'd thought. Another growl had him rubbing the area to shut it up. He straightened and glanced down. Hell, he wasn't wearing a shirt.

Looking over at Tessa, he noticed the slight flush brightening her face. Her gaze was zeroed in on where his hand rested. Was she embarrassed by his lack of clothing? Did she think he was a heathen coming to the table without a shirt?

I'll be right back, he signed.

Still holding the wall—damn, he was lightheaded—he rushed to the bedroom and jerked on the shirt she'd left for him. Not wanting to waste time, he hurried back, leaving the shirt unbuttoned. To show her he did have some manners, he eased over to the chair where she stood and pulled it out. Tessa hesitated, but settled into place.

He cautiously stepped to the chair across from her. With a wide smile, she waited expectantly for him to sit. Instead, he took a moment to button up his shirt. He looked up. She regarded him with an unwavering gaze, as if she was trying to figure him out. Uncomfortable with how she continued to stare at him, he motioned to her, *Thank you.*

For what? She shrugged.

The food. He pulled at the front of his blue shirt. *The clothes. The medical help. For everything.*

She tucked her chin and then covered her mouth for a moment.

Was she laughing at him?

You're welcome. Ready to eat? Her eyebrows rose as she waited for his response.

He dropped into the chair and nodded.

Smiling with a pleasant blush to her face, she started passing dishes his way. They ate in silence except for the clicking of utensils and an occasional hum of approval by him.

Odd that the quietness didn't bother him. Most likely it was because the expressions on her face said so much. The pure delight she took in biting into a biscuit, or the way she licked her fingers after eating a piece of bacon. He'd never become hard from watching a woman eat before.

He forced his gaze back to his plate and continued to eat. After a few bites, he stopped with his fork mid-way to his mouth when she knocked on the table. Resting his utensil on his plate, he lifted his eyebrows in question.

Is your arm okay?

After a shrug of his shoulder, checking the tightness of his stitches and the expected pain, he nodded while raising and lowering his fist. *Yes.*

She nodded back and hesitated as if she wanted to say

more, but then looked down at her food. Pinching off some bacon, she popped it in her mouth and glanced his way.

His eyes narrowed as he held his hands out in question.

What?

Do you have a girlfriend?

Surprise did not cover it. He hadn't expected that question.

No.

Why?

What could he say to that? Most of the women he'd been with weren't what a person could call girlfriend material. Those of good families were barred from dating him because of his dad, or his trouble-making brothers, or his Asian heritage. It never really bothered him until he met grown-up Tessa.

From what he'd learned, for the majority of her life Tessa had lived at a special school learning to cope with her deafness in a hearing world and ensuring a better education than Marystown or Sand County could provide her. He remembered seeing her once when she was around ten.

She'd worn a green satin dress with white patent shoes and lacy socks. Her hair was arranged in shiny auburn—darker color than now—ringlets down her back and shiny green ribbons in the curls. Quinn had stopped by Dick Whitfield's office to pick up his monthly stipend before church and brought Tessa along.

Sen had been vacuuming and cleaning the office as punishment for getting fingerprints on the old man's classic black El Camino. When they had walked in, he'd found himself fascinated by the little girl who looked like a fairy princess.

She'd sat in a chair near her dad waiting for Dick Whitfield to return from the safe in the other room. She swung her feet and looked around until she spotted Sen. Her eyes twinkled with curiosity. Unable to resist, he waved. She waved back and smiled big. His heart flipped. For some reason, he felt as if he was the luckiest boy in the world.

Then the old man came up behind him and slapped the back of his head.

"Get back to work, boy. That girl will get you an early grave if you touch her."

Embarrassed and pissed that the old man thought at fifteen he was so perverted to think that way, Sen balled up his fists and glared.

A smirk crossed the old man's face. "Yeah, boy. Swing at me. It's about time I whupped your ass again."

It had taken Sen two weeks to recover the last time Dick decided he needed corporal discipline. His mom had cried for days, afraid the old man would kill him next time. Without a word, Sen picked up the mop and bucket and walked down to the next room.

He'd seen Tessa over the years but stayed in the shadows. That was, until he showed up at Quinn's Funeral Home with a knife wound. She'd been all alone. Her glorious hair in a long ponytail he wanted to wrap his hand in.

After she'd sewn him up and Quinn had kicked him out, Sen decided the hell with the old men. He ached to put his arms around her and kiss her sweet little mouth. All grown up and so sexy, she stayed in his mind, his dreams. He'd seen the interested looks she gave him. They needed a chance to get to know each other, to see if their attraction could mean more.

So anytime he spotted Tessa without her dad, he would give her a flower or hand over a note, telling her how pretty she was that day. Never doing more than that. There was so much he longed to say, but how could he? It wasn't like he could talk with her. It wasn't until much later he learned she could read lips. By then his desire to fluently communicate with her had pushed him to take ASL lessons. There was something about being able to "talk" with her without everyone knowing what they were saying. He rather liked that idea.

Knocking on the table brought his attention back to the present and the woman smiling his way. Her lovely face with eyes wide waited for his answer about a girlfriend.

A bolt of need shot through his body straight to his groin. For some, the freckles across her nose and scattered all around her lovely face would be a big turnoff. Not for Sen. He found the freshness she portrayed hot as hell. She had the girl-next-door look. For a bad boy, she might as well be a drug. He knew he was already addicted.

Yeah. He craved everything about her.

He carefully signed, *Busy. Work. No time to meet new people.*

That was only the partial truth. No one else had fascinated him until her. If truth be known, he'd been waiting for them both to grow up.

His little fairy princess.

CHAPTER 7

*H*is mom had taught him manners. So he started to clean the table by placing leftovers into the refrigerator and dishes into the dishwasher. Steady on his feet, he'd felt so much better with a full stomach.

Tessa tried to tell him to have a seat and let her handle it, but he stayed busy, not looking her way.

As he turned to grab a skillet to soak, he bumped into her, nearly knocking her down.

"Whoa." His hands clasped her upper arms and he looked into those lovely green eyes. Damn, her skin was soft and smooth. The swell of her breasts rose and fell beneath her T-shirt. Her lips parted slightly in a silent sigh.

Unable to resist any longer, he slowly leaned down. He wanted her to have time to protest. When she closed her eyes and lifted her sweet face, he finally touched his lips to hers. Heaven. Unable to hold back any longer, he deepened the kiss and took what he'd wanted for so long.

His fairy princess was not shy. Her tongue darted between his lips, and it was like she flipped a switch. His dick swelled and lengthened so fast it hurt. He even expected, if he glanced down, he would see the tip peeking above the waistband of his pants. If she would slide her hand down his pants, he would be hers to do with as she wished. He craved her touch that much.

Pressing her back against a pantry door, he slipped his hands down to her waist, and then spread his fingers to the front, over her ribs, up to massage her breasts. Oh fuck, they felt so good. Perfect size for his hands. Hooking his fingers into fabric, the sound of tearing didn't sink into his brain as his hands met soft skin. He dipped into her bra and lifted her breasts out. His thumbs flicked the tips.

A squeak escaped her lips. He leaned his head back and smiled.

From the ASL classes, he'd learned a deaf person wasn't necessarily unable to make sounds or talk. It sounded stupid now, but he'd known so little about her world. He'd learned if they were a child when they lost their hearing, they usually had an easier time learning how to speak. Not saying those born deaf couldn't learn, many did with the right methods and teachers. He wanted to ask her about that.

All thoughts of asking questions evaporated when Tessa grabbed his hair and her mouth met his again. He grinned into her kiss. Her aggression turned him on big time. She tasted like heaven.

She deftly unbuttoned his shirt and spread the material open for her touch.

He slid a palm to the small of her back as his other hand lifted her with a firm grip on one butt cheek. Hauling her up, nearly chest to chest, he thrust against the warmth at the apex of her legs. She quickly spread them wider, and he clasped the back of her knee, encouraging her to wrap those beautiful legs around his waist.

Yes. This was perfect. Felt so good.

He began to rock against her. Groaning, panting for

breath in between exploring her hot little mouth, he hungered for more. Damn, he loved the way she went wild, biting, licking, wiggling in his arms. He never expected her to want what he wanted or be so...hungry for him. She'd always been nice to him, but she was kind to everyone. He was one of those bad-seed Whitfields.

Danger and bad boys must be her catnip. Fuck yes! He mentally gave a fist pump.

She rubbed her hard nipples against his chest.

Unable to resist, he held her in place as he stooped to kiss a trail down to one sweet puckered nipple. Yes, the woman's skin was so soft. He released the snap and zipper of her jeans. Then he dipped his hand down the front to press a palm against her pussy. She was hot and wet. Groaning, he stopped when someone started pounding on the front door.

He rested his forehead on her shoulder.

Damn it, damn it, damn it.

After he moved his hands off her, straightened, and took a step back to help her regain her footing, he signed, *Sorry. Someone's at the front door. You stay here.*

No. My door. I'll go. She shook her head and pointed at a red bulb flashing in the upper corner of the room.

There must be a motion sensor at the front door. How had he missed that? A warning signal. She made him crazy and blind.

He shook his head. He understood her need for independence, but the power behind the knock indicated an angry person, most likely a man. Even if it was her dad, he wanted to prove he could look after her and stand up to her old man.

The look she shot him said he wouldn't win. Stubborn woman. Compromise. Otherwise, they would be standing there all day.

Okay. We'll go together, he signed.

Bam, bam, bam, bam.

The light blinked again.

When he tried to help her straighten her clothes, she slapped at his hands. Raising them in surrender, he smiled as she looked up and frowned.

I'm faster, she explained.

Nodding, he indicated for her to go ahead of him.

Thankfully, during the time they argued and she straightened her clothes, his dick had deflated despite the sight of a small tear at her neckline. He'd done that in his frenzy to touch more of her. He tucked the piece of fabric, hoping it appeared part of the style. No need to advertise what they were doing. He buttoned his shirt one more time.

Being a good bit taller than Tessa, he stayed close to look over her head. So when she opened the door, he stared almost eye-to-eye with Cutter Hightower, the president of the local chapter of the Brothers of Mayhem. Despite being a vicious man, Cutter and Sen had managed to sustain a mutual respect of each other's territory. The club's chapter was headquartered in Sand City, a few miles north, and they knew to keep any disruptive business out of Marystown. Anyway, Tessa's lake house was southwest in Cullman County. Certainly, in neutral territory as the area didn't belong to either of them.

How did he find him here? Besides Ethan, there was only one other person who knew his whereabouts. Why in the hell couldn't people keep their mouth shut?

"So Digger was right. I can't believe you thought so little of your life, man." Cutter smirked at Tessa and returned his attention to Sen. "From what I heard, her old man's the type to cut off your tallywacker if he catches you with her."

"Go fuck yourself." Sen glared at the big man while moving Tessa by the shoulders to the side, easier to protect. "What do you want? It's too early in the morning for you to be out and about."

Almost six-three and what looked to be around three hundred pounds, Cutter chuckled as he filled the doorway and craned his neck to look inside.

At the same time, Sen checked outside to see who had ridden with the man. A few yards away, another kutte-wearing Brother sat on a motorcycle. The kutte, pronounced cut, was a vest with patches and lettering indicating their club name and position along with important events. The man lifted his chin Sen's way. The Brothers' sergeant at arms, enforcer, and all-round savage son of a bitch, Kick was the usual bodyguard for the big man. Actually, no one in the MC ever went anywhere alone if they could help it, and certainly not their president.

"Are you going to invite us inside?" Cutter's brows shot up. "You know that's the polite thing to do." The glint in his dark eyes said he wasn't going anywhere fast.

With a sigh, Sen stepped back.

"Kick can stay outside," Sen said in exasperation.

"No problem." Cutter leaned back and spoke to the Brother. "Have a smoke. I won't be long."

The man nodded and pulled out a rolled blunt from his shirt pocket and lit it, taking a long draw.

Closing the door, Sen tried to maneuver Tessa to stand at his back as he ignored her hand movements. She kicked him in the shins.

"Damn it. What was that for?"

Before he remembered to sign, she did. *What does he want?*

No idea. He raised his palms up.

Actually, he suspected the MC leader was there to encourage Sen to fight at the Barn that night.

"You two better not be talking about me," Cutter said teasingly in his gravelly voice, but his face appeared dead serious as he made his way into the house.

Along with his hulking size, a lot of people became

nervous on seeing the tattoos of death vignettes on his arms that went all of the way to his neck, a vicious scar slashed across his nose, and the long black hair in a braid trailing down his back. Someone had told Sen he was of Native American descent, but never said what tribe. One fact was known, he'd been in the U.S. Marines and no one messed with him.

"She's asked me the same question I asked you," Sen said.

"Yeah. When did you start understanding all those hand signals?" Without waiting for an answer, he wandered into the living room. He picked up a vase, looked it over, and set it back down. "Nice place."

"If you came about the Barn, I'm not fighting anytime soon. I have more pressing things on my mind."

"I bet." Cutter eyed Tessa with a little more interest, giving her a smirk when she crossed her arms pulling the material together to hide the tear in her blouse.

Sen's fingers itched to pull out his gun and remind the man why he should tread carefully. Tessa was his. If the asshole kept looking at her that way, Cutter might get his fight, but not at the Barn.

"Cutter, look at me, not her. Or I will shoot you in the gut." He added between gritted teeth, "What do you need?"

The big man's eyebrows shot up. Not many people had the guts to threaten a Brothers of Mayhem member, no less the number one man in the chapter. But he nodded and examined a lamp, fingering the fringe on the shade before turning his attention to Sen.

"I heard you were shot yesterday." Cutter scrutinized the correct shoulder. Sen put it down to the mound of bandages pressing against the sleeve of his shirt. He hadn't told Digger which arm. "You're not on your death bed. Anyway, you owe me. I lost a lot of money last time."

"I didn't tell you to bet against me."

"What can I say? The bastard was a big motherfucker." Cutter shrugged. "Turns out his brother is here and will sponsor Grizzly to have another round with you. You know, to defend his honor. Turns out he's with the Brute Force MC and my club owes them a favor. They want the fight to happen tonight. So here I am. Besides, I want a chance to win back my money."

"Don't tell me, you're betting against me again." Sen glanced at Tessa.

She stared intently at his mouth in an effort to read his lips. He really wished she wouldn't learn about his fighting. The last thing he wanted was for her to be afraid of him. The way she smiled and teased him, chances were she had no idea what he did for a living, and for sure what he did to release stress.

"Fuck no. I want you to beat his ass." Cutter chuckled with a glint in his eyes. "When they are stupid enough to think they can come into Mayhem territory and have someone beat one of our people, they deserve an ass kicking."

"Marystown isn't part of your territory and I'm not one of your people."

"You know what I mean." Cutter's eyes narrowed. "We stay out of each other's business, but we've found ourselves on the same side during different…difficulties," he carefully said the last word. "We claim you as a trustworthy associate. Hell, I thought we were friends."

"Yet, you bet against me."

"Ah, come on, man. I made a mistake. You got to let it go." Cutter chuckled.

An idea popped into Sen's mind. With so many people in attendance, someone should have the information he needed. Who was involved with his old man's and the Tally patriarch's deaths? And who was trying to kill him and his brothers?

"You sponsor me and I will." Sen held out his hand.

"Deal." Cutter shook it with a big grin on his face. "Digger is going to shit his pants. He swore up and down you wouldn't do it. He'll get over it when you show up and ticket sales and betting skyrocket."

Minutes later, Sen closed the door behind Cutter and turned toward Tessa. The scowl on her face slowed his path back to the living room. The sound he'd ignored earlier filled the room as the men cranked their bikes and zoomed down the long drive.

Tessa glared, shaking her head in disgust. *Think about what you're doing. You're stupid. Your stitches will break. You will bleed. Stupid. Stupid.*

You lip-read really well.

Do not change the subject. She narrowed her eyes.

I need to go. People might show up who can answer my questions. He shrugged his shoulders in apology.

Then Tessa's hands moved so fast, Sen could only get a few words. Some of the signs had not been used during his classes, but were easy to guess. Between shooting him a bird and other lewd movements, one indicating a person sucking a cock, he understood she was plenty mad about his decision.

Sen raised his eyebrows. He'd never been cussed out in ASL, but her tears were the final blow. Unable to refrain from doing so, he wrapped his arms around her even as she struggled, but he didn't let go. Rocking her back and forth, he kissed the top of her head. Though he cared for her opinion, he remained steadfast in his decision. When her body relaxed, he loosened his hold, but kept her in his arms.

Looking down into her face, he enunciated each word and said, "I promise, I will not get hurt. Only my opponent has to worry about that."

She leaned back, forcing him to drop his hands to her waist, and huffed. Then she signed, *I've never been and have always wanted to go. So I'm going with you. Besides, I can tend to your wound when it starts bleeding again.*

She tapped his arm and he winced. Her eyebrows rose in challenge. She'd done that on purpose, the little hellion.

He threw up his hands and then signed, *Fine. You won't like it. It's a rough and bad crowd.*

I don't care. I'm going. She crossed her arms and narrowed her eyes.

Expecting her to stamp her foot any second, he chuckled.

Okay. Okay. Let's rest up and then tonight after supper, we'll head over there. It's going to be a long night.

CHAPTER 8

Tessa held onto Townsend's belt loop. He'd placed her fingers there when they exited her car, and signed, *Don't let go.*

They presently stood in the middle of a field with about sixty sedans, trucks, and SUVs, and almost as many motorcycles. He claimed he didn't want to lose sight of her. But she knew he worried for her safety with so many opposing groups wandering around. The Brute Force and Brothers of Mayhem were only two of many outlaw motorcycle clubs in attendance.

So this was the reason no one would ever bring her. Not her type of crowd or fun, but she refused to be separated from Townsend.

Tugging at her gray V-neck T-shirt, she was glad she resisted dressing up. The way the men ogled and molested the few women in attendance, with their spangly and barely there outfits, would have made her a nervous wreck if she'd been alone.

Thank goodness for Townsend, despite the way he glared

at everyone who came within touching distance of her or stared a second longer than necessary.

In a way, she found his attitude such a turn on. If he'd wanted her so badly, why hadn't he finished what they had started in the kitchen? Since neither of them had wanted a nap, they'd instead watched old movies and cuddled throughout the afternoon until time to eat and then leave. Sen had teased and kissed her during the commercials, but during one in particular that showed an Asian woman selling purses, he became still. She asked if he was all right.

My mom loved purses. It was one of her obsessions. He grinned. *And shoes. I guess all women have those urges.*

She'd nodded, hoping he would say more. Anything he had to say about his family she found fascinating as she suspected he didn't talk about them often.

The only time I remember going to a fair, I think I was seven, maybe eight years old, the old man took me and my mother. I don't know why my brothers weren't with us. I didn't like the place that much. Too many tall people and the old man was walking too fast. Mom was almost running to stay with him. But I fell behind because there was so much to see. The color and smells were fascinating. Then I lost sight of them. I was too afraid to cry. The old man would punish me and complain about me acting like a baby.

Oh, no. You were a baby, she signed, a little pissed at his parents.

He patted her hand and lifted it to his mouth, pressing a kiss to her palm.

It got late and a security guard came across me sitting in front of a booth that sold purses. I had hoped Mom would come by and find me there.

Did she? She hated the thought of a little Townsend sitting alone and waiting for someone to come searching for him.

No. The security guard took me home. The housekeeper we had at the time let me into the house. No emotion betrayed what he thought about the memory.

I don't understand. What kind of people wouldn't look for a child? Her heart was hurting for him.

The old man had forbidden anyone to go looking for me. He said I had to learn a lesson.

That adults are stupid?

Townsend had chuckled and shook his head.

The movie's back on. Don't worry. It was a long time ago.

She wanted to ask more—he had so many layers—but their moments on the couch were going to be short and she felt it best to keep it lighthearted. So she'd snuggled closer and hoped he knew she would come looking for him.

Though she enjoyed their time together, it was a little frustrating. Stretched out together on the couch, his hard cock pressed against her ass, she couldn't concentrate on the movie. Each time she'd pushed back, encouraging him, he would grip her hip and hold her still. Oh man, that had the opposite effect. Instead of making her behave, she'd craved more, until he slapped her butt. Then she had teasingly glared at him over her shoulder, and he'd merely smirked and shook his head.

Whatever his problem was—it wasn't her saying no—she would solve it later. Currently, excitement zinged through her. She was about to see the fights she'd always heard about. It was a good thing she was never brave enough to go alone. She was no daredevil.

Out of the corner of her eye, a blur of red caught her attention. A woman in a short red skirt and sequined crop top ran by and flung herself into the arms of a long-haired, bearded man near a monstrous wooden building where the crowd congregated. The man wore a leather vest with a skull logo similar to the man who'd visited them earlier. More dangerous-looking men, wearing various alarming words or pictures on their backs, entered the structure behind him.

The massive, two-story weathered barn stood near the open field being used as an impromptu parking lot. Two food trucks, parked against an exposed wall, pulled in hungry attendees and infused the air with scents of hot dogs and tacos. Towering trees sheltered the farthest end, giving it a bit of camouflage from the main road in the distance. It was doubtful anyone worried about the local law showing up. It was well known Digger Turner's cousin was the new sheriff of the county, and the sheriff had a young wife who loved new shiny things.

Thinking of shiny things, she was glad to see the June sun had sunk behind the treetops, giving everyone a break from the smothering heat. Beneath the denser tree branches, a few lightning bugs flashed and danced, unaware of the activity nearby.

Townsend stopped and she almost bumped into him. He draped an arm over her shoulder and pulled her closer to his side. She looked up, confused by his unexpected PDA. Why had he decided her hold on his belt wasn't enough?.

His expression changed from frustration to stone.

Glancing around, she spotted the big man from earlier weaving between a line of motorcycles. His long strides ate up the distance as he headed in their direction. He smiled and his mouth moved the whole time. Once he came closer, she could read his lips.

"Took you long enough. I started to send Kick after you." The biker smirked.

"I'm here." Townsend's face remained stone-like.

She tugged at his sleeve. His questioning gaze met hers before dropping to her moving hands.

You never told me his name.

He dropped his arm from her shoulders and signed, *Sorry.*

This is C-u-t-t-e-r. He must have spoken out loud as Cutter smiled and waved at her.

She dipped her head in acknowledgement, but couldn't match his smile. The man wasn't handsome in a typical way, but in a manly type of way. Being a bit oversized, he appeared well-muscled instead of fat, and his confidence around women said he was used to having plenty of female attention. Even so, she felt uneasy. Not as if he'd harm her—Townsend wouldn't allow that—and it wasn't the scar on his face or the thick braid down his back proclaiming his uniqueness. It was those dark eyes. Even while smiling or laughing, they exuded sadness and anger. Not anger at her or Townsend, but at the world. A wildness surrounded the man, ensuring a woman would have her work cut out to tame him.

Maybe the same could be said about Townsend, though he rarely smiled unless they were alone. She'd noticed people staring at him with apprehension—usually men—or hunger —usually women—on their faces as they passed by. She squeezed his arm. He patted her hand absentmindedly as they entered the barn. His gaze searched the crowd as if he expected a threat at any minute.

Despite the industrial-size fans twirling above their heads, she wrinkled her nose as they entered the building. It certainly had been used for hay, feed, and animals at some point after its construction. Parts of the walls showed lighter strips of wood where stalls had existed, but the over-whelming smell was of unwashed bodies and sweat, not of animal waste.

A few feet beyond the door, she hesitated as the crowd rose to their feet, clapping and what appeared to be shouting. The vibrations surrounded her. She noted the light pink on Townsend's cheeks, and suspected with the way people spoke with their teeth together, they were saying his nick-name. "Sen, Sen, Sen..."

The fighters inside the cage, situated at the center of the floor, hesitated for a few seconds to see what had changed, but then returned to pounding on each other.

Townsend ignored the accolades and held her elbow, whisking her through the crowd until they came to metal stairs against the side of the cavernous room. At the last level, they opened a door into a long room. A buffet table, covered with shrimp and several other mouthwatering dishes, was set up against one wall. Two oversize, black leather sofas faced a solid wall of glass. The viewing suite being near the barn roof provided the occupants a clear view of the cage and the crowd surrounding them. She guessed it could be considered a skybox, country style.

Her gaze landed on a tall, broad-shouldered man standing at the other end of the people-filled room, laughing and pointing at the activity below. Digger Turner. Her heart squeezed a little. A year had passed since she'd last seen him and that had only been from a distance. A little rougher than she remembered, not as soft around the edges. Age would do that to a person. He and Townsend were about the same age, while Digger was an inch or two taller.

Pulling her gaze from him, she noticed a man in a khaki uniform, drinking a beer, with a huge smile on his sun-wrinkled face. It was the sheriff of Sand County. The older man laughing and bumping shoulders obviously enjoyed the illegal event. No surprise that Digger had the man in his pocket. Besides being related.

Digger leaned in to listen to what his cousin said and joined in the laughter, shaking his head. His grin lit up his whole face, bringing back memories of their time together. Goosebumps ran down her arms. He'd been a wonderful and kind lover. That was when she was eighteen. A little over a month after she graduated high school. She'd been a headstrong teenager, determined to have the older neighbor she'd been crushing on since she was twelve.

Digger's well-washed, tight green T-shirt defined every muscle along his shoulders and arms. The worn blue jeans his shirt was tucked into accentuated a taut butt. From what she could see, his body was still in fine form for a man on the downhill slide to thirty. What could she say? She had a thing for older men. His wavy, sun-kissed brown hair softened the harsh masculine features of his jawline and high cheek bones. Those light blue eyes were so striking, they would make any girl question her morality.

With a silent huff, she turned abruptly toward the sofas and sat. Townsend looked down at her, curiosity stamped on his face. No way could she say she was checking out an old lover. With a shrug, she pretended interest in the fight below.

She no longer had a crush on Digger. He was a womanizer and had broken the hearts of many women in Sand County. The man always acted unfazed by his notoriety.

Most of her life, she'd lived next door to him, but only saw him during the summers for she attended an out-of-county specialized school. Not long after their time together, he'd moved to his grandparents' farm. Then they'd seen each other occasionally around town, but he'd pretended she didn't exist. Pointedly ignoring her. The bastard.

Unable to resist, she glanced again toward Digger.

His gaze caught hers, and he froze, ignoring the sheriff's babble. Then he slapped the sheriff on the back and said a few more words. With a bright smile, he excused himself, and headed toward her and Townsend.

"Glad you could make it, Whitfield." Digger grabbed a beer from a tub of ice. *"Here, have a beer. Your fight isn't for two more hours. Eat. Plenty of food."* As if he decided on what to say to her—she held on to her stoicism—he finally greeted her. *Hey,*

Tessa. You look well, he slowly signed. She had taught him a few words and phrases in ASL when he lived near her.

She shot Digger a bird and then glared at Townsend. She bet he recognized that sign. Digger certainly had received it from women often.

One corner of Townsend's mouth lifted with a pleased look before changing to curiosity. His dark brows rose higher as he carefully said to Digger, making sure she read his lips, *"So you know Tessa."*

"Yeah, Tessa and I were neighbors at one time." Her old neighbor's smile widened.

"You obviously must've been a terrible one."

"Oh, I wouldn't say that." His smirk irritated Tessa.

She refused to rise to the bait. Instead she leaned into Townsend and gave Digger a big smile.

Townsend rested his arm over her shoulders. Then he stretched over to set his beer on a side table. He looked down into her questioning face. *"No beer for me before a fight."*

Digger's smirk disappeared. So he finally realized she was with Townsend. She fought the urge to stick out her tongue.

"One beer won't hurt," Digger said, keeping his gaze on her.

"Alcohol thins a person's blood, makes it run freely." Townsend squeezed her to his side.

"So you expect to lose?" He glanced toward Townsend, a devilish look on Digger's face indicating it was a taunt.

"You don't have to lose to bleed." Townsend's eyes narrowed as if he wanted Digger to be in the ring instead of Grizzly. *"Maybe that's all you know, losing and bleeding."*

Tessa looked from one man to the other as if she watched a tennis match. Were they friends? They didn't look tense with anger. Men loved to talk trash to each other.

"Fair enough." Digger chuckled and his gaze briefly touched on Tessa. *"Why did you bring her?"*

She gasped. She'd caught each word. Rude. He knew she could read lips.

Fed up with their pissing contest, she decided to shut them up. Before Townsend could reply, she spoke up, "Because I want to make sure he doesn't bleed to death, alcohol or not!"

Satisfaction lightened her mood upon seeing Digger glance at Townsend with a mixture of worry and anger creasing his face.

Digger always had a hair-trigger temper. Too many times she'd seen him get in a fight whenever people made fun of her voice. She never really cared what others thought. So what if it sounded flat and weird like they said, but her dad and Digger always got worked up in her defense. To keep arguments down and fists from flying, she rarely said anything unless alone with her dad. She still worried about modulating her volume.

Townsend grabbed her shoulders and turned her toward him as he pulled her against his chest. Facing each other, she looked up as his chin dipped down. She patted his chest in an effort to quell the confusion flashing in his dark eyes and tightening his lips.

"You can talk." He cupped a cheek and spoke slowly. She grimaced and rolled her eyes to convey "duh," and he added, *"Of course, I suspected you could when I made you squeak this morning."*

As heat spread across her cheeks, she could imagine what Digger was thinking. A warmth covered her back. Digger had stepped up behind her, into their personal space. Between the two tall, hard male physiques, her body quivered with the temptation to take a deep breath. How would it feel for both of them to rub against her? No, no, no. She shouldn't think that way. Yet, the image continued to grow as they remained motionless.

Looking up into Townsend's beautiful face, lust shone in those mysterious eyes. She caught her breath. Was he imagining the same thing?

He blinked. Then his hands dropped away.

Unable to resist, she glanced over her shoulder and peered into Digger's face. His sexy lips moved. *"And what did you do to make her squeak?"* The menace on his face revealed his reaction to what Townsend had said.

Damn, she was getting a headache from all of the testosterone being sprayed by the two cavemen. Though she admitted to a little tingle of excitement. Men never fought over her.

"None of your fucking business." Townsend's eyes changed from a warmth like aged whiskey to a cold, black bottomless pit. Chills raced down her spine. Not a man to cross when angry. Since his anger wasn't directed at her, again, she didn't feel guilty about how turned on she was at the moment.

She turned her head to catch Digger's response.

"I see." Digger met her gaze, his expression softened, and then he backed off.

That was surprising. She never remembered seeing him back down from anyone. He wasn't afraid. So he understood Townsend didn't mean her any harm. She returned her attention to Townsend.

"If you'll excuse us, I would like to talk with Tessa privately." Townsend's grim countenance said he didn't give a fig if Digger cared or not.

She looked back at Digger.

"Sure." The questioning look in Digger's eyes conveyed he wanted to make sure she was okay.

She lifted an eyebrow. So he wanted to be a hero all of sudden? Besides, she was a grown woman and hadn't asked for his help and actually didn't need it. Townsend would never hurt her. Deep inside she felt that.

On a lift of his chin, Digger walked away.

Callused fingers lightly brushed her cheek, redirecting her attention.

Blinking to clear her vision as he leaned down, almost too close to see his lips, she waited for Townsend to explain his bad mood. It was clear something bothered him.

"Why?" He frowned as he searched her eyes.

She opened her mouth to ask what he meant, but stopped. Of course, it had to do with her outburst. Clearly, he wanted to know why she kept her ability to speak to herself.

Unsure of the timbre of her voice, she decided to sign instead. So she pushed at his chest, forcing him to give her room. *I was going to tell you.*

When the f-u-c-k were you planning to tell me?

She really needed to teach him a few shortcuts for curse words in ASL. Spelling out the word appeared to irritate him and he even winced when he jabbed his finger into his chest.

Soon, she signed.

Soon? Is that all you have to say?

It's the truth. What more is there?

He brought his hands up as if to grab her shoulders and then stopped, creating fists instead as he gritted his teeth, frustration apparent. She could tell he wanted to shake her.

I should turn you over my knee and spank you. He glared at her.

When did you pick up your older brother's habit? she sassed back.

Who told you about— He shook his head and then gave her a strange look. *You deserve one.*

You and what army?

She was actually enjoying their sparring.

He lifted his palms in exasperation, took a deep breath, and then carefully signed, *What is Digger to you?*

Her eyes widened. How could she explain?

We were neighbors when I was a kid. We're friends, she signed, giving him a questioning look. She had no idea why he asked about Digger. It wasn't like he had anything to do with her ability to speak. Then again, he might could tell she was still attracted to the Lothario.

Nothing more? His face showed no emotion.

Hands on hips, she narrowed her eyes, trying to glean what he wanted to know. Maybe whatever was bothering him wasn't about her voice. No way would she talk about Digger being her first. Not at that moment.

Never mind. He shook his head and started to turn away, but she placed a hand on his arm to stop him. Before she could ask any questions, he signed, *I need to sign in. I'll be back.*

We'll talk about this later.

He gritted his teeth again. *No, we won't. Just forget it.*

She glanced toward the ceiling.

Men.

CHAPTER 9

*D*igger stared sightlessly down at the fighters. He had no doubt Sen would beat the shit out of Grizzly. His calm, quiet manner threw people off-kilter. Strangers underestimated him, what with his pretty face and being different from most individuals in the small county. But at six feet with many years of martial and weapons training, the man was a stone-cold killer.

And a damn good friend. Sen had pulled his ass out of the fire so many times. During their teens and early twenties, they partied hard and shared most of the women they were interested in, one after the other, in the same room or bed, and most, at the same time with one woman. Though Sen wasn't interested in sex with another man, as Digger enjoyed on occasion, Sen ignored the necessary touches caused by the closeness of fucking a female.

But why in the hell had he brought Tessa? She wasn't that type of girl. Then again, from the looks of her, she'd changed over the last few years. He also realized he was still attracted to her.

Staying away from her had been challenging. Hell, her old

man even liked him, despite suspecting they had hooked up the month after she graduated high school. And really, there was no way Quinn had his head in the sand when it came to how Digger made his living. But his lifestyle wasn't one she'd understand or enjoy. Most likely.

Hmm. But with her showing up with Sen, it was a good sign she'd obviously matured to the point she might enjoy an unconventional relationship. Everyone knew Sen was a freak in bed. Didn't she?

His tongue swiped his bottom lip, thinking of how adventurous Tessa would be in the sack. She'd been pure temptation as a headstrong teenager. Now as an adult, he suspected, she'd become sin incarnate with her reddish-brown hair, green eyes, and well-curved figure. The sexual power she exuded brought men to her, like bees to honey. He'd planned to wait for her to truly reach adulthood before he became involved with her again. Less of a chance of getting shot by her old man if he decided to open his eyes. But more time had slipped away as he built his businesses.

If he remembered correctly, in another month she'd be twenty-four. Plenty old enough for him to sink his hard cock into Tessa's soft, hot body once again without any repercussions.

Yet now, Sen showed up with her.

What the fuck?

Yeah, yeah, yeah. Same old, same old, sharing a woman, but Tessa was different...special.

Tessa was the first woman his friend had ever brought to the fights. Hell, Digger couldn't remember Sen taking a woman anywhere no matter how many times she spread her legs for him.

Yeah, she was special to Sen. As she was for him.

Well, wasn't that fucking perfect? He guessed it was destined, considering they had identical taste in women.

So they wanted the girl…hmm…woman and not just for their normal threesome. Or like he called it, *pas de trois*. Sexier sounding and less involvement for himself than a *ménage à trois*. By the possessive way Sen studied Tessa's every movement, he wanted her completely and totally. Digger preferred to love 'em, leave 'em. Sure, he wouldn't mind having more than one go at her, but he wasn't the settling down type. Too many warm bodies out there to try out.

Hell, she was the type who would want to settle down and have kids.

His gaze drifted over to her. She sat on the edge of the couch's cushion, biting her bottom lip. The giveaway was easy to read, she was worried.

He needed to find a way to get her alone and talk.

CHAPTER 10

$\mathscr{A}$bout two hours later, Tessa watched as Townsend pulled off his shirt and shoes, preparing for his match. Certainly not the first time he'd been shirtless around her, but she couldn't pull her gaze from his broad back and lean waist. The white bandage on his arm appeared bright against his darker skin. Muscles shifted and bunched as he walked over to her, leaned down, and kissed the living daylights out of her. Seconds later, he was jogging down the steps to the arena. As soon as he reached the bottom, Cutter, along with another man, pulled him to the side and started wrapping his hands.

She dreaded it. Yes. She had always wanted to attend a fight, but not with Townsend as one of the contestants. From what she'd seen of the nasty cuts and massive bruises, and way too much blood from the last two men, the brutality might be more than she expected.

Yet she surprised herself when the fighting started, something primal inside her kicking in. Maybe it being an organized fight, sort of, counteracted the terror. The place filled with testosterone and caused her body to tighten with need.

A mixture of shame and excitement flowed over and through her. Shame heated her cheeks for being excited by the slamming of fists against flesh.

Townsend played with his taller and larger opponent as if he was in no hurry to end the round.

Twice, she had to concentrate on releasing her bottom lip from between her teeth. The tender flesh was swollen and sensitive from her mistreatment. A bad habit of hers when she was nervous or worried. She was both, along with all the other spectators, as she watched the big bruiser swing his ham-sized fists at Sen.

As expected, the man called Grizzly looked like his namesake with a hairy chest and back and a bushy head of hair that extended down to an equally bushy beard. He easily towered seven inches over Townsend's six-foot height.

Sweat glistened on Townsend's torso beneath the bright lights. Each muscle shone to its perfection. His jeans rode low on his hips, revealing the indentions near his hips.

Her mind wandered to what he looked like without any clothes. Glancing down to his groin, she squeezed her eyes shut for a second. What had gotten into her? She'd never been so obsessed with a man's...whole package. Briefly ashamed of herself for letting her mind go there, she missed the final punch. Grizzly wobbled and then crumpled at Townsend's feet.

The crowd shook their fists, mouths open as they obviously shouted while stomping their feet in the excitement of the knockout, even the floor of the skybox vibrated beneath her.

A pressure on her arm brought her around to face Digger.

"Come to my office," he said, stooping down a little, making sure she read his lips. *"Sen will need to be checked out before he hits the showers. I'll send him a message to meet us there when he's presentable."*

"I want to see if he's okay." Her stomach clenched as she remembered the few hits Townsend received from the ham-size, hairy fist.

"A real doctor will check him out. Please don't worry. I want to talk with you without interruption." The pleading expression on his face convinced her to agree.

He led her to a door near one corner she'd overlooked. The office was the same length of the skybox, but the long window faced the dark woods and looked out over treetops. She bet the view was gorgeous at sunrise. The room included a long conference table near the door and a massive desk at the other end.

Before she could react, he grabbed her hand and swung her around, crushing her front to his torso. With a finger, he lifted her chin.

"I've missed you, Tessa," he said. His lids dropped half-mast as he searched her eyes. Was he hoping to see desire reflected back? *"Why are you with him? I stayed away because of extracurricular activities. But I'm a choir boy compared to what he does for his family."*

"That was your prerogative. But obviously you don't remember, you actually ghosted me." When his forehead wrinkled in confusion, she rolled her eyes. "Whatever." With a tilt of her head, she added, "I thought he was your friend." She hoped her voice was low enough for the empty room.

He nodded.

"We are. We have many of the same interests." His grin she'd always loved, with a dimple in one cheek, spread wider. *"And it appears that includes you."*

She slapped his arm. "Behave. Townsend and I are friends."

"A special friend. Like me, heh? You couldn't keep your eyes off him." He caressed her cheek with a knuckle. *"You call him Townsend. Only you could get away with it."* His other hand slid

up her shoulder and clasped the back of her neck. *"I'm jealous."*

"Of him, or what I call him?"

"Silly woman. Both."

Then his mouth covered hers.

How had she forgotten what a great kisser he was? His tongue slipped in when she gasped. Heat raced through her body. For a moment, she relaxed and enjoyed memory lane as he deepened the kiss.

She sensed a shadow dimming the light on her face. Opening her eyes, she pushed Digger back. Her cheeks scalded from her inappropriate curiosity. It had been so long and she couldn't resist finding out if she remembered correctly. She had been more than correct.

Only thing was, Townsend stood across the room, damp hair hanging in his face as he warily studied her and Digger. Then a flare of anger flickered in his eyes before he looked away. What? Did he think she initiated the kiss and not the other way around? Sure, she hadn't fought Digger. Townsend didn't own her. Men were so frustrating. Couldn't they ask at least one question. And then believe her? She would tell the truth.

Sure, Townsend had been flirting with her for months and slept at her lake house, but he'd kissed her just once. That was all. Though she admitted Townsend's had caused her pussy to throb.

Well, hadn't Digger's kiss been on the way of doing the same? So what? That didn't mean she was a slut. Just lucky enough to kiss two hot-as-hell men.

She glared at the dangerous man until she checked on Digger. He had a furious stare leveled at Townsend. Unable to hold back the humor—the whole situation was crazy—she smiled and covered her mouth. She held back her laugh. Her dad had always said it sounded more like a huff or a pant, as if she'd been running. Not a lady-like sound at all.

But how could anyone not see the humor? Who would have ever thought two men wanted her, especially at the same time? She sure never imagined that.

Townsend signed, *Let's go.*

His face was stone-cold. No expression. Giving nothing away. A chill ran down her spine. Was he truly angry?

She nodded and turned to Digger. "Despite your ghosting me, it was good seeing you again."

Hopefully, she'd softened her voice in an attempt to convey her tender thoughts. She did care for the man. He grinned at her, his gaze softening as he lifted his chin. That wonderful sparkle in his blue eyes. One he'd worn often when they lived next to each other.

"Don't be a stranger. I've missed you," he said as distinctly as he could. Then he cut his eyes toward Townsend. *"Down, boy. She's going home with you."* His grin widened. *"This time."*

Really? No one owned her. She looked over toward Townsend. He turned toward the door before she caught his expression. With a quick glance at Digger, she raised her eyebrows in question. He said something she couldn't read for he was laughing too hard. She shook her head and shrugged.

Digger then painstakingly signed, *He g-r-o-w-l-e-d.*

She blinked in surprise, covered her mouth to keep from giggling, and then waved goodbye as she followed Townsend out the door.

CHAPTER 11

$\mathcal{D}$igger lifted his hand in farewell though she'd already turned her back. The look Sen gave him over Tessa's head warned that Sen was a little irked in finding Tessa in his arms and his mouth on hers.

They had never fought over a woman before. Of course, it never had been a problem when it came to men. That didn't count as Sen was hetero while Digger swung both ways. Men merely spiced up his sex life. Damn it. How many times had Digger tried to get Sen drunk or high enough to try it? The closest he'd managed was when they fucked a woman at the same time. A stray hand or mouth could not be helped, especially when thrusting caused their balls to slam against another as they drilled into the same female. Digger preferred the back entrance.

The possibility of having Tessa between the two of them was a delicious thought. Remembering how Tessa had been such a willing student in her first experiences, he suspected she would be excellent in a trio. He rubbed a hand over his hardening cock.

Two people he loved.

"Yo, boss. Someone here to see ya!" One of his security men knocked on the door and waited for an answer.

"Who is it?" Before the man could answer, Digger opened the door. "Oh, it's you. What do you want?"

CHAPTER 12

Sen fisted the gear shift as if he drove a manual instead of an automatic. He needed something to keep his mind busy and had insisted on driving back to her lake house. All types of emotions roiled in his gut from what he'd seen moments earlier. The picture of Digger and Tessa kissing refused to dissipate.

The hell of it was, he'd noticed she hadn't fought him off and had returned the kiss. Fuck, his body, especially his dick noticed. She enjoyed it so much, she'd been unaware of his return. He was aware his buddy, Digger, had been the instigator. Tessa wasn't the type of girl to play one guy against another. Had she heard stories of how they'd shared women?

Up until two years ago, Sen and Digger had shared because of the alcohol and drugs they experimented with. A drink or pill would lead to another and then some crazy shit would go down. One girl between the two at the same time, or at different times while the other watched. Hell, they'd done it numerous times and in many different ways. The women often begged for a return act. It was one of the perks of having a savage Whitfield or Turner in their bed. Most females loved bad boys.

But Tessa wasn't one of those easily swayed to the wilder side of fucking. Or was she?

She was known for being a good girl, went to church on Sundays, helped out with the elderly at the senior center on occasion. He'd never seen her at the bars or nightclubs he frequented.

When he'd seen adult Tessa, at the time recently returned to Marystown, he abruptly ended his wild partying. He had never wanted a woman like her. A do-gooder. If she was his, he would do anything to keep her happy.

But he'd seen the sensual look wash over her face when he and Digger had sandwiched her between them. Yeah. She likely had heard the rumors. Had she wondered how it would be to share? He would have to think on it. There were many layers to Ms. Tessa Quinn and he was ready to peel each one back.

Damn. His dick stiffened a little more behind his zipper. He yearned for her to want him for himself, not the thrills he could provide by his name or the life he'd led. He really needed to know how she felt. Maybe they should have a heart-to-heart talk about their feelings.

Hell, when had he grown a vagina?

So disgusted with the emotional shit coming out of his brain, he yanked his attention from the woman next to him and checked the road ahead and behind.

The headlights in the rearview mirror caught his attention. The road they drove on held a small number of houses and he ignored his premonition. Maybe the car would turn before they arrived at the T-intersection not far from Tessa's place.

By the time the yellow sign with the black double-headed arrow reflected his headlights, Sen rejected the idea of leading the tail anywhere near her house. He'd like to stop and pull out the asshole and beat the person to a bloody pulp, but he had to protect her. So he turned in the opposite direction and kicked in the big SUV's engine while keeping an eye on the rearview mirror, waiting to see what happened next. Mere seconds later, the silver truck—Sen caught a glance of it in a street light—squealed its tires as he hit the turn without slowing.

Tessa's sharp intake of breath caught his attention. Her fingers were digging into the edges of her seat and the door armrest. Eyes wide, she glanced his way and gave him a weak smile. Unable to release the steering wheel, he switched from watching the road ahead to face her so she could read his lips lit by the dashboard lights.

He tried his best to explain quickly.

"We have a tail." He checked the road and then looked at her again. "Someone following." The SUV hit a dip in the road, and he straightened, eyes back on the road as their heads almost hit the overhead liner. Once more, he faced her long enough to add, "I'm trying to lose them."

She nodded. Damn, he didn't want anything to happen to her. Unable to resist, his gaze quickly scanned her body. Damn, he liked her soft, full figure. He breathed in deeply. Now wasn't the time to think of that. Glancing her way one more time, he nodded. She looked as if she was handling the craziness like a pro.

Then she squealed, pointing ahead. He returned his attention to the road to see they were hitting a curve a little too fast. Thankfully, the Ford Explorer wasn't known for flipping. He felt two wheels lift, but they quickly returned to the asphalt, and he pressed the gas a little harder. That was when he heard a pop. He checked the rear window. A good-sized hole and the webbing of cracked glass around it told him the truck's driver was shooting.

"Down!" He reached over and shoved her head down.

Even though she didn't hear him, his action ensured she became less of a target.

Another pop followed and a larger hole near the original one was created and the glass shattered more, pieces falling in. The opening was the size of a soft ball.

Before he pulled out the gun hidden in his ankle holster, Tessa unbuckled her seat belt and reached between his legs and under his seat. What the fuck was she doing? She pulled out a pink-and-black pistol. He would laugh but from the looks of the Beretta, she could still do damage to the asshole behind them, despite both being in moving vehicles.

She lowered the passenger window and began firing.

The truck swerved. She must have hit the windshield, but it didn't stop the asshole, and from the way the motherfucker was speeding up to the driver's side. Tessa had made him mad.

Sen lowered his window, pressed his shoulders back, and nodded toward the advancing truck. He hoped like hell she didn't accidentally shoot him. Just as she leaned over to fire, he saw danger ahead and lifted his foot from the gas pedal, preparing to stop. When he checked the side mirror, he noticed the truck driver had slammed on his brakes and completely stopped. Smoke billowed from the truck's tires.

"Oh fuck!"

In the middle of nowhere was a railroad crossing gate coming down, the warning lights flashing red. He could see the train coming at full speed. Damn. He'd forgotten about the crossing. Trains only came through late at night in that area. What was he going to do? Even in the movies, the automobile didn't always make it. But he didn't have an option. If they stopped, they would be sitting ducks. Of course, with both of them armed and firing at the truck, they had a chance of getting out of it alive, but it'd be easier if they placed the train between them, cutting off the asshole's path.

Tessa, being the smart girl he knew she was, quickly buckled her seatbelt back on and then began stomping her foot. He guessed that was the signal to put the gas pedal to the floor.

As they drew closer, Sen was relieved to see the opposite side of the gate missing. Someone had already busted through before. If he timed it right and put enough space between them, the truck would have to stop again or risk being torn in two. He hated putting the train engineer in danger along with Tessa, but he really had only one course of action.

They hit the raised area on the left side of the road full force as the train's headlights lit up the interior of the SUV. The train horn blasted so loud, Sen wished he could clap his hands over his ears, but kept the SUV pointed straight. Tessa covered her eyes with an arm. Once again, their heads almost touched the headliner when they topped the slight incline, and they bounced in their seats as they landed.

Heart beating so hard, he was sure it would bust through his chest. He considered stopping, but felt it best not to press their luck. There was no sound of metal crunching and twisting and brakes screeching unless the horn had damaged his hearing. Curiosity overtook his good sense, and he slowed a little to check the side mirror again. The rearview mirror was useless. The spiderwebbed cracks in the back window, despite the softball-sized hole, blocked most of the view. The train was still moving and no one was behind them. That was what counted.

He pressed the gas once again. Relief eased the ache between his shoulders. The SUV shot forward past a couple of dark buildings and into the night.

One glance over to Tessa brought the tenseness back. Her

eyes squeezed shut in a pale face, with one hand over her heart, indicated she felt the same way; lucky to be alive, but wondering if her chest might bust open from the pounding inside. He hoped she wouldn't ask to be taken back to her father's house.

Stretching his arm out, he placed a hand over hers.

She opened her eyes, blinked, and grinned.

In the odd voice that was part of her uniqueness, and he was beginning to love, she said, "I don't know if anyone would believe me if I told them about the last couple days."

He chuckled and shook his head. Amazing how well she handled not only the damage to her SUV, but the danger from the gunfire and train. Without thinking, he clasped her hand and brought it over to kiss the back of her slim fingers and then placed them on his thigh, his hand covering hers.

For the next thirty or so minutes, they sat like that. Sen holding her hand in place as he drove down the dark roads. They couldn't take a chance of going back to her lake house. So he decided to take her to one he knew about. The owner had left home for a couple of weeks. It was on the other end of Smith Lake and only a handful of people knew about it. Not as cozy or fully stocked as hers, but it should give them some time to clean up and contact Jake. Plus she would need to attend to his arm.

The asshole had nicked him. At least, he hoped it was a nick. He'd felt the sting—like a son of a bitch—a couple of inches farther down the same arm already wounded. Who could claim they were shot two different times in the same limb in less than twenty-four hours? He hoped the wound wasn't as deep. He would know for sure soon.

He turned off the road and down a long, curvy cement drive. He peeked over at her. She raised her brows at the two-story building.

As he expected, no cars were parked out front on the

half circle near the double doors. The man who owned the place hadn't built a garage yet. Sen suspected the man didn't worry because most people wouldn't traverse such a long drive. Most everyone who lived on the lake owned a gun or two, and they didn't think twice about shooting trespassers.

Stay here. I need to get the key. He waited for her nod.

Instead she signed, *Whose place is this?*

A friend's. No need to upset her. Chances were she wouldn't understand why he was breaking in.

She nodded and relaxed in the seat.

Tired and aching all over, he hated to admit his body could no longer take the beating it once endured. That was one of the reasons he no longer fought at Digger's on a regular basis. The couple of blows he received earlier were unpleasant enough. With bruised ribs and one cheek swollen, he pushed hard not to hold his side or wince from pain. Anyway, time would heal one and ice would help the other. But he needed Tessa once again to check his arm.

When he'd stopped by to collect the money owed a few days ago, he'd noted the cheap lock. Spend thousands of dollars on a cabin, decor, and certain items that were illegal for civilians to own, but go wimpy on security. Didn't make sense.

With his back to Tessa, hoping she was looking the other way, he kicked the door knob. As he expected, the pieces fell off. With a simple twist of his pocket knife, it creaked open. Two steps in, he pressed in the code, one-two-three-four, on the alarm pad hidden behind an artificial plant. Yep. Last time Sen had been there, he'd noted the man had a cheap-ass alarm and used a stupid code too.

Stepping outside, he waved Tessa in.

He sauntered through the foyer and open living area and turned into the kitchen. Slapping at the switches on the wall, he activated several recessed lights and brightened the room. Another switch activated the back deck lights.

She walked up to the window and shook her hand near her face. *Wow.*

He smiled at how mesmerized she was by the view of the lake spread out beyond the deck. It was a prime spot. The full moon glistened on the choppy water as the wind swayed the silhouetted pines.

While she stared at the scenery, he pulled a large, white metal box with a red cross painted on it from a cabinet beneath the sink. He had helped the guy doctor his cuts and bruises. He wasn't a total asshole when he collected funds. After he unlatched the box, he examined the supplies. The man had crappy taste in security, but he had high-quality medical supplies.

Sen and his brothers were experts at sewing each other up when it came to minor cuts, but they were all so busy handling their own part of the Whitfield businesses, they were rarely at home at the same time. And they learned not to involve Miss Jimmy Sue in any of their misadventures. She was such a soft-hearted soul and worried too much. That was one of many reasons they went to Quinn's place.

He pulled out a couple of gauze pads, bandages, and petroleum jelly. If she needed to put in stitches, there was a proper needle and thread for that too. Soap and water should be plenty to wash out any germs left behind from the bullet and fibers of his shirt.

Her light touch on his shoulder brought his gaze up.

Did the fight cause your arm to bleed? Stitches okay?

He shook his head. *Not the fight. Stitches good. In the car. New hit.*

Unsure how much to explain and what words to use, he held up a finger for her to wait. He then pulled off his shirt, turning his shoulder toward her.

The horror and concern flashing across her face warned he might have misjudged the seriousness of the wound. His arm burned as if it was about to burst into flames, but he'd assumed it was the combination of two bullet wounds within inches of each other.

You were shot again? What are you? A bullet magnet? More stitches.

He knew better than to laugh at her comment, what with the deep concern showing on her face. She held up a small mirror so he could see. Yep. She was right. Instead of a graze needing a stitch or two, it was more of a gouge. Looked as if it would take twelve. He examined his shirt. Blood soaked the sleeve and down one side, and most likely the driver side of her car too. What a mess. He really needed her to stay far away from him. Until he could stop whoever placed a contract on the Whitfield boys. It was dangerous to be around any of them.

Luckily, once again, the bullet had continued on, probably lodged in the dashboard. His vision blurred red with the thought of the bullet hitting Tessa instead. The bastard who shot at them would need to die.

CHAPTER 13

essa finished tying off the last stitch. The box of medical supplies included Lidocaine to deaden the area. There were a couple of other items only an ER usually had on hand. All of that work to sew him up confirmed what her dad often said about the Whitfield boys. It was hazardous to be seen with them. She hated he was right.

She dropped the surgical needle into a small disposable container and reached for more gauzes to clean his arm.

When she glanced up, she realized his eyes were closed. He cracked them open, cut his eyes her way, and smiled.

How was the man still conscious? Two nights in a row he'd lost blood from bullet wounds, bruised and battered after fighting in an event, but still awake with shoulders back and head held up. No longer able to resist, she brushed a strand of his black hair behind his ear.

Over the last few years, she'd seen his hair long—below his shoulders—and short—almost military length. She had to say middle length suited him best, hair over his ears and brushing his collar. About a week ago, she'd spotted him walking into the Italian restaurant on Main Street. He'd pulled the top portion into a silver clasp. Somehow, he looked barbarous, foreign, wild, savage—bundled together—he was so damn sexy.

Do you have a rubber band? She bit her bottom lip to prevent from smirking.

A questioning look wrinkled his forehead as he signed, *I think I have one in my pocket. Why?*

Maybe you want to move your hair from your eyes. She kept her gaze on her hands as she gathered the bloody gauze pads. Her cheeks warmed. Would he think she was weird?

He leaned to the side and dug into a pocket. Cracking a grin, he pulled out a black ponytail holder.

Put it on, she encouraged.

His gaze softened. With his attention remaining on her face, he scooped up his hair and twisted the holder in place. A wince squeezed his face.

Ashamed for not remembering how lifting his arms would hurt because of his wound, she mouthed sorry, but couldn't take her gaze away. Heat seeped into her cheeks and another type of warmth spread down her body.

He was so hard to resist. With his hair brushed from his face, those cheekbones stood out in stark relief. He was handsome, but with his hair like that, he was devilishly so.

For goodness sake, she wanted to kiss him again. In fact, she wanted more, wanted to touch him all over. Without thinking it through, she cupped his face and pressed her lips to his. He didn't respond.

Was he still mad at her for kissing Digger? Actually, Digger had kissed *her first.* She couldn't help responding. Her last relationship was with a boy at college and had ended months prior. It had been a long, dry spell.

She drew away and moved her hands away.

Had she ruined her chance with him? Was she the only one feeling the attraction? Why couldn't she read this man?

Was he the type who preferred to always be in control? She knew he was macho and all, but nothing indicated he was a male chauvinist.

No, he wasn't. He wouldn't have leaned back and encouraged her to shoot at the truck. He would have taken the gun out of her hand and shot at the truck himself.

A little embarrassed at her brashness, she hung her head, pretending an interest in the floor as she stuck her hands into her blue jeans pockets and regained her common sense. What she needed was sleep. Anything to help rein in her horny thoughts. Sure, they had kissed and more that morning, but it could mean nothing to Sen.

Had it only been that morning? Hard to believe it had been less than twenty-four hours. Maybe she screwed up by kissing Digger back. No matter what, she refused to say she was sorry for kissing him or Digger. Straightening her shoulders, she gave an arrogant lift of her chin and stared into his beautiful midnight eyes.

A heated look crossed his unsmiling face. She stepped back.

With a lightning-fast move, he clasped her upper arms and jerked her against his chest. Her toes barely reached the floor. He glared down into her eyes. Vibrations from the chest pressed to hers warned he'd said something she missed. A little afraid but so turned on, she dropped her gaze to his lips.

"Yes. Watch my lips. You are driving me insane. I want you. I want your taste on my tongue." His mouth shaped the words as if he was biting each one off. Strong hands squeezed and eased their hold as if he was fighting his desire to shake her. *"To feel your softness against my hard aching body. To fuck you out of my system."*

His last few words caused her to gasp so sharply, she started coughing. Finally, she regained her composure. Eyes wide, she looked into his again. The darkness in his gaze he normally projected was gone. Pure heat shone in their depths.

His mouth covered hers and everything around her disappeared. His tongue stroked hers in between sucking her tongue and lips. So erotic. It was as if she'd never been kissed before. Sure, Digger's kiss had been delightful, but that was like comparing sweet tea to a fine wine. Both were wonderful, but Townsend's kisses were like sipping a dark burgundy that went straight to her head.

Had she ever felt so needy? The musky male scent beneath the soap he'd obviously used after the fight filled her senses. Struggling in his hold, she wanted to wrap her arms around his neck and hold on tight. She whimpered with a stronger need. Then he dropped his hands to her ass and lifted her until she spread her legs around his waist and crossed her ankles at the small of his back.

The length of his cock beneath the black denim and zipper pressed into the right spot. She began to rhythmically move, taking pleasure from each roll of his answering hips.

With long strides, he carried her along a short hallway and kicked open a door. Taking her down with him, he landed above her on the soft bed, keeping most of his weight from crushing her. Happy that she finally had him in bed and her body beneath his, she wiggled, hoping to regain the lovely rhythm from seconds ago.

Instead he held himself off her, not touching, but nibbled at her earlobe.

Oh hell. She never knew such a simple thing could arouse her from head to toe. Breathlessly, she opened her mouth, trying to take in as much air as possible, unsure it would ever be enough. Dizzy and craving a firmer, possessive touch, she clasped his head and found his mouth again.

His big hand slid beneath her shirt and over her ribs. He

shoved the material over her head and threw it to the side. Ready to do some of her own touching, she slipped her hand beneath his shirt, up his broad chest, and stripped it away.

In a flash, he loosened her bra, and she shrugged out of it. Before she could feel self-conscious of her small breasts, he bent down and sucked in a turgid nipple. She groaned and he matched each draw with a thrust of his hardness against her tender pussy.

Yes. He made it feel so good.

Threading her fingers into silky hair, she soaked in the sensory overload of cool tendrils, hot mouth, hard cock, and scratchy stubble against her skin. His head eased away from her touch as he kissed and nipped his way down to her stomach. The strange sensation of her jeans becoming slack and then moving over her hips, taking her panties with them, added to the magic of the moment.

Without warning, a warm tongue delved between her folds. Yes. Warmth flooded her limbs and rolled across her torso. Her knees fell to each side, giving him more room. He clasped her thighs with strong fingers to ensure she kept them open. She closed her eyes, arched her back, and rotated her hips, immersing herself in the pleasure he gave with each swipe.

No sooner than he rotated a thumb on her clit, the waves of climax shook her. She dipped her hands into his hair, wanting him to crawl back over her and thrust his beautiful cock inside her. Even before that she would love to lick his cock. She wanted more, but he rolled away and off the mattress to stand near the bed.

Sleep. I'll wake you later, Townsend signed. Then he pulled on his shirt, tucking the ends into his pants.

No. Come back to bed. She crooked her finger and wiggled her eyebrows. The view of his rigid cock outlined alongside of his zipper was a beautiful sight. So damn hot. She wanted to touch, stroke, toy with, squeeze, taste, and possess what he had under that denim. *Let me help you with that.*

I need to check on your car and call a few people. Rest.

Frowning for a moment, she watched Townsend turn off the light, walk out of the room, and softly close the door.

What the hell?

He was confusing the crap out of her. Didn't he want to do more? He'd kissed her back. Everything pointed to his wanting her. Goodness, his cock had been rock-hard. He'd even gone down on her. So surely he wanted more. He was taking being a control-obsessed sort of guy to the extreme.

She yawned. He'd given her a wonderful climax.

He did have such a nice butt. She was so tired.

Her eyelids weighed a ton. They drifted closed. Her body felt limp, contented. It had been an exciting, scary, climactic day. Emphasis on climactic. The corners of her mouth lifted in a pleased smile as she fell asleep.

CHAPTER 14

"You've got to be the biggest chicken shit in the world," Sen murmured beneath his breath as he quietly closed the front door and stomped over to Tessa's shot up SUV.

He was losing his mind. The woman had him talking to himself. Hell, to be honest, it wasn't her fault. He felt guilty for touching her, but fuck, the feel, smell, taste of her drove him to nothing short of insane. Even more so, how crazy was he to have the girl he'd dreamed about for the last two years stretched out on a bed, naked, begging for more, and he walked away?

His plan had been to ask her out. Once he got his guts up to ask. There had been a chance she'd turn him down. It would've killed him to see her date someone else. He'd been wanting her ever since she came back from college. Not that it hadn't crossed his mind to kill anyone who dated her before then. She had returned home to stay. He didn't kid himself into thinking she was untouched. Even if it was only a local community college, all college kids were the same. They loved to party. With her dad over an hour's drive away, she had probably explored her freedom thoroughly. Possibly more than one lover.

And there was Tessa's reaction to Digger. Sen had known they'd been neighbors, but had no idea how close before Digger moved away and Tessa left for college. The kiss had been more than a friendly peck. Sen had never experienced jealousy before. The anger tightening his chest mixed with curiosity was new to him. Was he jealous of Digger kissing the woman he was interested in? If yes, it never happened until Tessa. He needed to figure out what it all meant.

Squinting his eyes at the stars as if he could find an answer in the sky, he shook his head and breathed in deeply. Time to bring his mind back to the more pressing problem. They needed to leave before whoever tracked them down again.

First on his list was to check her vehicle for bugs. The model was too old for a GPS. So he searched the interior, front and back, along with the cargo area and beneath the hood. No tracking devices.

He started the SUV to check the gauges. It spit, spluttered, then backfired and died. Damn. He popped the hood again. Using a flashlight he'd found in the cabin's kitchen drawer, he checked for bullet holes. Everything looked fine. No holes in the front end.

Next, he walked around toward the back. He examined the holes, small and big, around the busted back window and cargo door. Then he stooped down and aimed the light toward the gas tank.

The potent smell of petroleum filled his lungs before he covered his mouth. Coughing, he stepped back and his light reflected off a pool beneath the gas tank. One of the bastard's bullets had likely ricocheted off the pavement into the tank. Unlike what television and the movies prefer people to believe, the conventional automobile's gas tank would not explode. The issue was, even if Sen could locate more gas in the shed behind the cabin, the leak would prevent them from getting far. The nearest repair shop was out of range for the amount of gas needed. They were fortunate they'd made it the distance they had.

They needed a ride out of there. Calling a tow truck would be like hanging a neon sign above their heads. People talked, especially about a Whitfield with a female, the Quinn female no less.

No way was he about to call Jake at this time of the morning. He would text instead. A short one would do.

He searched the SUV for his phone. During all of the acrobatics, it had fallen onto the floorboard. The glass was smashed but it flickered on. Most likely the tracking app was useless. All of the brothers tracked each other as a safety factor. The phone acted like it was barely receiving, let alone sending.

He needed it to work well enough to get a couple of texts out. There was no other way to contact someone for help, the cabin didn't have a landline.

Taking a chance, he sent: Wound. Hiding. Cabin. Later.

As soon as he pressed Send sparks flew from the phone. He dropped it. Glass shattered. Did it go through? Fuck it. He had more to worry about and still had Ethan to contact if possible. But how?

Tessa's phone! Of course. He'd seen it inside on the kitchen counter. As soon as he walked in, he snatched it up and went back outside. It barely had a charge. With luck, that should be enough.

Earlier, he'd noticed she didn't have it password protected. Though helpful at this point, he'd have to talk to her about that later. Then he punched in another number— thankfully he had a knack for remembering numbers—and stared at the stars as he listened to the cell phone buzz over and over again.

"Pick up the phone, asshole." Instead, Ethan's voicemail was full and Sen couldn't even leave a message. "I swear he does that to irritate the hell out of me," he muttered beneath his breath. "How fucking easy is it to delete voicemails?"

Taking a deep breath, he punched in a number he wanted to avoid at the moment, but kismet was determined to bring them all together again.

"Tessa?" the deep male voice asked.

How the fuck did he know it was her number?

"It's me. I'm using her phone. It's about to die on me."

"Well, if it isn't Mr. Townsend Whitfield, the fists of fury himself, calling me so soon."

Digger could be such a pain in the ass. Why did Sen stay friends with him, especially when he'd kissed his woman? And dammit, the worst part was—her body language had given it away—Tessa had enjoyed it. Now wasn't the time to dwell on it. So he ignored his asshole of a best friend's comment.

"Fuck you. We need a ride and a place to stay for a few days." He lifted his eyes to the stars.

Digger's voice softened. "Tessa okay?"

"Yeah. And I'm not sharing."

"Ah, man. Some days you don't play fair. It's not like we haven't played before. Maybe you'll change your mind. Have you not thought that she might want it?"

Before Sen realized it, he growled.

What the hell? That was the second time that sound had emerged from his throat in the last twenty-four hours. He never acted liked a damn Neanderthal. He was well-known for being level-headed and in control.

Digger's laughter echoed in his ear.

"Damn, man, you got it bad." Digger choked as if he was

making an effort to stop laughing. He cleared his throat. "Where are you?"

Sen hesitated. Maybe he could find a car to steal from a neighbor.

"Hey, can you hear me?" Concern filled Digger's question.

"Yeah." What was he thinking? He needed to find a way to keep Tessa safe. One thing about Digger's house, it was about the safest place to be in the whole county. She needed a secure place until Sen figured out who was trying to kill him and his brothers. He gave in and provided directions.

"I know where you're at, but I'm on my way to Tennessee presently. I've business to finish later this morning before I can pick you and Tessa up. You should be good there until I arrive in the afternoon."

"We'll make it work. See you then."

"Tell Tessa I'll be there to protect her."

"Fuck you." Sen disconnected the call as Digger cackled. Again, he wondered why he was friends with the bastard.

CHAPTER 15

$\mathcal{A}$ hand gripped her shoulder, almost painfully, and shook her.

Jerking awake, Tessa blinked several times to clear her vision. Darkness greeted her. Heart beating fast, she looked around. Thick curtains covered the window. What time was it? Had the shooter found them? A light from the open doorway lit Townsend's easily recognizable tall, lanky frame near her bed.

He stepped to the side and flipped a light switch.

She shield her eyes for a few seconds until they adjusted to the brightness.

Townsend grimaced. *Sorry.*

It is okay. She signed, *What's the matter?*

We need to get out of here. Our ride should arrive in about an hour. Are you hungry? I've heated up some canned beans I found in the cabin. Not much. Cabinets nearly empty.

She rubbed at her eyes and stretched. *Sure.* Why was she so stiff?

Unmoving, he stared at her.

Frustration pushed her to sit up and then she used her voice. "What are you staring at? Is my hair sticking up? Dried slobber on my chin?"

He slowly shook his head. Then he leaned down, grasped her beneath the arms, gathered her body to his. Her torso skimmed his the whole way to her toes reaching the floor and his mouth taking hers. She melted into his warmth. Finding a little balance, she wrapped her arms around his neck and kissed him back.

Screw morning breath.

Blasted man, he tasted of toothpaste and his skin smelled of fresh soap.

Large hands cupped her ass and pressed her groin to his. The strong vibration from his chest and his mouth heated her blood. Made her remember the day before when Digger said he'd growled. Had he? Sexy.

She rhythmically met the hardness pressing against her mons.

Seconds before she did something stupid, she released her hold. He pulled away at the same time. They gazed into each other's eyes. His chest rose and fell at the same rapid pace as hers.

Sorry, but we need to get ready, Sen signed. *Digger will be here soon.*

He handed her clothes to her and then turned his back.

Okay. He had a good excuse to stop, but sometime they were going to finish this. She tapped him on the shoulder and asked, "Do I have time to take a quick shower?"

He looked over his shoulder and nodded. "*Yeah.*"

After a short time, she'd showered, dressed, and entered the kitchen.

He stood from the table and reached for a pot on the stove.

Beans are ready. The sad look on his face worried her. It sure wasn't because they were going to eat beans for supper. Or was it breakfast?

She glanced out the window, through the open curtains. Rain poured, blurring the view. Vibrations traveled up her legs. The house shook. Thunderstorm.

Another look his way, he still looked concerned about something. Before she could ask what was wrong, he clasped her hand and led her to the table. He was probably worried about whoever was chasing them and how they needed to stay on guard. Making love would make them vulnerable at this point. They needed to keep their minds on protecting themselves. At least, she could spend more time with him. With her free hand, she smoothed down her damp hair, tripping a little behind him. She smiled big. So this was how it feels to be happy and maybe falling in love.

Even the beans smelled lovely.

Before she pulled out a chair, he handed her a spoon and bowl, and nodded toward the stovetop. She dished out a portion and sat at the table. He slid a bottle of soda in front of her.

After blowing on the hot mixture, she tasted it. Nothing fancy, but she tasted several flavors and a little of cayenne pepper. Hot! She gulped down a long swallow of her drink.

Sorry. I meant to warn you, he signed. He brought her hand to his mouth and kissed the tips.

You like spicy food? she signed after regretfully pulling her hand from his.

Hotter, the better. His devilish grin had her blushing.

Well, then. In between smaller bites, she watched Townsend eat with gusto as he wrote on a paper.

What are you writing? She craned her neck, focusing on the words.

He turned the paper around.
She read,

I'll pay for damages.
Sen Whitfield

Damages?
I broke the doorknob.
Oh, okay. She grinned. It had been quite noticeable when they had entered last night.

After her last bite, she pushed the bowl away and sipped on her soda. Full and well-rested, what woman could resist staring at the hot man across the table? The heat in his eyes had her swaying toward him. He reached out and brushed his knuckles across her cheek. She closed her eyes and leaned into his touch. He tapped her cheek and pointed when she opened her eyes. She was facing the window. The view was gorgeous with trees outlining the lawn that spread out to the lake in the distance, misty from the light shower. She bit the side of her upper lip. What a beautiful scene.

She glanced over at Townsend. *What time is it?*
A little after four in the afternoon. He grinned.
You're kidding? I slept fourteen hours? With the clouds and drizzle, it appeared to be early morning, just before dawn.
You had a stressful day. You needed sleep.
No wonder my muscles are sore. Why is it so dark? Bad storms?
Thunderstorm coming through. Will be gone soon.
Tornadoes?
Maybe.
Did you sleep?
Yeah, he answered.
Before she could ask where, he leaped out of his chair,

knocking it backwards. He stooped down, gun in hand, his other hand making motions to get down.

What was going on? She looked around, out the kitchen window, and then caught a movement across the sloping lawn near the trees.

Townsend pointed to the floor and grabbed her ankle. From the seriousness on his face, she understood, and without further hesitation dropped onto the floor and stretched out beneath the table. Her palms spread beneath her, she felt vibrations as glass scattered nearby. Had the person in the truck found them?

Head down, Townsend waddled over to the light switch and turned off the overhead fixtures. Now whoever was outside would have difficulty seeing inside.

She'd seen the damage before the lights went out. As she suspected, someone had fired through the beautiful windows that overlooked the lake. Her eyes adjusted to the dim room. The motion-activated light several yards down the drive near the line of trees should help to spot anyone coming near the cabin. Tilting her head to see around a table leg, she watched another pane fill with holes and cracks spider across the surface without falling out of the frame. That didn't last long. With one more shot, the glass shattered and sprinkled across the floor.

Movement in the room brought her attention back to Townsend. He hurried out of a deep pantry carrying a M110 sniper system.

The only reason Tessa knew about that type of rifle was from her cousin. He'd served in numerous hot spots overseas with the Army Rangers and believed in teaching women about guns in order to protect themselves. He'd been the one to give her the pink Beretta. Thank goodness he had. And besides, she was a southern girl. They learned stuff like that from their fathers, brothers, and cousins, even if they didn't shoot.

She knew that the sniper rifle wasn't normally sold to civilians. How did he know the weapon was there?

As if he felt her staring at him, he looked her way.

What kind of friend owns that?

A dangerous one, he signed after he cradled the rifle. He then lobbed something her way. *Here. Put these on and look away.*

With one hand, she caught what she guessed was a noise-canceling headset as he already had a pair on. What in the world was in that closet? If she got the chance, she would be checking it out. It had to be insane.

She slipped on the headset. Her cousin had warned her that, though she was deaf, the pressure from firing a powerful weapon inside a closed space could hurt and the flash blind her, especially at night. Even her small handgun had bothered her. Luckily she had fired it in intervals. It had been loaded with low-flash ammo, so it hadn't blinded her.

Placing the headset over her ears, she was unable to resist a couple of peeks. The weapon jerked with each shot he squeezed off. Beautiful but deadly. Kind of like Townsend. He probably owned several handguns and rifles, maybe even an assault type or two. No one could stop a Whitfield from finding a black market dealer and purchasing one. She hated that part of his life. The criminal side. He was a good guy deep inside. Closing her eyes and sighing, she hoped she was right.

She no longer felt the vibrations. No new glass sprayed across the floor. It appeared the shooting had stopped for the moment. With less light in the room, and the shooter in the trees, he would be uncertain where they hid in the house, especially without a flare from Townsend's rifle muzzle.

He shoved a table beneath a small, undamaged window

near the back door. Then he set up the rifle with a stand and drew a chair behind it. Taking a seat, he pressed a cheek to the pad near the shoulder stock and adjusted the scope.

Did he see the shooter?

He remained still for several minutes. Her attention never strayed. The headset pinched her ears, so she slipped them off to hang around her neck.

Fascinated by his patience, she took advantage of the respite to drink him in. Even hunched over the gun, his shoulders appeared wide and the faded, navy blue T-shirt he wore stretched over lean muscles. Where had he found a clean shirt? The short sleeves showed off his forearms with a light sprinkle of dark hair. She'd never realized a man's forearm could be so sexy. Dropping her gaze down to his jeans, she admired his fine ass. She bet even bare they would be firm and perfect to dig her heels into.

Not since her time with Digger had she been so aware of such a dangerous man or so obsessed with wanting to have sex with him. Yes, she'd known about Digger's extracurricular activities.

A weird burst of air pressure came from Townsend's direction. She jerked the protective gear over her ears again and shook her head. A cartridge rolled past her on the floor. She looked up and noticed the rifle danced on its stand a little each time he pulled the trigger. He was firing through the glass to the outside. He stopped and sat back, adjusting the headset to hang around his neck as he brought her phone to one ear. What was he doing with *her* phone? She hadn't even thought of texting for help.

He nodded. Obviously talking, as his chin moved, but she couldn't catch the movement of his lips in the dimly lit room.

Turning to face her, he signed, *We need to go. Digger is here.* He reached out a hand.

She carefully crawled out from beneath the table with his

help. A shower of glass fell around her feet. Oh my goodness. She had glass shards on her.

Eyes wide, fighting the panic trying to take over, she stood and stepped away. She leaned over, hands on her knees, to shake her hair. Then she dug her fingers into the strands, checking to make sure all of the glass was gone as she tossed the headset to the side.

Strong hands caught hers.

She lifted her gaze. Townsend shook his head.

Don't rub at your scalp. They will cut. Wait. I'll help soon. First, we must go before someone else shows up.

Okay.

Noticing more glass on her shirt, she shook herself like a dog before Townsend tugged on her hand, leading her toward a door opening into a storage room, opposite side of where she suspected the sniper had set up shop. She snatched up her purse on the kitchen counter on the way out. They rushed through the empty area to the small exterior door on the far wall and exited.

Sitting behind the steering wheel of a large black truck with oversized tires, Digger waved them into the opened passenger side of the cab—lights turned off inside—as his gaze searched the surrounding trees.

She looked around too, but with the storm picking up and wind whipping the heavy sheets of rain, her line of vision had dropped to mere feet. Hopefully, it would keep the shooter from firing on them or following the truck.

Townsend grabbed her by the waist and nearly tossed her inside. The truck's cab had to be four feet off the ground. On her hands and knees, she scrabbled in the rest of the way. She moved over to the center, making room for Townsend.

No sooner than she was settled, he reached across her and pulled the seatbelt over her lap, buckling her in. He did the same with his. Digger shifted the truck into drive. It shot off the cement driveway into a dirt track between large pines. As they talked over her head—she couldn't tell what they were saying even by the light of the dashboard—they bounced and swayed at an ungodly speed. Just as she was about to ask where they were going, Townsend placed his arm across her chest as if she were a child. Before she could protest, the truck slid to a stop. Her chin almost slammed into the dashboard. She patted Townsend's arm, thanking him, as she glanced his way. Then she checked to see why they had stopped so suddenly.

The truck's headlights radiated off a tangle of wet limbs. A massive tree trunk resting on its side blocked their path, and with numerous trees surrounding the area, they would need to back up to the last fork and go down another dirt road. Not unless they preferred walking. In the middle of a storm, that wasn't an option.

Digger twisted around, resting one arm on the back of her seat, and looked out the rear window as he drove nearly as fast in reverse as he had forward.

The back of her head slammed into Digger's muscular biceps when he applied the brakes again. She reasoned it was better than hitting the rear window. When he shifted the gear into drive, Digger glanced down and gave her a wicked smiled, returning his arm to his side. The man enjoyed driving like a crazy man.

Townsend stirred next to her. Then she felt his arm slide over her shoulders as he pulled her nearer. A glance up at his face confirmed what she'd guessed. His jealousy clearly shone from his dark eyes as he stared at his friend. She snuggled against his side, resting her head near his heart, hoping he understood her unspoken feelings. Maybe he did. His heartbeat thumped in double time.

With a tap on his chest, she drew his attention to her hands. *Where are we going?*

With her heart beating a hundred miles per hour, it would take too much concentration to talk.

Digger's place, he signed in the dim dashboard lights.

He turned away and stared straight ahead, squeezing her tighter to his side.

She frowned. For those two were friends, Townsend acted awfully unhappy about it.

CHAPTER 16

"*D*amn, man, you got a boatload of people hunting you." Digger fought the steering wheel to keep the truck on the pothole-riddled, three-wheel dirt track.

"Yeah. I've been told someone has a contract on me and my brothers." Sen rubbed Tessa's upper arm and then squeezed her to his side once again. He would have put her in his lap if it had been safe enough. Her warmth seeped into his body despite the coldness drifting down his spine. Was he making a mistake taking her to Digger's house? Like the voice in his head kept saying over and over again, wouldn't she be better off far, far away from him? He kept preaching it to himself, but he couldn't carry through.

He was a selfish bastard. Yet no matter how much he wanted her, once he was certain no one could harm her because of him, he had to give her a choice: return to the safety of her dad's house or leave town. Either way she'd be out of his screwed up life.

"I bet Jake is fit to be tied," Digger said. "Speaking of people tied, I tried calling Ethan yesterday and couldn't get him to answer." With another jerk of the steering wheel, Digger avoided a deer as it bounded across their path, barely missing the truck's wide grille. "Fuck. I just got this to running again after the last deer I hit."

"I sent a message to Jake last night…this morning, early. Not sure if it went through. Tried calling Ethan, too, but as usual his voicemail is full."

"Your brothers hadn't checked in on you?"

"Humph. A day or so ago. We've all been busy. Anyway, my phone is a goner. It got smashed. I was lucky Tessa's had enough juice to call you." He shifted and pulled out her phone from his back pocket. "I need a charger for hers. I bet her dad's going insane."

"I have plenty at home. Fuck Quinn. Tessa's grown. He needs to get over it." Digger glanced his way. "So you haven't heard the latest about your brothers."

Sen disagreed with Digger's attitude about Quinn. If he had a daughter, he would be tearing the county apart looking for her.

He raised his eyebrows at Digger. "Obviously not."

"Yeah, what I thought." Digger shook his head. "Someone burnt down your big brother's garage night before last. All of the classic cars and bikes are goners. And he got married to a fucking Tally today. Crazy, right?"

That was the news Ethan was probably trying to call him about the other day. Jake did it. Married Angel. Nothing like taking a bullet to keep the peace. Sacrifice was a common occurrence for Sen and Ethan, but unusual for Jake.

"Strange to think of a Tally married to a Whitfield. Yep. Crazy time we're living in." Relief loosened Sen's shoulders. Thank fuck, it wasn't him.

"There was a shooting after the vows were said, and they got the sniper."

"Know who it was?"

"Nope. But your brother and his new bride are okay." Digger shook his head. "Not sure how you Whitfields aren't all dead."

"Fuck you."

"Hey, I'm not wishing, but you fellows have so many people pissed off."

Tessa shifted a little and Sen looked down and signed, *You okay?*

A frown divided her forehead as she stared first at Digger and then him. *Who is crazy?*

It had to be hard to know there was a conversation within inches of her ears, and not be able to hear. And she sure as hell couldn't read anyone's lips well enough with everyone facing forward and the heavy rainclouds outside enveloping them in darkness.

Guessing it was safe in the woods, he turned on the overhead light long enough to sign, and explained what Digger had said.

Her worried eyes glanced up to his.

"There's more," Digger said with a grimace. "They found a body after they put out the fire. They believe whoever killed him set the place on fire."

Sen dropped his hands for a moment, shaking his head. "Damn. Have they identified the body?"

Who's body? Tessa signed.

"Matt Bodine." Digger turned onto a paved county road and the ride smoothed out.

"Big Judd's nephew?" Sen asked as he slowly spelled out the answer for Tessa.

"Yeah."

Sen hated to hear that. Matt wasn't the brightest bulb in the pack, but he did what he was told, and was good-natured about the shit work he was handed most times. He wondered how Big Judd's son, Tick, was taking it. They were not only cousins, but best friends.

"Funny thing was, not only was he burnt to a crisp, but he had two fingers missing." Digger shook his head and glanced over to Sen.

His look confirmed to Sen that he suspected the same group of miscreants. The Savalas mob was notorious for taking body parts, but Sen was unsure if two fingers would interest their killers as souvenirs; they tended to be more gruesome. All of that he kept to himself. No need to upset Tessa with that tidbit.

By the time they turned off the two-lane road and traveled down a long cement driveway, the rain had tapered off. The trees lining both sides thinned out and the truck came to a stop. Well-placed exterior lights showcased the large, red-brick parking area and the pink, blue, and yellow flowers blooming on both sides of double doors. Every time Sen visited, he was amazed it all belonged to Digger. The man wore faded T-shirts with liquor brands printed across the chest and equally faded jeans with holes at the knees. Sure, he'd grown up in an upper-middle-class neighborhood, but this was several steps higher than that.

About ten motorcycles sat beneath a massive oak tree. The flaming skull on the saddle bags of one warned Sen who was waiting inside.

"So Cutter and his crew still hanging with you?" Sen never understood why Digger let the Brothers of Mayhem hang around. They brought nothing but trouble. Kind of ironic considering the trouble following Sen, but it was an exception and not the rule like it was for the MC.

"Yeah. Cutter's chill and he keeps his boys in line, and they know how to party." Digger sauntered into the foyer with its twenty-foot-high ceiling and waved Sen and Tessa on. "Make yourself at home. I'll be right back." He turned down a side hallway that led to his office.

Sen walked into the living room with his hand pressed lightly to the small of Tessa's back. Eyes wide, she peered around, awe brightening her face as she took in the luxurious surroundings.

A long, curvy bar stood before the length of one wall and supported the leather-clad backs of several MC members sitting on stools. Cutter lifted a half empty beer bottle in greeting. Wolf, the club's recently voted treasurer, a lean muscled, much younger man, grinned and waved. Most of the other men he knew slightly. Each nodded and checked out the woman next to him. Sen hooked Tessa's waist and pulled her closer. From the numerous empty bottles on the black marble top, they'd been drinking for a while and that spelled big trouble. Through the back French doors, Sen spotted a few more Brothers standing around talking on phones, or smoking, or both on the large patio and surrounding the large pool. A flash of lightning lit up the tops of pines and oaks at the end of the large backyard.

Sen stopped and faced Tessa to sign close to his chest, not wanting to draw attention.

You need to rest? You want to go to bed? Sen wanted her away from the unruly men.

Are you asking? Her eyes twinkled.

Unable to resist, he leaned down, almost nose to nose, and caressed her cheek. Damn, she was the sexiest woman he'd ever been around. Gutsy, daring—remembering the pink gun she used without hesitation—ferocious, yet so sweet.

"Hey, you two. Get a room." Cutter howled with laughter as if it was an original joke.

Sen straightened and coldly stared at the MC's president.

What's his problem? Tessa rolled her eyes as her hands moved.

He's an idiot. Before Sen signed anything more, Digger returned, carrying a bottle.

"Your favorite wine." He lifted the bottle of chardonnay, showing it to Tessa.

She clapped her hands and smiled. Then she glanced toward the men in the room and then the window. Her shoulders sagged.

Thank you, but I think I need water, regular food, and maybe another shower.

"I didn't catch it all, but I got the gist. We'll save it for later." Digger placed the bottle down on the bar. Eyeing Cutter with uncertainty, he slid it behind a cabinet door under the bar. The bikers were known to drink anything unattended. "Sen, your usual bedroom. Tessa can sleep in the one across the hall." When Sen raised an eyebrow, Digger added, "Or not. Just let me know if there is anything you need."

"You have a charger for a phone?" He held up Tessa's phone.

"Yeah." He reached over to an end table, pulled out a drawer, and tossed a white cord to Sen.

"Thanks." Sen turned to Tessa. *It'll be safer for you to stay in my room. Okay?* Her cheeks turned pink. So adorable. *Don't worry. I'll sleep on the floor.*

Who said I didn't want you in my bed?

Maybe it shouldn't, but that surprised him. They'd kissed and he'd gone down on her. He wanted to take it slow, but he admitted enough was enough. Maybe tonight... Damn, thinking about tasting her again was the wrong thing to do. Having a hard-on in the middle of that crowd would be asking for their relentless heckling.

Okay then. This way. He held out his hand toward the

opposite direction Digger had gone earlier. She walked past, taking in the luxurious surroundings.

He adjusted his cock. Then forced his gaze to stay off her beautiful ass and followed. When they came to the open bedroom door halfway down the corridor, he stepped next to the opening and waited for her to come through. Her hand brushed his groin as she slipped by.

He was in hell.

Had she done it on purpose? Unable to take his eyes off her as she surveyed the room, even pushing down on the mattress, he struggled to control his breathing. Then she looked over her shoulder. Her big smile told the story. Fuck. His cock might explode for real this time.

He hesitated when he heard footsteps behind him. Gritting his teeth, he turned around.

"Hey, wait up. Digger was telling me about your situation. I have some info for you, man." Wolf hesitated, staying in the hallway when he spotted Sen's face.

Sen took a deep breath to mentally work at deflating his cock and temper. The fucker better have solid info to make it worth not diving between Tessa legs in the next thirty seconds.

"Give me a sec. Let me get my lady settled." He jerked his head toward the living room.

"Sure, sure. I'll go back down to the other end of the hall." The young Brother sauntered away.

What's going on? She lowered her hands, her forehead creased in concern, as she walked back to the bedroom door.

Nothing. He needs to tell me something. Go to bed. I'll be there soon. He leaned down and kissed her gently on the lips.

Her eyelashes fluttered and lips parted as she stood head back with a dreamy expression. Then she glanced in the direction Wolf had gone and nodded. She closed the door between them.

His chest ached with such yearning to follow her. But what if Wolf had knowledge of who placed the contract? Then again, the biker's info might involve his old man's death. So much craziness swirled in his head. Determination filled his chest. Somehow, he would make certain his ugly mess never touched Tessa again. Enough was enough.

<<<>>>

As Sen strode by Wolf, he waved his hand toward the French doors. Whatever information the biker had to pass on, he wanted it pronto. No need to waste time. He sure as hell didn't feel comfortable leaving Tessa alone. Especially with Digger in the same house.

He and Digger had done a lot of crazy shit since becoming friends after that bar fight as barely adults. On occasion they drank until neither could stand. They made bets on who could get a certain woman in bed first, and sporadically, they shared one. But through it all, they'd protected each other's back. So he did trust the man with his life. He was uncertain how he felt with the woman who would one day become his wife.

What the fuck?

Hard to believe he even thought that. Only his feelings were different with Tessa. The other women had meant a crazy night of sex, but he wanted more with her. Yeah, wife. Mother of his children, if she wanted them too. Damn.

Besides, he finally understood Digger's late night drunken ramblings about the long-ago, cute young girl. His friend had never divulged the girl's name, but after yesterday, Sen had no problem putting two and two together. It had been Tessa.

On seeing their reaction to each other, Sen realized the ramifications of bringing Tessa around Digger, and possessing a newly discovered jealous streak was no help.

When the hell did that happen? He'd never been proprietorial toward the women he fucked. Women had been a means to an end—released sexual tension—and nothing more. But every time Digger came within feet of Tessa and looked her way, Sen wanted to flatten his nose.

"Sorry, man. Didn't mean to take you from your old lady."

Sen snapped his attention back to Wolf as they moved from where other Mayhem Brothers smoked and talked. They crossed the patio, walking away from the pool to a more private area with an unused fire pit and metal bench.

"She's not—" Remembering he'd referred to Tessa as *my lady*, he decided it best to rush the conversation along. Hell, he liked the possessive word. He sternly regarded Wolf and said with a lift of his chin, "Tell me what you have."

"I went on a run to Atlanta for the prez this week. While there, you know, I bumped into an old buddy." Wolf hesitated and glanced around, making sure no one eavesdropped. Sen made a get-it-rolling motion with his hands. Wolf nodded. "Yeah, right. Anyway, he said Mikolas Savalas's been bragging that the Whitfield boys' days were numbered."

"You think he's behind killing the old men?"

"Doubtful," Wolf said confidently. "He respected the old guys. Same generation and all. The bragging didn't include he was taking over. Anyway, if he'd changed his mind, he would've used his own enforcers, but they've been handling a problem in Nashville. So it has to be someone local with a grudge or someone new. Mikolas doesn't believe you motherfuckers have what it takes to handle your territory." He shrugged.

"How do you know where Savalas's enforcers are?" Wolf had told him nothing new when it came to what the old bastard had or hadn't believed. There was a long line of doubters and Mikolas would need to wait his turn.

"I keep in contact." Wolf grimaced. "They're family. Me and my cousins look out for each other."

"Hell, remind me to never cross you," Sen said, half joking.

Considering Wolf's last name was Savalas and Mikolas was his great uncle, he could easily have asked for a dark favor and seen it done.

Wolf chuckled. "Yeah, my family's fucked up. We can play cops and robbers without any outsiders."

Besides the mafia uncle and cousins, the biker's older brother was formerly an undercover cop, and last Sen had heard, he wore a U.S. Deputy Marshal's star.

Smiling at the good-humored jest, Sen let his gaze drift toward the French doors. Was Tessa finished with her shower? Through the glass, he spotted Digger sauntering toward Tessa's hallway. Where in the hell did he think he was going?

"There's an alphabet chick hanging around Sand City and Marystown," Wolf stated out of the blue.

That grabbed his attention.

"Say what?" He knew for a fact the locals wouldn't ask the Feds for help in their investigation.

"As in FBI. She's been hanging around and snooping into the old men's deaths. Rumor is she also met up with Jake." Curiosity lifted the biker's eyebrows.

He'd have to keep wondering. Sen had no idea what his brother was up to. The man often kept his business close to his chest, and the same for Ethan, and for that matter for himself. The old man had taught the brothers to do what was needed and not talk about it. They were all self-reliant.

"You got a name?"

"Special Agent Alex Carleton."

"Wait. You said chick."

"That's right. Could be short for Alexandra or Alexis." Wolf shrugged as he lifted a blunt and lit it.

"Yeah." Sen wiped his hand across his mouth and narrowed his eyes. "You know where she's staying?"

"Her plain-ass blue sedan has been seen parked at the Mountain High B and B off the interstate."

"I know the owner. Thanks." Sen nodded and slapped Wolf on the back. "Let me know if you hear anything else. Okay?"

"Sure. Give me a few days and I should have more info." Wolf offered Sen a toke.

He shook his head. His mind had to be clear to piece together everything Wolf had said.

"I should be here, but if not, call Digger. He'll know how to get in touch with me."

"Will do." The young biker nodded and ambled over to a small huddle of Brothers.

Sen headed back inside. It wouldn't hurt to have a few days to recover from his wounds. In the meanwhile, Digger better not be disturbing Tessa.

When he reached her bedroom door, hand on the knob, he heard moaning, followed by whispering and more moaning. What the fuck?

The air turned red as he slammed the door open. A picture fell from the wall with a thunk and tinkle of broken glass. He glared at the couple on the bed. Looking all innocent, sitting next to each other at the end of a rumpled bed, Tessa wide-eyed, and Digger with a smirk. Both had clothes on. Nothing undone. Their hair neatly combed.

The moaning started again. Something familiar about it.

His attention rested on the remote in Tessa's hand.

Sen turned. A huge television on the opposite wall showed three bodies writhing on a massive bed. Oh hell no. He stepped in front of Tessa, blocking her view of the screen, and reached for the remote. She twisted away and hid it behind her beneath throw pillows.

What is your problem? Then she placed her hands on her hips and lifted one eyebrow.

Instead of answering her, he grabbed Digger by the shirt, and leaned down into the man's face.

"What the hell are you doing showing her that?"

"Actually, she found the flash-drive in the TV. You know my house isn't kid friendly." The smirk remained on his face.

How many times would it take hitting the asshole before he calmed down? Friend or not, he knew it was no accident she discovered the video.

Tessa slapped at his shoulder. When he ignored her, the next hit jarred his chin. Had the little fireball used her fist? Still clutching Digger's shirt, he scowled at her in warning.

"Let him go." Her face flushed with anger as she continued to speak. Each word said loud and clear. "It was my decision to watch it. I wish I was the girl you and Digger were fucking." She jabbed her chest with a shaking thumb.

A little shocked by her vehemence, he dropped his hold of Digger and straightened. He glanced at the TV and then Digger and then her.

"Hell no," he said and signed, making sure everyone understood his feelings on the subject. Did she not have any idea how he felt when another man touched her?

"I told her you'd say no," Digger leaned back on his elbows at the edge of the bed. "You were always a selfish prick."

The asshole shifted his hips, ensuring Sen noted the bulge in his jeans. Fuck him.

"Leave," Sen growled.

"This is my house." The grin on Digger's face grew, flashing white teeth.

"Leave the room before I decide to gut you." He was certain icicles hung from his lips with his cold tone.

"You could try." Chuckling, Digger stood. "But think about it. She wants it. Better you and me than two other assholes. You know I care for her. It's not like we haven't done this before. If you're worried, even I can tell she wants you more."

Knowing he needed to regain his sanity, Sen remained motionless, except for his fists opening and closing, as he stared at Tessa. She was unlike the perception he'd always had of her. A Goody-Two-Shoes. Naive about what men really wanted. Was that really like how he wanted her? Bringing her down to a level that he would be her superior in experience.

Yet, the thought of watching her coming apart in another's arms tore him in two. Half hating it, but the other half burning with the image of Digger going down on her. The scene had played out many times over the years, but with Tessa in the middle, he almost ignited with hunger. Her beautiful breasts pressed against his chest, her spread legs clasping his hips while Digger drilled her ass. Fuck, they would go wild.

She would like that. She was angel and demon mixed together into the perfect woman. The perfect woman for him. Even a perfect woman for Digger.

Was that why he was acting so unlike his normal self? He'd never been the jealous type. Maybe it wasn't all jealousy but a fight against what he really wanted. He enjoyed threesomes. Women benefited from having more than one man at a time. It ensured they had several orgasms. Maybe it was also the wickedness of it all. It was mind-blowing.

He was recognizant of Digger fucking men too. Sen fucked only women, but whenever they shared, he was aware Digger often took advantage and rubbed against him. There were other times it couldn't be avoided. Being truthful, he admitted it added to the spice.

He groaned when Tessa reached down, cupped and squeezed his semi-hard dick. Damn.

Her face confirmed how desperate she was for his touch.

"Fine. Come back in twenty minutes," Sen said to Digger, his gaze on Tessa's face. "But make sure she still wants both of us." She needed more time to think it over. He wanted no doubt she was all in.

When the only sound in the room was the "home" video, he looked up to make sure Digger was still there and had heard. The man smirked. Asshole knew he'd won. Sen wasn't fooled, the man had planted it for Tessa to find.

Tessa released his hard dick to move away. Without looking her way, he covered her hand and showed her how to stroke him through the material.

Digger looked at Tessa and back to Sen. "She won't change her mind. I'll be back." His friend strolled out, softly clicking the door closed.

He moved his hand from hers and signed, *Do you have any idea what you're talking about?* With each word, he struggled with the frustration rolling through him.

She narrowed her eyes and jerked her hand back. *You're a coward.*

Damn, she was something, all spit and vinegar.

Just make sure this is what you want. He jabbed a finger at her chest. *What about birth control?*

Got it covered. I swear. I have a IUD. She held her hand up like a Vulcan on Star Trek.

That's not what that means.

You get the idea. Besides I'm not a Boy Scout.

Yeah. But to keep you safe, we'll use condoms.

So you'll cover it.

Smartass. A huge grin broke through his sober mood.

Better than a dumb one, she teased back.

Damn, he loved it when she was sassy. Unable to resist any longer, he attacked.

Then it wasn't until he had her spread out on the bed, naked, holding her wrists to the mattress, he realized his solid as steel dick hung out of his jeans. The woman had unzipped and pulled him out.

He released her and quickly stripped the rest of the way. Then he leaned down for her to catch each movement of his lips.

"I'm going to fuck you so hard, you're going to taste my dick in your throat," he said slowly.

"Yeah, right," she said, taunting him further by leaning up and nipping his bottom lip. Her green eyes bright as if from a fever caused by anticipation. "In your dreams, big boy."

He ran his tongue over the pounding tender skin. No blood. A bit of a surprise.

"Shut the fuck up," he said before bending down to take her mouth. His tongue dived in, immersing his senses with her flavor. Sweetness and a bitterness from the beer she'd had earlier twined with the scent of lavender in her hair. This woman wasn't afraid to make it known what she wanted. Her bravery and sassiness were bigger turn ons than the thought of sharing her with his best friend. Bottom line, he would do anything to ensure her happiness and the possibility of staying with him forever.

CHAPTER 17

A short distance from his bedroom, hands on the wall, Digger pressed his forehead against the sheetrock. The coolness helped his oncoming headache. Damn, he wanted his friend and his friend's girl. As a kid, he'd been taught a hard lesson. Just because he wanted something didn't mean he deserved it. No matter how much he lusted after Sen, he couldn't make Sen feel the same way. He was satisfied they'd learned to compromise.

Anyway, he could dream.

Years ago, he'd come to terms with his feelings for both sexes. He understood Sen didn't travel the same road. That was okay. Not only was the man his best friend, but he owed his life to him. Drinking buddies. Business pals. Every aspect of a friendship including his being the second of a threesome, fucking a beautiful woman between them.

To think of it, Tessa was the perfect solution to his dilemma. Sen was falling for her. Digger already loved the girl—no, correction—woman. Sharing her with Sen made sense. Besides, he loved watching Sen fuck. The man had moves. There were always moments they touched, rearranging the female between them, fucking the same hole or different ones an inch or so apart. He likened it to a game. Touch just enough, but not overaggressively and pissing off his best friend.

He rubbed his lengthening cock beneath the denim. Unable to hold back the half smile, he closed his eyes. Two of his favorite people were in his bed. Fuck yes.

Digger grinned. He straightened, rearranged himself in his jeans, and headed toward a room in the back of the house where he stored a few toys and plenty of lube. He had a feeling it would be hours, maybe days, before they got each other's fill. Then maybe he could show Sen how this trio could be perfect for each other.

CHAPTER 18

Tessa arched into Townsend's embrace. His hard body heated every inch of hers. He cupped her face and covered her mouth with his. She brushed her hands over his chest, along his ribs, up his arms, exploring the muscles she'd admired for days. Feeling daring, she dipped a hand past his stomach until she squeezed his scorching, hard cock.

His chest vibrated against her breasts.

The corner of her lips tilted up.

Maybe she was crazy to push him to do something so wild and naughty, but the two men had played important roles in her life and fantasies. Just one time, she wanted to experience what she only imagined. It actually felt empowering. It was odd what a person could find on the internet, especially on social media, about their hometown. She'd read the rumors about Townsend and Digger and their exploits, in particular of the sexual kind. Those were the kind many of the women in Marystown were interested in and tempted by. Considering the aura of danger surrounding their fine, hard bodies, what confident, sane woman could resist the opportunity?

While stroking his enticing girth, she nipped at his tongue and laughed when she felt what she imagined was his growl. She ran her tongue across his bottom lip, swollen from her earlier bite. Her own kind of apology.

A tad nervous—how would she handle the sensory overload?—she released her hold and peeked up between her lashes at his expression. Her pulse increased when he narrowed his eyes and thrust his hips, reminding her to continue her caresses. Happily, she ran her hand along his cock down to his balls and gently squeezed.

Her chest rose and fell almost as fast as her heart rate. She pushed him away and slipped off the bed, shedding her clothes in record time. She grinned at the mixture of excitement and lust crossing Townsend's face. He'd always appeared to be a private person, his countenance so unreadable. That was, until they were alone. For whatever reason—did he let her see?—she could read his emotions when it was just the two of them. His earlier reluctance had changed to anticipation and her forwardness in wanting sex with him and Digger had heated his expectation. She'd wanted what their other women had experienced.

Over the years, she'd learned if she wanted something bad enough, it was up to her to go after it. Too many chances were lost when she hesitated.

She took her time in folding her top and jeans. Funny, she'd always imagined this part would be where they would tear each other's clothes off in a heated rush. Instead, they nonchalantly watched the other strip. So cool and collected. That was when she realized her hands were shaking. Maybe she was more than a tad nervous.

Townsend had always fascinated her, but her boring, book-obsessed self with her overbearing father certainly kept most men away. Then add in her profession and being deaf—some ignorant people acted as if it was catching or treated her as if she was stupid. Anyway, who would have imagined gorgeous Townsend Whitfield, enforcer, collector, all-round bad boy, would be interested in her? She was aware he normally stayed away from so-called good girls, especially those on the wealthy side of town. Considering the Whitfields lived in a brick monstrosity on the edge of that same town, he technically belonged in their affluent category. But the daddies of the debutantes would never accept him as marriage material because of his father and his heritage. Ignorant people. He was his own man.

Sighing, she paused to soak in the moment and the sight of his ripped body as he stretched out on his side. The bandages on his left arm only enhanced the other scars on his torso, presenting the body of a barbaric man. Oh, she liked that. A lot.

She should be ashamed. He'd gone through so much. The life he lived caused those scars. He deserved compassion and she did feel sympathy, but...he was still hot. He'd already proven he didn't want pity. for goodness sakes, he did want her.

Unable to resist, her gaze continued over his wide, defined chest. Ripples flowed down his torso as he inhaled. Beautiful. His stomach curved in and his boxer briefs dropped slightly, revealing the deep slashes of his Adonis belt and the tip of his cock peeking over the elastic band. A twinge of arousal gripped her stomach and shot down between her legs, taking away her breath for a second.

No, she didn't care what anyone thought. Townsend was the hottest man she'd ever been around, and if everything worked out, she would have the second hottest man join them.

You don't have any tattoos, why? she signed, tilting her head in curiosity.

My mom disapproved of them. He shrugged, giving her a lopsided grin.

How sweet. It said a lot about a man who kept his dead mother's wishes.

Turn. I want to see your tattoo, he instructed.

How did he know about her tattoo?

Digger. He probably told him.

She turned and arched her back, sticking her butt out, making sure he could see every colorful inch of the butterfly across her lower back. Looking over her shoulder, she soaked in the hungry look he gave her. She wanted to lick him from chest to cock.

A flush of heat flowed down her face and neck. The last couple of years, she'd sat on the sidelines and watched other girls have a shot at the dangerous duo. She didn't care what people thought or said, she deserved the experience.

While growing up she'd sat on the sidelines and watched people have so much fun. Her first daring move had been to make Digger her lover between high school and college. It had only been the last year she finally pushed herself to really experiment. Her time away at collage had helped her self-confidence, and she'd promised herself to say yes more often.

She finished stripping off her underwear and neatly folded them with her clothes, hidden in-between the layers on the nearby chair. Old habits were hard to abandon even when she was keyed up.

Her gaze returned to his.

Townsend's crooked smile took her breath away. He'd peeled off his briefs. His cock was beautiful, long and thick enough to satisfy any woman.

What happened to all the air around her? She had never understood the concept in novels. That was, until seeing him up close the other night for the first time in a year—and that was with clothes on—and again now while he was definitely naked. Goodness, she had to look away for a moment to regain her breath and let her face cool.

He waved his hand to grab her attention back to him. The smirk on his lips said he'd been trying to get her attention for a moment or more.

Crooking his finger for her to come to him, his devilish grin tempted her to obey every word and gesture.

Get on the bed. Hands and knees, he signed.

His dark hair had fallen over one eye, adding to his wicked looks. Oddly, he reminded her of an anime character she had the hots for as a teenager. Coincidence? Probably not.

Maybe she was allowing her imagination to get away from her.

We can leave him out of this, she signed back, referring to Digger. She lifted her eyebrows, letting him see she was sincere.

Why? Have you changed your mind? He sat up, his big, sexy feet landing on the floor.

Wow. Her brain was melting as he gracefully stood—still naked—and pointed to the bed. So freaking gorgeous. He signed something more, but she didn't watch his hands. Her gaze stayed glued to his cock.

Anyway, she understood what he wanted.

Pulling her attention back to his face, she managed to sign, *No. I want you and Digger. But I don't want to force you to accept it.*

He rolled his eyes. She'd never seen him do that before.

Once again, he pointed at the bed. She crawled into position, a little nervous, but crazy enough, fighting a grin.

Sure, she was a little embarrassed by the vulnerable pose, all exposed from her ass cheeks to heaving breasts. It hadn't been awkward to show him her tattoo, but that was different from waiting for a man to fuck her. He certainly was getting a closer look now.

A cool breeze stroked her skin. She looked over her shoulder.

Digger had reentered the room and stood next to Townsend. Already stripped and ready for action, his body was a little thicker than Townsend's, but still well-muscled. He stood maybe a couple of inches taller than Townsend's six-foot. His brown hair, tipped blond by the sun and slightly wavy, reached his shoulders. The edges of his lovely light blue eyes crinkled with excitement, revealing how pleased he was by her position.

Tessa found Townsend's dark eyes mysterious, and at the moment, they looked as if his soul shone through their depths. A warmth enveloped her heart and the apex of her legs. Two men she cared for intensely, who were determined to provide her with her crazy fantasy, were ready to fulfill all her fantasies.

It's important for you to let us know if you feel uncomfortable at any time. We'll stop. Townsend waited for her to nod. *Now, face the headboard.*

Townsend walked around the bed as he fisted his cock and stroked, stopping beside her.

Swallowing deeply, she shut her gaping mouth and did what he directed. He was so sexy, hot, banging, or whatever term her lust-filled mind could think up.

A movement in the corner of her eye brought her attention to Digger. He'd followed Townsend's lead, but circled to the other side.

Another deep swallow of air helped her lightheadedness. If she hadn't, she'd certainly hyperventilate in the next few seconds.

A slap to her ass vibrated through her body. She glared

over her shoulder at Townsend. She was beginning to feel outnumbered—glancing at each man—she mentally added, but in a good way.

Townsend's dark eyebrow lifted, and he calmly signed, *Look straight ahead.*

This was what she'd wanted. A fantasy come to life. Something she could mark off her bucket list. So she grudgingly did what he said. Besides, if they didn't hurry, she might attack both of them.

Hands touched her back and smoothed down her ribs to a trembling ass cheek. From the romances she'd read of reverse harems, the men would talk dirty, or encouragingly sweet, or both to the woman to help her relax. Since that wouldn't work as well for her, their light caresses and pinches helped. She closed her eyes, immersing herself in their sensual touches. One callused hand slipped under her and cupped a breast, fondling playfully before carefully squeezing. Tingles brought goose bumps up and down her whole body. Her pussy clenched. Then a hand traveled down her stomach and grazed between the moist folds below.

The bed dipped on both sides as warm bodies pressed against her thighs. They surrounded her with warmth as rough hair from brawny arms and legs stroked her skin. A hard cock glided along, leaving a thin trail of pre-cum along an ass cheek, alerting her to his readiness for more.

Someone gathered up her hair and arranged it to one side. Lips and teeth kissed and nibbled her neck and shoulder. Townsend. She recognized his ocean breeze smell. Funny, she hadn't consciously realized that about him. She wanted to ask if it was his cologne, or soap, or just him. Lips pressed to her bare shoulder. That answer would have to wait.

Hands continued to knead, tug, dip, and pinch different highly sensitive parts until her arms and legs shook. The world disappeared as her body drifted on the sensations they created.

A warm mouth covered her pussy from behind. She gasped with pleasure as a tongue laved her clit and then thrust into her. When her body tightened, about to climax, Townsend lifted her away and placed her in his lap. No! She slammed a fist into his shoulder. He smiled and then laughed at her when she began signing how she felt about him stopping.

You'll like this better, his hands moved.

A couple of adjustments and they were in the center of the bed. She looked down. His cock stood straight up against his taut belly. He had nothing to be ashamed of, for sure.

With a crook of his thumb, he lifted her chin.

Are you still okay? He raised his eyebrows as he waited for her confirmation.

She nodded.

Digger sat on the edge of the bed and handed a condom to Townsend.

Her gaze drifted over to her old lover. He'd already covered his length. He touched her cheek and she followed his lips as he said, "Are you ready?"

Digger's cock was as beautiful as she remembered. Since their time together, she had realized he was a bit over average, but not uncomfortably so. Unable to resist, she leaned over and kissed his delicious lips. Digger clutched her hair at the nape of her neck and crushed her mouth to his as if he was thirsty for her taste. The flavor on his lips and tongue confirmed he'd been the one between her legs a moment earlier.

Townsend's big hands covered her breasts and squeezed firmly enough for her to cut her eyes toward him.

The tongue-dueling kiss continued but her attention was split as Townsend's fingers trailed down her sides. Without pause, he lifted her, breaking the kiss as he notched his cock to her opening, and then slammed her down the hard length. Heat and fullness took her breath, causing her to gasp.

Thank goodness her body had been prepared for what she'd craved so badly.

Digger leaned over, grasped the hair at the back of her head, and kissed her again, thrusting his tongue deep into her mouth as if laying claim to her.

Needing air, she jerked her lips away, tossing her head back toward Digger's grip, saving her hair from being wrenched out. He released his hold and caressed her cheek. His blue eyes glinted with excitement before he eased behind her.

Then Townsend wrapped his arms around her and crushed her sensitive nipples to his chest. Her upper body on top of his and her knees spread to each side of his hips. His body stretched out beneath hers, keeping them attached. She didn't have to guess what would happen next. A slippery, thick finger inserted into the tight ring so close to where Townsend's cock throbbed in her pussy.

Thankfully, Digger had come prepared with lube.

It stung, but still felt so good. When his second and then quickly his third well-lubed finger thrust in, she groaned. Cool lube poured around the enlarged tiny hole brought a little relief from the stretching. The two men stopped their caresses. She opened her eyes to see what was holding them up. Their gazes met hers, concern clearly on their faces.

"Good," she said, knowing the two men couldn't care less about the sound of her voice, especially at that moment.

Townsend's crooked grin fired up her heartbeat. He was so beautiful.

Digger's warm torso slid against her back and then his cock sank gradually into her ass.

She whimpered. Exciting pain-pleasure flowed over her

entire body. Then he began to pull out and carefully push back in until the lube heated, giving her a little relief from the ache. Then his cock was completely in and he began a rhythm with Townsend. They pumped in sequence, one in, one out. The fullness engulfed her with all kinds of feelings. Fulfillment, gratitude, need, and a wantonness she unknowingly possessed. She never remembered being so desired as she felt in that moment between the two men. What a heady feeling.

Too many times in her life she'd fought the belief she might be less than other women. But always her inner consciousness screamed she was enough. Maybe more than enough. Maybe she was so much of a woman she needed two men. Not just any two men, but two specific ones. Her decision helped to confirm her self-doubt of the past was all a trick of the mind. She was all-powerful. She wanted two strong, dangerous men, and they wanted her. She was in control. There was no doubt in her mind that if she suddenly said no to their actions, they would stop, all from concern for her well-being. That was power. She felt better than she'd ever.

Having the right man wanting her, bringing her to the pinnacle of satisfaction made the difference. Having two men was a bit overwhelming, but a perfect solution to quell her self-doubt. Her mind, body, and soul were in heaven.

Hands constantly moving, caressing, tugging in all the right spots brought her quickly to a climax. The waves shook her from head to toes. The men kissed her shoulders, cheeks, arms, neck, never letting up as her pussy and ass squeezed their cocks.

Then she finally felt the men tense as their thrusts sped up, pounding into her.

Would she be able to walk or sit tomorrow? She didn't care. Well worth it. Then they tightened their hold on her hips and waist, slowing their movements. More bruises. Still okay.

Not realizing she'd closed her eyes, she gradually opened them and stared into Townsend's dark depths. Such tenderness shone back at her. She leaned forward and licked his full lower lip. Their mouths meshed as they tasted each other. Whiskey and heat.

A pulsing in her ass announced Digger's climax. She winced when he eased out of her, but she didn't stop kissing Townsend's wicked mouth.

With one arm securely around her, Townsend pulled her on top of his body and he brought his knees up, keeping her in one spot. His cock remained inside her. It felt right.

Their lips separated and she rested her head in the crook of his neck.

Minutes passed before she looked around for Digger. The room was empty. Sadness mixed with a strange relief crept over her as she nuzzled Townsend's heated skin.

Had Digger regretted their lovemaking? He'd climaxed. Why hadn't he stayed with them and cuddled?

Remorseful that her first time with Townsend included a threesome…no, not really remorseful, but worried a little. Yet, she enjoyed the wild sex. She hoped to enjoy many more interludes—she smiled at that word—before she left this house. Once she returned to what she now thought of as the real world, she'd find a way for Townsend to understand he was her main interest. Digger had been her first lover and he would always be special to her, but she wanted Townsend to be her last.

CHAPTER 19

Sen stretched his legs and then rested one over Tessa's. His hands roamed over her silky smooth back. Heat and desire flickered over his senses with her breasts flattened against his chest. Her nipples were taut. He wanted to suck on them again until she arched into him and spread her legs in a silent plea for more.

Maybe in a few minutes his stamina would return. In the meanwhile, he'd hold her, memorize the softness of her skin, the warmth of her supple body.

Her breathing tickled his neck. He sighed. What a sap. He was smiling at the ceiling. If his brothers saw him wallowing in post coitus, they would never let him live it down.

He lifted strands of Tessa's hair and inhaled. Like sunshine and lavender.

The last few days at Digger's, they'd partied, had sex, both one-on-one and threesomes. Tessa acted as if she couldn't get enough of him and Digger. Hell, how long had it been since he indulged in such a marathon?

By yesterday evening, he had enough of sharing and kicked out Digger from the man's own guest bedroom. He'd

"

wanted Tessa to himself. He knew their time together was coming to an end. She'd talked with her father using Digger's burner phone. The old man demanded she return home, or at the very least, to work.

She'd misled Quinn into believing she'd left Sen days ago to his own devices and had gone to visit friends in Birmingham. There, she claimed, someone had stolen her car and phone. She'd added they'd found the SUV the next day a total wreck and had reported it to the insurance company.

Though the truth was she hadn't reported it. No need to involve the police. Sen had promised to replace her a car. Her pangs of conscience about lying to her father was soothed a little.

In truth, he refused to think she claimed those lies because she was ashamed of being with him. Instead, she was saying it to keep her father from blaming him for what all happened. He would go ballistic on hearing people were shooting at them. It would be hard to explain the bullet holes. All of it happening because of Sen and his family. And heaven forbid Quinn learn she'd been shooting back.

Actually, he understood her father cared about her, and she lied mainly to stay with him. For a good girl like her to lie to a dad she loved had to mean Sen was someone special. He never had a person to care so much or worry about what other people thought of him.

Nothing like his old man. Dick Whitfield had never worried about Sen or his brothers' whereabouts or how they received a bullet or knife wound. For that matter, the only time he acted as if he cared was when they had screwed up a job. Maybe if the old man had a daughter, it would've been different.

Sen was happy to spend more time with Tessa. They were safe at Digger's compound. He wanted her any way he could keep her for now. Tessa had guts. From what he'd seen so far, she could handle her old man.

He gave her a light squeeze as he kissed the top of her head and quietly chuckled.

The woman not only had guts, but a sex drive that rivaled his. Before daybreak, they'd gone at it again. Without Digger. She'd whimpered a couple of times while he hammered into her. Not from pain—she had murmured "more"—but from a massive orgasm. Fuck, how had his heart not stopped?

She looked up and grinned. "Morning."

"Morning to you."

Unable to resist, he swiped his tongue over the sexy freckles on her cheeks and kissed the top of her nose. How could they taste sweet like brown sugar?

Squeezing her eyes for a second as she shook her head, she smiled even wider before she wiggled off the bed and ran to the bathroom. Damn, seeing that sweet peach-shaped ass brought on an urge to take a bite.

Tranquility seeped into his bones as he listened to the running water. It was one of her funny habits. She turned on the faucet while she peed. She didn't like thinking people could hear her. Considering what all they'd done and been through, her little habit was endearing. Who had taught her that?

He chuckled again when he heard the faucet water stop and the shower come on. One day he'd tell her the shower made more noise than the sink.

Every moment he spent with her, he wanted more of her.

When would their luck run out? Was she really safe with him? Any minute things could go to hell and she could be hurt.

His eyes closed. Damn, he would protect her with his life.

Stretching, he yawned. The woman had worn him out. Pure indolence caused his body to sink into the soft mattress.

A shuffle woke him. Unsure how long he'd dozed, he blinked to clear his vision. A delightful view came in focus and roused his body. Tessa stood in the middle of the room in a towel wrapped from breasts to knees. Digger supplied his bathrooms with beach-towel-sized ones.

After crossing his arms beneath his head on a stack of pillows, Sen watched from the bed as Tessa dropped the cloth and pulled on underwear and then a pair of jeans Digger had somehow uncovered in her size. The overlarge, tie-dyed blue-and-aqua T-shirt obviously came out of Digger's closet.

The question of where the redneck got the underwear and jeans ate at his brain. Had Tessa been there before? Before he could ask, shouts echoed from the other side of the house. Then the doorknob jiggled.

He reached for the gun on the nightstand. His fingertips merely grazed the grip when Digger burst into the bedroom and slammed the door shut.

"You two might want to get your shit together. The FBI will be here any second. The MC's spotter just notified Cutter and they're clearing out the back way."

The MC didn't trust any government alphabet not to harass or arrest their members. Besides, too many of the men carried firearms illegally—past felony charges—and had narcotics, or outstanding warrants.

"How does he know it's FBI?" Sen asked as he signed for Tessa to get her stuff together, trouble was coming. Damn, he was getting good at this ASL stuff. He jumped out of bed, naked and uncaring. Hell, everyone in the room had seen all there could be seen of each other.

"A female agent has been pestering Jake." Digger bit off each word with frustration.

"Alex Carleton," Sen said with a grimace. He jabbed each

leg into his pants, glaring at no one in particular, merely the situation.

"They said it was a woman." Digger tossed Sen a clean shirt.

"I thought a dude too. Alex is a woman. If she's already harassed Jake, I'm sure he's told her some bullshit to throw her off whatever she's looking for. There isn't any reason for the FBI to be involved in the old men's death." Sen had been recently apprised by an informant about the special agent snooping around Marystown.

He hadn't heard anything from his brothers about it, and it would be unusual for a Whitfield to deal straight with the government. The family had too many illegal operations to trust nothing would be leaked at some point if a government agent hung around.

"Fuck, man. You Whitfields are demented."

"Pot, kettle, black." Sen pointed at Digger and himself.

Digger chuckled and then his forehead wrinkled as he squinted his eyes. "I'm guessing you're not running with your tail between your legs like my other guests."

"Nope."

"What about Tessa?" Concern washed over each word.

Sen contemplated his best friend. Was he in love with Tessa too? Did it matter? Digger could be trusted. Yet, an urge flowed through him to shoot the man in the head despite their years of friendship. The last few days had been crazy and he needed time to think it all through. One moment he was okay with seeing Digger and Tessa making out and fucking—it was hot as hell—and then next he wanted to yank her out of his arms and beat the hell out of him. Yeah. He was insane.

"Stay with her and make sure she doesn't leave the bedroom. No need to put her on the FBI's radar. I'm taking her home this afternoon."

Digger's head bobbed. "Yeah. Good idea. It's getting crazy out there." He glanced over at Tessa and flashed her a smile. His obvious attempt to keep her from worrying.

What is going on? Tessa then placed her hands on her hips, her glare moving from Digger to Sen.

Maybe too obvious.

Some unwanted company. It's best you stay hidden until we leave for your dad's.

Her eyes narrowed and she raised her middle finger.

Dammit. Sen snorted, cutting his eyes at Digger who was laughing his ass off. Then he signed, *Please*, to Tessa.

For a few seconds, he held her gaze. Then her shoulders dropped. After a quick nod, she grabbed her purse and pulled out her pink gun, checked the clip before tossing it back in.

He loved her attitude, but resisted the urge to show it. Sen placed a hand on the doorknob and slowly opened the bedroom door, keeping his back to her to hide his lips' movement. "If the agent's here for me, for some stupid-ass reason, and takes me into custody, you get Tessa gone."

"No worries, bro."

Then Sen closed the door behind him with a firm click.

CHAPTER 20

"What can I do for you, Special Agent Carleton?" Sen strode to the bar and leaned over it, grabbing a couple of glasses and then a half empty bottle of Jack Daniel's. He poured a shot and lifted it to her.

The blonde woman stood in the middle of the room acting as if she had the right to be there. She wore a cheap navy blue suit with a white shirt and red tie. Despite her shitty taste in clothes, she was nice looking, her body had all of the right curves.

"I need to speak to you," Agent Carleton said, unsmiling.

"Digger hides his good stuff, but Jack is good when you need a nip." His eyebrows rose in question as he again lifted the glass.

She wandered by the sectional couch, manhandling the odds and ends sitting on tables, while taking in the disorder left behind by the Brothers. Sen gritted his teeth as he glanced around surreptitiously for any forgotten illegal substances. Last thing he needed was a drug rap.

"No. I'm on duty." She crossed her arms over healthy-sized boobs. "Do you need alcohol so early in the afternoon, Mr. Whitfield?"

Shivers almost shook his body. He hated it when people called him that. It made him think of his old man. "Whitfield will do." Normally, he'd suggest Sen—Townsend was only for Tessa and Miss Jimmy Sue—but something told him she wasn't the type of woman he wanted to be on a first-name basis. He drained the glass, the liquid burning going down. "Alcohol comes in handy when I have to deal with objectionable situations."

"What is objectionable in meeting with me?" Her well-trimmed brows rose. "I'm sunshine in a suit." The grin she gave was evil to say the least.

"Wherever the FBI go, they seem to stir up trouble." He craved another swig of the whiskey, but keeping his senses would be for the best.

"That's one way of looking at it. The way I see it is, we hunt for those who cause trouble."

Frustration built in Sen's gut. He wanted Tessa miles from the suffering the agent appeared to have planned for the Whitfields.

"What trouble are you tracking here?"

"Actually, I figured I'd ask if you wanted the same deal as your brother?" The crooked grin on her face warned she was as vicious as he'd sensed.

"What deal?" He suspected the answer, but wanted to hear her version.

Jake had once talked about playing the long game and offer the FBI evidence against others to have his record cleared. To go legal. Sen had told him no. Besides, it wouldn't work. No one should believe a word out of a special agent's mouth. Only the higher ups could offer such a deal and their small outfit wouldn't be worth the trouble. It would be easier to just shut them down.

The agent slid a hand inside the jacket, flashing a holster and gun beneath.

Sen stood straight, prepared to duck and grab the gun in his back belt holster. Thank goodness Digger had thought to hand it to him while he'd dressed.

She slipped a long envelope out of her interior pocket.

"Here's the evidence you'll need to track down the people who killed your old man."

What the hell? Then it struck him. If she knew, she wouldn't bother with the Whitfields. She would arrest the man or men and take all of the glory.

"Same evidence you provided to my brother?" He'd tried calling Jake last night after he spoke with Wolf, but without success. Tessa's phone wouldn't even connect to voicemail. He wasn't sure if it was the tower or her phone screwing up.

"Yeah. Same." She eyed him with suspicion.

"Are you so sure my brother'd do anything to harm this family and our organization?" Gambling wasn't his favorite activity, especially when it involved jail time or their lives.

She chuckled, not a nice one, and leaned against the bar. "I've been told to watch out for you three. That you guys are dangerously smart. But if you were truly such geniuses, you'd provide me a list of your suppliers. It would be the first step to becoming legit."

Over his dead body. The Whitfields along with the Tallys were the only reason the county's crime statistics hadn't exploded like many in Alabama. Keeping out the big crime syndicates was their number one issue.

Before he could answer, a mobile phone rang. Hers. She palmed it out of her pants' pocket and frowned.

Damn. He spotted Tessa peeking around the corner of the hallway. Digger pulled her back just as the agent looked up from her screen, barely missing the sight of Tessa.

He nodded toward her phone. "Time for you to skedaddle?"

Did he actually say skedaddle? Maybe he better not drink anymore whiskey. Lately, he'd drank more alcohol than he had in years. Between booze and sex, he was so loose he wasn't weighing every word coming out of his mouth like he usually did. Touching his face, he confirmed he was smiling. So out of character for him.

It was all Tessa's fault. Seeing her for a mere moment was enough to brighten his mood. During his time with her, despite the danger and being shot at, nothing bothered him. Tessa had shown she wanted him as much as he wanted her. Damn, that thought felt so fucking good.

"There you go, another Whitfield brother hurting my feelings," she said with sarcasm. "Trying to push me out the door."

As if she had feelings to hurt.

"But yet, you're still here." Rudeness to women didn't come naturally to him, but he wanted her gone.

Her mouth straightened in a line of irritation. "We have the man who shot at you the other day in custody."

"No one shot at me." Who had told her about the assassin's attempt? Did she know about the contract out for him and his brothers? He and his brothers sure as hell didn't require the FBI's help.

"Uh-huh. I've been told there's a contract out on your head."

So she knew. Someone locally had been talking. The old man's cousins, Rat Boy and Teddy Bear? That sounded like them. He could ask, but it was unlikely she would give them up.

"I never said I was popular." He rested a hip on a barstool. "Is that all, Special Agent Carleton?"

She stared at him for a few seconds.

Expressionless—he made sure of it—he stared back.

"Fine. All you Whitfields are assholes." She handed him a business card. "Call me when you want a deal. And officially report the shooting. I'm sure your pawn shop manager would appreciate it."

No worries there. Despite threatening to fire him, the man who ran it had been with the family for more than twenty years. Sen had already made a call and set everything to rights, the broken glass and all.

With a long sigh, she turned toward the front door. "I guess I'll…what did you call it? Oh, yeah, skedaddle."

He followed her to the front door and locked it behind her. Peeking out of the narrow beveled glass lining the doorframe, he frowned as she strode to the unmarked sedan.

That was too easy. What was she up to?

CHAPTER 21

Tessa glared at the door after Townsend strode out of the bedroom to the FBI agent. He'd ordered her to stay. She didn't like the hard stare he gave her. What did he think? That she was house-trained and would follow his every order?

Digger cupped her cheek and grabbed her hand, pulling her attention to his smiling face. A guilty twinge shot through her.

He treated her as if she was number one in his life when they were together. She should never feel guilty about enjoying the two men. She loved them both, but Townsend edged out Digger when it came to her emotions. Digger enjoyed bed-hopping too much. She'd come to terms with that during that special summer.

And there he sat beside her, trying to keep her mind off Townsend's unexpected guest. Though Digger's handsome face fascinated her, her gaze returned to the door.

Once again, he turned her face until she noticed his lips moving as he spoke to her, *"I don't know what you're thinking, but it's best to stay here with me."* Then a devilish grin spread across his face. He leaned in and kissed her.

His tongue skimmed her bottom lip. Heat engulfed her whole body. She opened her mouth enough for him to thrust inside, causing her heart to flutter and her pussy to tingle. The vibration from his humming brought a smile to her lips while they still kissed. She'd forgotten his little habit. It was sexy and endearing. Her fantasy hadn't come to an end yet, despite the real world interfering in their idyllic time.

With a light push, she leaned over Digger and rubbed her hand over his hard cock. Nothing more of a turn on than a man hardening beneath her touch. He started to sit up but she shook her head and pressed his shoulders to the bed. Within seconds, his jeans were unsnapped and the zipper down. His tight red briefs surprised her. When they were younger, he'd been a commando type of guy. The fire-engine red underwear he wore was actually hot on his narrow hips, his large, long cock pulsing against her dancing fingers.

Again, he tried to sit up, probably to tell her something she didn't want to know.

Following the blond trail beneath his waistband, she clasped his hard length and swiped her tongue around the crown, heat and silk over a rock-hard cock. His whole body jerked. A quick glance ensured he was okay. His eyes were closed and mouth open, broad chest and flat stomach rising and falling rapidly, as if he was working on regaining his breath.

She dipped back down and sucked him in deep, choking a little as she attempted to take him all the way. He smelled like the lavender body wash they'd used earlier along with the musk of a fervent man. As she enjoyed her control over Digger, sucking and licking, even reaching the curly hairs at the base of his shaft, she expected that he would explode soon. Then a hand in her hair pulled her away from her enthusiastic treatment.

Sure it hurt some, but at the same time his treatment turned her on. Digger had finally decided to take charge. Using his thumb and forefinger, he kept her mouth open as he carefully pulled his cock out of her mouth. Her gaze shot to his.

"I rather be miles deep in your pussy when I come. Let's make sure you're ready."

He pushed up her T-shirt and bra in one quick move and licked one stiff nipple. She arched her back as he sucked hard on the tip. The mixture of pain and pleasure brought a whimper. She whispered—hopefully—"More."

He continued to pull and release the nipple as he tweaked the other one with his fingers. When it almost became unbearable, he switched to the other one.

She reached down, trying to reach her clit and gain a little relief.

He shifted and slapped her hand and then pussy.

One moment she gave him a threatening look and then she sat up and clasped his chest hairs between her fingers and kissed him as she tugged.

His chest vibrated. Yeah, it hurt didn't it, fellow. She leaned back and grinned.

"You're playing dirty now," Digger said.

"Not. Dirty. Enough," she said, carefully spacing out the words, and wiggled her eyebrows.

"Fuck."

"Yeah. Now."

So he did.

CHAPTER 22

"**I** don't give a fuck what you think I should do, I'm coming with you." Digger squared off with Sen. "Don't you understand how dangerous Quinn can be?" Sen shook his head, but Digger continued, "I'm not saying he's dangerous to his daughter, but to you. Sure, the old man has mellowed over the years and it's not your fault Quinn's dad died in a country you'd never lived in or visited, but a person doesn't poke a stick at a wounded animal. The old man likes me. Maybe I can help defuse the situation."

Sen knew what Digger meant, like bringing his daughter home after she disappeared with that Whitfield, and her lying about where she'd been the last few days.

"You think everyone loves you. But no," Sen said and then turned his back, looking at Tessa.

Her hands moved so fast, even Sen became confused.

"What's she saying?" Digger muttered. "Damn, I need more lessons."

"I believe she wants to help."

"To help find the one paying for the contract, or who killed the old men?"

"Yeah," Sen answered with his gaze remaining on Tessa as his hands moved.

Are you wanting to do both?

She nodded.

"Which?" Forehead wrinkled, Digger glared.

"Both," Sen answered on a sigh.

"Fuck no." Digger pulled back and turned his glare at Tessa.

"That's what I keep telling her." Sen shook his head and tapped his thumb to two fingers on the same hand as if making a sign of someone speaking.

"Apparently not strong enough." Digger pointed at her and said, "No!"

With one eyebrow raised and hands on her hips, she stepped toe-to-toe to the blond country boy.

"She can read your lips without you shouting. Damn, man, don't make her any angrier than she is." Sen decided Tessa was the most stubborn woman he'd ever met. Not a wimp by any means.

Digger ignored Sen and leaned down close to her face. "No. We're taking you home."

"I'm going with you!" she shouted back, giving up on signing.

Sen held back his laughter when Tessa pushed Digger's chest, making the sad excuse of a bad-ass take a step back. The woman wasn't afraid of anyone. He knew how Digger felt. Hard to say no to her and stand his ground. Literally and figuratively. The only solution was to protect her to the best of their abilities.

Giving up, he chuckled and headed toward a side door, leading to Digger's garage. He kind of felt sorry for Digger, but he loved Tessa's mettle. Hell, she was a better shot than most men he knew.

And oh, he felt sorry for the assholes they were after.

Tessa was a power to reckon with. He was glad she was on his side.

CHAPTER 23

No sooner were they on the road to Sen's home in Digger's more sedate—that was, for him—double cab dually, when his phone rang.

During their time together, Digger had offered Sen one of his extra, new phones he kept in a drawer, waiting to be set up. He'd said it came in handy, what with the way he constantly smashed his. They simply switched out the SIM cards, followed a few simple instructions, and he had his old contact list and phone number. No matter how often he thought of punching Digger's face in, he was a good friend.

"Yes?"

"Hey, Sen, I've got you some more information on that FBI chick—" Wolf's voice was drowned out by someone revving their motorcycle, and at the same time, a hard rock tune started on Digger's truck radio.

He covered the opposite ear from the one with the phone to cut down the noise.

"Say it again."

"The FBI chick. She ain't FBI anymore. She was fired for insubordination."

"Interesting. How long ago?" Sen winced, the last three words came out too loud because Digger had switched off the radio.

"Not sure, but pretty certain it's been around thirty days."

Sen glanced over to Digger. Wolf's voice blasted into the cabin. The furious look on his friend's face, which probably matched his, said he heard it clearly.

"Is there anything else?" Sen asked.

"Yeah. Just a minute." The sound of wind hitting the phone was followed by shouting—he must be holding the phone away from his mouth. "Move that piece of shit away from me, I'm trying to have an important conversation here, asshole." A second later, everything became quiet. "That's better. Stupid ass. Not you, man, inconsiderate mother-fuckers here. Anyway, where was I?" Before Sen could remind him, Wolf said, "Oh, yeah, she had a visitor last night. I don't know his name, but I've seen him in Nashville before," Wolf said.

"Who? Wait. Are you following her?"

"Ha! Not likely. I recognized him from a couple weeks ago. There's a Chinese restaurant my wife likes down the block from the B and B we stay at whenever we're in Nash-ville. This rangy dude got out of his cage…you know, car, and shook hands with an associate of my Uncle Mikolas. My old lady and I were sitting at a table on the restaurant's patio and noticed them on the sidewalk across the street. That associate handles some of the dirtier business for the Savalas organization."

"What did the visitor look like?" Sen desperately wanted to talk to the man.

"A rangy-looking dude, under six foot and wears a ponytail."

"Do you know his name?"

"Nah. Only that he drives a black Camaro that appears fully loaded. Really sharp for a cage."

"Got anything else?"

"Nope. But the dude must be trouble to have met with anyone in my uncle's organization. Sorry, man, I wish I could help you with more."

"Where's the agent staying?"

Wolf gave him the name. It was the nicest motel in Marystown and near the interstate.

"Thanks for the info. If you hear anything else, let me know."

"Sure." Then Wolf clicked off.

Sen repeated the conversation to Digger in case he hadn't caught it all as he signed the info to Tessa.

Digger U-turned in the road.

"Do you really think Carleton or the man is still there?" Sen continued to sign for Tessa's sake. Her frustration was clear as it was impossible for her to read the men's lips fast enough on each side of her. She was probably getting a headache.

"Probably not. Best to check." Digger's fingers whitened on the steering wheel. His itch to catch the two apparently as great as it was to Sen.

When they arrived at the motel, no blue sedan. Only an old couple sitting near the pool.

"Stop and I'll run inside the office and see what I can find out." Sen fingered the door handle, anxiously waiting until Digger parked before hopping out. When he turned to shut the door, Tessa stuck one leg out, ready to follow him. "No. Stay safe in here. I'll be back in no time," he said as he signed.

She glared.

Please. Sen gave her a pleading look.

She bared her teeth and brought her leg in. With a huff,

she folded her arms over her chest and sat back to stare out the windshield. He took it to mean she'd hang with Digger.

Damn, she was cute when she pouted. He wanted to kiss those pooched, hot lips.

Within moments, he'd returned.

"She checked out. The attendant said she hung around and had lunch with a skinny guy with a ponytail. They drove off in separate cars."

He hadn't signed the information because she was concentrating hard on his lips. Unable to resist any longer, he wrapped his arms around her and kissed her. She gasped in surprise and he took full advantage. He lifted her onto his lap and squeezed her against his chest. Heat flared from his groin as she wiggled perfectly. His hand covered a firm breast and massaged as the kiss continued. Then he pinched the hard nipple and drank in the release of air from her silent sigh. The chuckle from the other side of the cab brought Sen's attention to the here and now. He carefully released Tessa and helped her back into her seat between them, making sure she buckled the seatbelt.

"Whoa. I'm all for asking about an available room we can rent for a couple hours. This truck is huge, but I can promise it's not as comfortable as a bed." Digger's crooked grin said he was only half joking.

Tessa hit Digger in the arm. She obviously picked up the conversation.

"Shut up and drive to Scene 69." Warmth flooded Sen's cheeks. Damn, it wasn't as if Digger hadn't been involved in their lovemaking for days now.

"Sure, boss," Digger teased. Then he asked, "You plan to interrogate Karma?"

"No. But I heard Ethan had been spending a lot of time there," Sen answered, making sure to sign for Tessa. "I figure he might have seen the dude."

"I don't blame him. Karma is something."

"That's the new manager, right?"

"Yeah. Your old man did good when he hired her."

"Anything I need to know? If she's good at her job, the last thing we need is for Ethan to be bothering her. He knows better than to fuck the employees, especially with him being their boss." Sen left off the last sentence in his signing. Tessa had no reason to know that.

"She's the type who can handle big boys like him," Digger stated with a smirk.

Sen looked over Tessa's head. Eyebrows raised, he nodded. So the manager at Scene 69 likes to play rough. Ethan was six-four and loved dishing out pain and receiving it. Not Sen's cup of tea, but so far his younger brother hadn't crossed a line that would create trouble.

"Besides, she might be the one who can confirm Mikolas Savalas had placed the contract on your family's heads," Digger said.

"She connected?" Most people he knew in the nightclub businesses were connected to one mob or another.

"A Savalas through marriage. That is, former marriage to his sister's kid. He was one of Savalas's numerous nephews. So even though the nephew got killed, Savalas keeps a tab on her because she had a kid by the nephew. But I've heard her family is well connected in Nashville." Digger shrugged. "You know how those families are, they marry each other as a way to control the area."

Just like the nightclubs, when Digger talked about connection, he wasn't talking necessarily about money, but high-up mafia. The southern mafia, which the Whitfields in Sand County were part of, were more dangerous than any Yankee mob could imagine. Hell, one county west of Birmingham was rumored to be the best place to find a hit man or dispose of a body, and they were still not as savage as Sand County.

Tessa then slammed her fist into Sen's shoulder. Damn, the girl had a punch. He rubbed the spot.

What? Sen signed.

You forgot to sign the last part of your conversation. She narrowed her eyes in fake anger.

Just about my brother and his latest female. Nothing you would be interested in.

Who is she?

Karma. The manager at Scene 69.

I'm not familiar with her.

She's new in town.

How do you know her? She squinted her eyes as if she could see into his brain.

I don't. Just what I've been told. The old man handled the hiring before he died.

With a nod, obviously satisfied she'd been given all of the facts and was assured his interest had been merely business, she crossed her arms and leaned back. She yawned.

I'm tired. Wake me when we get there. She closed her eyes and snuggled against him, resting her head carefully above the healing wounds on his shoulder, her face tilted up. It had been a rough few days, not counting all the sex they had indulged in. He lightly traced one arched eyebrow. She smiled with her eyes still closed.

Relief eased through his chest. The thought of explaining his brother's strange proclivities to Tessa was daunting. Considering how she surprised him the last few days, she might ask to try a few. Whips and chains weren't his kind of kink.

By the time they arrived at Scene 69, the neon sign sitting on a tall pole was on and flashing at the cars driving by on I-20. Still early, with the sun low in the sky, there were already several cars in the parking lot. The large white building sat at the edge of a cornfield. Not impressive, but the interior made up for the sterile exterior.

"I don't see Ethan's car anywhere." He pulled out his phone and called his brother. It went straight to the recording. Frustrated, he disconnected the call without leaving a message. Ethan's voicemail was still full. No surprise. "I'll go in and see what Karma knows."

Just as Sen turned to order Tessa to stay put—fuck, it did sound like he was telling a pup to obey, good thing she couldn't read his mind—he saw out of the corner of his eye a black car pull in and park a few spots from Digger's truck. What were the chances? What could he say? He was lucky that way.

A skinny man with a ponytail, wearing jeans and a green checkered shirt, stepped out of the car.

Damn. Perfect timing.

CHAPTER 24

*H*ow dare the guys tell her to stay put.

Screw them.

She wrestled with the seat belt until a big hand covered hers. Her gaze shot up, ready to fight, but Digger's concerned look made her hesitate.

He shook his head.

"It's safer for you to stay here." He lifted his chin in the direction Townsend had taken. *"See. He won't take long."*

Sure, she'd watched Townsend fight at the barn, but this was different. It was not a controlled environment, but one where guns and knives could be involved. Chewing on her bottom lip, she followed him with her gaze. He sauntered up to the man as if he was about to walk by. Then he swung a right, left, ending with an uppercut. The man wobbled and finally went down before he could defend himself.

From the higher advantage of Digger's truck, she watched Townsend rifle through the man's pockets. He then stood and dragged the man by the arm to the back of the Camaro. With a key fob in hand, he popped the trunk and stashed the unconscious man inside. For several minutes, he leaned over the trunk—she suspected he was tying the man's hands and feet, possibly gagging him with whatever he found back there—and then slammed it shut.

He pulled out his phone and began talking. After a few minutes, he pocketed it.

Then several my-balls-were-bigger-than-his strides later, he stopped below Digger's window. Tessa leaned over Digger. What did Townsend plan to do next?

His lips moving at the same time, Townsend signed, *I'm headed to Atlanta to have a word with Savalas. One of the Brothers of Mayhem has gotten me an okay to visit and a guaranteed safety.* He aimed the next to Digger. *"You've got Ethan's number. Text him, and let him know. If he gives you anything new about the contract or killer, let me know."*

Tessa wasn't concerned with Digger's answer. Instead she didn't waste any time. She unfastened the belt and was hopping out of the truck before anyone could stop her.

No, no, no. Go back, Townsend signed. He grabbed at her arm, but she was faster and dodged his hand.

With one eyebrow lifted, she raised her chin, ignored him, and headed toward the black car. He obviously planned to drive it to Georgia.

The passenger door was unlocked. She slid in and buckled the belt. For some strange reason, the interior's appearance shook her. She wasn't sure why she thought a contract killer would have loose beer cans and the smell of cigars or cigarettes lingering in the air. It smelled brand new without a crumb on the floorboards. A chill slid down her back. She'd always heard serial killers were mostly neat freaks. Digger kept a neat interior, but there was always signs of use like grass or dirt on the floorboards, along with a cup or two in the holders. She hadn't been in one of Townsend's automobiles. Whatever, at least he would protect her if the man somehow escaped the trunk.

She closed her eyes for a few seconds.

Why was that her only concern? Shouldn't she be worried about what Townsend planned to do to the man? So far, he hadn't lied to her. The probability of the restrained man being the hired assassin sent to kill him and his brothers was great. Maybe the man was even involved in Townsend's father's death. So sue her if she didn't care about the man's safety.

After tossing their bags of odds and ends they'd scrounged up at Digger's into the backseat, Townsend slid into the car, stared out the windshield for a few seconds, and then tilted his head her way, glaring.

It would be safer for you to go home, he signed.

Like I told you, I was due for a vacation. My dad believes I'm visiting friends in Birmingham.

He looked up at the ceiling, his broad chest heaved in a sigh. When his gaze landed on her again, she smiled.

You are one stubborn woman.

And you like it.

A rare smile broke across his face.

Yeah. I do.

Townsend shifted the Camaro into reverse, tires squealing—she knew this because the reflection from her side mirror showed a long streak of rubber on the road and a large amount of smoke dissipating behind them—before hitting the gearshift to drive, and then they were headed to Georgia.

They didn't stop throughout the night. Only idiots would stop with a live, trussed up man in the back. Considering all the racket he could make, someone would call the police.

Tessa slept most of the way until she woke to ask him to pull over for a potty break at a rest stop. There was only one truck in the parking area. She nodded to the two men as they passed her on the sidewalk. Later, Townsend had told her the men hesitated, glanced at the Camaro—they'd heard bumping noises coming from the trunk—and stared wide-eyed at him leaning against the driver's door. Then broke into a run for their truck, leaving the rest stop at top speed.

She woke again when the car came to a stop. Opening her eyes, she was greeted by armed men dressed in black and a large iron gate. An oversized, fanciful S was designed into the metal.

They'd arrived at Mikolas Savalas's home, a well-known crime boss, and possibly the man wanting Townsend and his brothers dead.

Never in her life had she seen such a large house. The main section stood three stories tall and the wings on each end of the house were two stories and disappeared behind trees. For sure, it qualified as a mansion. It made the Whitfield house look like a quaint cottage.

Townsend lowered the window to speak to one of the guards. She had no idea what he'd said, but the man talked on a mic at his shoulder before waving them through the opening gate.

Her body shivered. It all gave her the creeps.

More armed men met them as Townsend pulled to the curb of the wide sidewalk leading to the double doors. As they exited the car, one of the men patted Townsend down, taking the pistol from his back holster. When another man with a smarmy grin on his face reached out to do the same to Tessa, Townsend pushed him away, glowering, and said something. Fists balled up, he was ready to fight. The man backed off.

Wild. The creepy feeling left and the shiver turned into an ache in her pussy. Was she an awful person for being turned on by that? That was so hot.

A third man, in what could only be described as a butler's

uniform, tails and all, opened the front door and held his hand out for them to enter.

"Mr. Savalas is waiting for you in the breakfast room," he said as Tessa read his lips.

Later, Tessa would have to ask Townsend if the man had an English accent. She'd bet a month's salary he did. From what her hearing friends had told her, it was a sexy sound.

Breakfast room? Who had breakfast rooms? Rich people, that was who. She wrinkled her brow. She wondered why they didn't call the dining room, the dinner room? Or did they? Shaking her head at her silliness, she let Townsend's hand at the small of her back move her in the butler's wake.

Trying to rein in her curiosity, she walked through a twenty-foot-tall foyer with a black-and-white marble floor to a long hallway without breaking her neck staring at the painted ceiling. No need to act like a bumpkin, though truthfully she felt like one. She'd only seen houses like this on the internet and television. The room they were led to was bright from the morning light. Walls of pale yellow with light green and pale blue trimming complemented the furniture and table setting. It looked like a picture.

The man seated at the head of the table leaned back and patted his mouth with a cloth napkin. A burly fellow, he sported thick white hair and had a booming voice—she'd felt the vibrations. Despite the smile and gracious manner, Savalas's treacherous personality filled the room.

She inhaled the different delicious scents. Certainly her stomach growled, as she'd felt the rumble.

"Grab a plate and dish out anything you want. It's difficult to negotiate with an empty stomach." She watched his mouth. *"I've been told you're excellent at reading lips, Ms. Quinn. May I call you Tessa? Please sit here."* He pointed to the second chair on his right. *"And, Townsend...oh, wait, you prefer Sen, right? Have a*

seat beside me. As we talk, this round table will make it easier for her to read both of our lips."

She had no problem with him using her first name, but he didn't give her a chance to agree or not.

Tessa looked at Townsend. Should she start thinking of him as Sen instead of Townsend? Perhaps so, especially since they had a lot of sex. A marathon kind. The man was sin incarnate, considering all the things they had done. Warmth flooded her cheeks. Turning her back to the room, she hoped they hadn't noticed her blush. No way would she explain it.

Sen—yes, it felt right with their current relationship—lifted his chin. Was he considering turning down the man's offer? She ignored him and grabbed a plate and dished out scrambled eggs, bacon, grits, and gravy. At the end of the buffet cabinet were small bowls filled with jelly and jams and a large platter of biscuits. Perfect.

When she turned around, Sen stood near the door. He hadn't moved.

He regarded her with one dark eyebrow lifted.

She shrugged and set her plate down where Savalas had instructed. Food was food. If he wanted them dead, the armed guards would've handled that by now, especially the two standing behind his chair.

CHAPTER 25

One thing Sen had learned a long time ago, when offered food, accept it, even from the enemy. It would be rude otherwise. Besides, the old man was not known for poisoning his enemies.

With only a hesitation—watching Tessa's enthusiasm in loading up her plate was a sight to be seen—he'd followed Tessa's example and filled a plate. His cook or chef was excellent. Once he finished the food on his plate, he pushed the dish away, signaling he was ready for business.

Savalas offered Sen a cigar. He declined. How dangerous would he look coughing up his lung? He'd never picked up Jake's or Ethan's smoking habit. Ethan's was mostly pot.

"So what brought you here so early in the morning?" Savalas asked as he leaned back in his chair, taking a long draw from a fat cigar.

Sen folded his arms on the table and leaned toward the man.

"I have a present for you." He tossed the key fob to the nearest guard. "Look in the trunk. I'm sure your boss would like to see what I brought."

Savalas eyed him before he nodded. Less than five minutes later, they dragged in ponytail guy. He looked rather rough. Hair falling over his red face. It had to be hot stuck overnight in such a closed-in space.

The guards held onto him as the gag and ties were gone. Probably weak from sweating and no water.

"You son of a bitch!" Ponytail guy tried to lunge at Sen, but the guards held tight. Apparently he wasn't too weak.

"What's this all about?" Savalas asked, staring at the man.

"It's the assassin you sent to kill me and my brothers."

"Nope."

Sen studied Savalas's expression. He was either an excellent actor or innocent of—hard to read his face—contracting the killer.

"Did you announce a price on my family's heads?"

Savalas pursed his lips and shook his head. "I hated your father, but have no reason to kill him or his children. You have nothing I want. I have bigger fish to fry. You and your family are minnows in a puddle."

Squeezing his fists, he suppressed the need to attack. True. Compared to Savalas, the Whitfields were specks on a map. If Sen had his way, it would stay that way. Easier to handle the businesses without outside interference. He forced his hands open.

"Well, it appears we have a problem."

"We do?" Savalas's thick, white brows rose.

"Yeah, it was an associate in your company who paid that guy." Sen nodded toward Ponytail.

"Is that right?" Savalas stood and walked up to the shaking man.

Was he afraid or had heat exhaustion? Hell, probably both.

Cool fingers touched his arm and he turned to see Tessa

standing next to him. Damn, how had she moved without his noticing? Good thing she wasn't a guard with a knife.

So Savalas isn't guilty of the contract? she signed.

Doesn't appear so. Sen wasn't going take Savalas's word on it. Yet.

He turned his attention back to the crime boss. Before he could ask anything further, Savalas waved away the guards.

"Take him to the basement and find out who gave him the orders," Savalas commanded. Then he turned and picked up a small bell and lightly rang it.

Seconds later, a maid walked in. "Yes, sir?"

"Show our guests to the Palm bedroom." Savalas turned to Sen. "It may take a few hours to get answers. In the meanwhile, your young lady appears tired. Take a nap, or enjoy the pool out back, or you can leave, but I figured you would want to help in obtaining the answers we need."

Sen understood what Savalas meant. First, he looked at Tessa, checked her coloring and stance. She looked dead on her feet. It had been a stressful and strenuous week.

"I'll be back," Sen said to Savalas without looking at him. His gaze remained on Tessa. He then lightly grasped her hand.

"I'll be waiting. My men can get him prepared," Savalas said, ignoring their tender moment.

The bedroom they were shown to was as large as Sen's condominium in Marystown. With the six-foot palms sitting on the balcony and a huge oil painting on one wall of palm trees with the ocean in the background, he understood the name of the room.

How beautiful, Tessa signed.

He nodded and opened the French doors leading out to the balcony. A few steps off the balcony was a small kidney-shaped pool. Perfect size for a couple to have a private swim.

Of course, palm trees and flowering plants in huge pots towered over one end to give occupants privacy.

Wow. Tessa stepped up next to Sen. *Wow,* she signed again.

Clasping her arm gently, he led her back into the bedroom and pointed at the bed, where their bags now rested.

Take a nap. Don't leave this room until I return. It might take most of the day. Check and see if they found your gun. If not, put it under your pillow. If anyone comes here who isn't me, shoot him. Sen was glad they were using ASL, in case they were being monitored. *When I return, we'll head back home.*

Where are you going? Are we safe? Maybe we should stay together.

Her worried face bothered him. He wanted her to feel safe. For now, he believed Savalas wouldn't turn on them. He was banking on honor among thieves.

They're questioning the guy with the ponytail. You'll be fine. I've never heard of Savalas harming women. Still, keep your gun nearby and everything'll be good. And lock the door behind me, including the one to the pool. I want you to be safe, you're important to me.

The words appeared to settle Tessa's nerves somewhat. Sen would never allow anyone to hurt her.

He pulled her into his arms and kissed the top of her head.

She stepped back and signed, *Okay. I'll take a shower and then a nap. Don't leave me too long.* Her hands stroked his chest as she looked into his eyes, waiting for a reply.

I promise. I'll be back as quick as I get answers. He traced her lips with his thumb.

His chest rose and fell as he worked at calming himself. Frustration at the whole situation and Tessa's involvement was worrisome. He girded himself for what was to come. Torturing someone for information had always been grueling on his body and psyche, but necessary, especially to protect everyone he cared about.

He caressed her face and then turned to walk away. She pulled on his shirt sleeve.

"Kiss me," she said, one eyebrow up. She teasingly pouted.

Amused, he nodded and then dipped his head. He showed her how much he wanted to do more by ravaging her mouth with his. Unable to resist, he thrust his hand down her jeans and between her legs. Rubbing the hard nub until she soaked his hand with her desire. He continued to stroke her tongue with his as his fingers rubbed until she came apart in his embrace.

He searched her face. How did this woman cause him to lose control of his senses? Even make him do things he never imagined doing? For most of his life, he'd controlled his libido, not the other way around. But with her...fuck, with her, he couldn't keep his hands off her, his mouth off her, his dick out of her. Too much was at stake for him to allow his body to call the shots.

He picked her up and placed her on the bed. She grinned at him and patted the mattress beside her.

Determinedly, he shook his head and walked out.

CHAPTER 26

Tessa swiped at the tickling trailing down her cheek. Squinting, she spotted daylight shining in from the French doors and across the floor at the foot of the bed. She rolled to her back. Gorgeous blue eyes stared straight into hers.

Surprised, she clasped his handsome face, smiling with glee.

"What are you doing here?" She hoped her voice wasn't too loud.

Digger sat on the bed beside her. *"Sen called and said it was taking longer than planned and I was needed to keep an eye on you."* She glowered. He added, *"No. Not that you're doing anything wrong, sweetheart. He wanted to be sure no one bothered you. That you remained safe."*

"From our host?"

"Savalas?" he asked.

She nodded.

"Probably. Anytime you're in a mob boss's house, there's danger. Someone is always out to kill him and his people."

"How much longer before we can leave?"

"No idea. The contract killer appears to be a tougher nut to crack than they expected."

With eyes narrowed, she asked, *"How did you get in my bedroom?"*

"Really, you have to ask?" He smirked.

Eyebrows raised, she grinned wide, waiting for his answer. He probably knew a hundred ways to get into a locked room.

"I could say I picked the lock, but I won't." He lifted his hand and opened his palm. A key rested in the middle. *"Savalas had given it to our friend."* Pocketing it, he looked over her shoulder and blew out his cheeks as if he was releasing the stress inside. With a small smile, he dropped his gaze down her body. *"Go, and after you take a quick shower, change into one of the swimsuits I left on the counter. They're bringing breakfast to us in twenty minutes and then we'll take a dip in the pool."*

She hesitated, unsure of what she really wanted to do next. One thing was certain, she didn't want to be involved in torturing another human being. Shooting another person when they were shooting back was one thing, but being cruel for information? No. Best for her to stay put and do as Digger asked.

Despite feeling like a coward, she realized Sen—wow, using his nickname now came easy for her—needed to find out who was behind all of the attacks.

Slipping out of bed, she walked into the bathroom. As she shut the shower door, it reopened and Digger, bare-ass naked, stepped in with her.

"Sen figured I could keep your mind off what is going on else-where in this monster of a house." Droplets ran down his face and over his chest as he leaned down to kiss her. His big hands clasped her butt and lifted her to eye level.

She wrapped her legs around his waist as he thrust into her. Oh, yes, he knew exactly what to do to keep her mind occupied until breakfast.

Sen was so good to her. In a weird way, sending Digger to occupy her showed how much she meant to him.

Maybe it was the movement of air under the hot Georgia sun, or she had a sixth sense when it came to Sen. Stretched out in a neon blue bikini, Tessa shielded her eyes to glare at his silhouette.

Coming closer, he kneeled next to her lounge chair. His hair was mussed with shadows beneath his eyes. He looked tired and maybe a little sad.

He carefully signed, *You look relaxed. Everyone treating you right? Digger kept you safe?*

I'm good.

A lopsided grin lit up his face.

Yes. You are.

She gave a brief smile at his teasing.

Did you get what you needed? She tilted her head.

Yes and no.

Who set up the contract?

Later. For now I need a shower and a short nap. Want to come with me?

She grinned. *Yes. But it'll be up to you on whether I come or not?*

He was so tired, it took him a second to understand the double entendre. His grin widened. Some of the tiredness in his eyes disappeared.

Yeah. I think I can make sure of that. Anyway, why wait?

He leaned over her. Before she could catch her breath, he

snapped the string at her hip and yanked the bottoms from her. His mouth covered her smooth pussy, his tongue divided her folds, and he quickly found her clit. He flicked the swelling bump. Her breath caught as she promptly came.

Never had she ever come that fast. Instead of being satisfied with the result, she wanted more. She grabbed his hair and pressed her mons against his face. The vibration of his chuckling pushed her over again. Damn, he was like magic.

Cupping his hands over hers, he gently loosened her hold and untangled her fingers from the warm strands.

Opening her eyes...when had she shut them? She watched as he stripped out of his clothes. What a glorious sight. The man had to exercise and work with weights sometime, what with his well-formed chest, V-cut torso, defined muscles along his arms, legs, and abdomen. Was she drooling?

He covered her with his body, and at the same time hooked her legs with his arms, lifting her butt up until the head of his cock rested at her opening. A smirk crossed his face as he thrust into her. She inhaled sharply. Not from pain, but from the pure joy of being filled by him.

While thrusting, he bent down and sucked in one nipple. She released a moan of immense pleasure. Had the whole house, goodness, the whole neighborhood heard her? Whatever it sounded like, Sen had liked it, as his thrusts sped up. He switched to the other nipple and drew in harder.

She surely would fall apart, splinter into a million pieces.

He pulled his mouth off of her and cupped her breasts, pinching the hard, beaded tips.

She screamed. She didn't care who heard or how strange it sounded, she couldn't stop it. The pleasure-pain zinged through her body, needing to be released somehow. Then a deep, prolonged climax shot through her, wave after wave radiating from her core.

Weak, unable to move, she felt a hand brush hair from her face. She gazed into the pleased look shining from his dark brown eyes. His lips pressed to hers in a sweet kiss. As if he was saying thank you.

He moved away and tossed her a beach towel. She signed, *thank you too.*

From the way he threw back his head and laughed, she knew he understood it wasn't for the towel.

By the time she showered—alone—and got dressed, Sen was sitting at a small table at one end of the bedroom with Digger, and they were eating from several dishes. A chair and place setting were waiting for her.

She tugged at the oversized T-shirt she'd borrowed out of Sen's bag. So many of her clothes were becoming damaged by the men's urgency in disrobing her. She smiled. Not that it was a totally terrible thing, but even washing and drying her clothes at Digger's forgave the mistreatment only so much.

Come and eat. Our host had to leave to handle some business. So we have the house to ourselves until we leave tomorrow, Sen signed, before digging back into the mound of food on his plate.

Why not this afternoon? she asked.

I've been up for over twenty-four hours. I need to rest tonight. We'll leave in the morning. Sen crammed in another mouthful.

She had never seen him eat so much.

The dishes looked delicious. After she dipped out a little of everything—Greek chicken, lemon rice, and strawberry salad—she wasn't sure she could eat it all. She gave it her best shot. By the time she pushed the plate away, most of the platters and bowls were empty. Wow! Men ate a lot.

Digger pushed his chair back, staring down at his phone. *"I need to answer this."* After a quick kiss to Tessa's cheek, he exited out the French doors toward the pool.

Tapping the table top, she caught Sen's attention.

Where next? She frowned and wiggled her finger.

Home. Ethan called earlier and he's searching for info in Nashville. No need for us to go there. I have a friend at Langley I need to call and my info should be there.

A spy?

At one time, maybe.

To your home?

Yes. Though you probably need to go to your home.

No. I'm not ready yet. If you don't want me at your home, I'll go with Digger.

Sen reached across the table, fisted her blouse, and pulled her toward him across the table. He met her halfway with her feet dangling in the air. Whoa! She sometimes forgot how strong he was.

"*If you refuse to go to your home, then you stay with me,*" he said as she watched his sexy masculine lips.

She slapped the hand holding her top. He released her. As she slid off the table and walked around to his side, she caught the flash of anger mixed with concern and embarrassment coming over his features.

Are you jealous? She smirked.

His gaze searched her face.

Yes. Sen bobbed his fist up and down as he nodded.

She leaned over, grabbed his T-shirt, and jerked him nearer, imitating his earlier action. Their lips, tongues, and even teeth came into play with the ultimate panty-soaking kiss, though technically she wasn't wearing panties. She wanted to make sure he understood she liked his answer.

When they parted, she was breathing hard and was so horny—how could she be horny again? It could be a case of the more she indulged, the more she wanted. Digger had his own talents in bed, but there was something special about

Sen. Eventually, she would have to decide between the two. No way could she handle being with two men at the same time. It was exhausting, and truthfully, there was times she wanted Sen all to herself. What a dilemma. Granted, one every woman should have at some point in her life.

CHAPTER 27

"So, we're heading back home?" Digger asked when Sen stepped out of the bedroom hours later.

Digger had enjoyed the couple of days relaxing at the infamous Savalas estate, but there was work to do. Between his fight club and ganja farm, he was a busy man despite people claiming he was a lazy bastard.

He took another long inhale of his joint. While he waited for Sen's decision, he held out the smoke to his friend.

"In the morning," Sen answered as he typed something into his phone. Glancing up, he shook his head at the offer.

His friend rarely indulged in vices. If not for Sen's sexy as hell looks and dangerous edge, Digger would be suspicious of why he hung out with him. Vices were his trade. Hell, vice was Sen's trade too.

Now it appeared his two best friends were in love. From what he could tell so far, they hadn't admitted it to each other. In a way, it made him sad. The ending of an era. Sen was loyal to a fault. He would refuse to team up in bed again, and probably would no longer share her. He had no doubt she would choose Sen. The way she stared at him and watched his every move. That morning at the pool had proven it. They had completely forgotten he was sitting next to them as Sen went down on Tessa.

He gritted his teeth. Once again, he'd been left out in the cold.

With a sigh, he pushed off the wall he'd been leaning on. Self-pity wasn't one of his indulgences. Time for another dip in the pool. He enjoyed swimming in the clear water—not a fish-filled pond like on his farm—the last couple of days. Chances were good he would pull out his excavator when he returned home and prepare a place for one hell of a pool. One of the benefits of having acres and acres of pasture and woodland. It would be fun to do something constructive with it, instead of burying his enemies on his property.

CHAPTER 28

Sen walked out to the pool area the next morning to tell everyone it was time to pack up and return to Marystown. He stopped and stared.

Legs spread on each side of the lounge she reclined in, Tessa arched her back as Digger thrust into her and covered a nipple with his mouth.

Immediately, his cock pulsed. She was beautiful in the throes of an orgasm.

He tugged at his pants, giving his cock room to stretch. His chest rose and fell with the decadence of the scene. Jealousy no longer caused a sharp pain to shoot to his heart. He knew Digger loved Tessa as much as he did. Tessa loved Digger. He only hoped she loved him as much if not more.

Every time he saw her, he wanted to fold her in his arms and protect her from all of the evil in the world. She made him happy. He hoped he could always do the same for her.

Sen loved her.

Yep. He was madly and deeply. He just wasn't ready to tell her. He wasn't sure why he kept it to himself. Pride maybe.

Fear certainly. Not physically of the woman, but her emotions, her affection.

And his brother of choice, not blood, Digger Turner, had always protected his back. Work and life in general would keep them apart months on end, but Sen knew Digger would be there if he called. The same with him for Digger.

Fuck, that was some sappy thoughts.

The groans coming from the couple heated his blood to the point he needed a respite or he'd explode where he stood. Unzipping his pants, he pulled out his hard cock. His thumb traced over the tip and rubbed the fluid down his shaft. Squeezing and sliding in his tight clasp.

Just as he about to climax, Tessa turned her head and stared straight at Sen, and what he was doing. Her eyes widened and then she licked her bottom lip as if she imagined tasting him.

Without thinking, he covered the space between them in a few long strides. Her mouth opened in invitation. He straddled her head on the lounger—good thing it was sturdy—adjusted her head back, carefully slipped his cock into her mouth and down her throat. She gagged, while cupping his balls, not letting him move away. She swallowed—oh hell, it felt so good—and then another thrust he came.

After he gently pulled his cock from her mouth, Sen remained on the lounger near her head as Digger picked up her legs at the back of the knees and pumped hard into her pussy, shouting her name. Tessa moaned and her body shook as they climaxed together. Fuck, it was so hot. His own private porno show.

So immersed by the scene in front of him, when Digger reached over Tessa and caressed Sen's cheek, he snapped out of a trance.

Sen slipped off the lounger, tucking himself in and zipping up. He refused to look at Digger. He loved the man like a brother, but he couldn't provide what his friend wanted so badly. His feelings didn't lean in that direction.

Tessa sat up and kissed Digger, drawing his attention. When she pulled away, she turned toward Sen. One auburn eyebrow lifted in question.

Sen gave her a crooked grin and signed, *Are you packed?*

She shook her head.

We're leaving in an hour. He tilted his head toward the house.

She nodded, picked up her towel, dragged it behind her as she strode toward the French doors, heading to their bedroom. Her unabashed nakedness stirred up every emotion in him. He wanted her more than he'd ever wanted any woman. He wanted her all to himself. He wanted her to have his babies. Fuck. Closing his eyes, he inhaled and exhaled slowly. No. They had too much to settle before he even could think of going that far. She might not want anything from him to last that long. Fuck. Time to regain his senses.

He turned to Digger. "When are you leaving?"

"I drove my truck. I'll follow you." Digger stood naked, wiping his face and shoulders with a towel.

"Fine," Sen said and then added, "Take her with you."

Digger stopped in the middle of slipping on his swim trunks. He eyed Sen with consternation.

"Don't you think she'd like to add her opinion to that?" Digger snapped the waist of his trunks and then adjusted his dick.

"It doesn't matter. She'll be safer with you for now. Take her home and I'll meet you at mine." Seeing his friend's glower, Sen asked, "What?"

"You want me to call some of the boys to ride along with you?" Hands on his hips, Digger's curious gaze changed to worry.

Sen looked off toward the pool in frustration at his friend's suggestion.

"If you're talking about the Brothers of Mayhem, you've lost your mind. They'd only make me a larger target. But wait until I leave before you and Tessa do. If anyone is following, they'll be on my tail."

"You're going to have one pissed-off woman on your hands later."

"She'll live with it." Live being the operative word. If she continued to stay around him, she would have to learn how to follow his orders. It could mean her death or, at the very least, being badly hurt.

Sen watched his speedometer as he drove on I-20. There were sections known for speed traps, and the last thing he needed was to be pulled over. As soon as he'd hit the interstate, he'd called his contact at the DMV to have the tag and registration of the Camaro changed into his name. Until that was done, if he were pulled over, there would be lots of questions.

Checking his rearview mirror for tails, he spotted a couple of cars that looked suspicious as they adjusted their speed to his. It could be coincidence. But in his business, he couldn't take a chance.

The next couple of hours went smoothly except for a slow down or two. One of the cars he suspected of following him had exited before reaching the Alabama–Georgia border. When he'd checked on Digger and Tessa earlier, they had stopped to eat at a Cracker Barrel restaurant in Bremen, Georgia. Tessa loved the little store attached to the dining room.

He tapped on his phone resting in its holder. The screen

lit up and showed Digger and Tessa were over thirty miles behind him, but off the interstate. Probably Tessa needed to stop and hit one of the rest stops. That was okay. At least, if anything happened, they would have time to divert.

The phone rang. Tessa. Odd, she normally texted. There were times she would use FaceTime, but not when she knew he was driving. Was it Digger?

"Hey, everything okay?"

"No. This isn't your suck buddy or whore." The deep voice wasn't anyone he knew.

Sen gritted his teeth and spit out, "You better not have hurt them or I'll cut your balls off and feed them to the dogs." All of his plans were for nothing.

"I'm shaking in my boots, asshole." A high-pitched chuckle came over the phone. "For now, they're still alive. When you get home, we'll be in contact again."

Then the phone went silent and returned to his home screen. He immediately checked their location. Nothing. Whoever had them had cut the connection on Tessa's and Digger's phones.

"Fuck." He squeezed the steering wheel, wanting to slam his hand down on it. Last thing he needed was to break it or cause the car to jerk and get pulled over, or bring about a wreck. "Fuck."

By the time he reached Marystown's city limits, the time had dragged by like days. He pulled in front of his condo and leaned his head against the steering wheel, trying to regain his common sense. He'd already called his people. Digger wasn't the only one who had people. They were putting out feelers for who had kidnapped his woman and best friend.

Instead of the expected staleness, his condo smelled of cleaning supplies from the service he used. Everything appeared to be in place. Nothing hung on the walls, no trinkets sat on the end tables. All was as he liked it. Bare and essential.

He stalked to and through his bedroom and into his closet. After placing his phone on a shelf, he shoved back a rack of shirts. Flipping a small metal plate on the wall revealed a keypad, and he typed in the code. Then a humming filled the small room as the shelves separated and moved out, exposing a wall of various weapons. He picked out a couple of throwing knives, a handgun, and a sawed-off shotgun. Nearby, he picked up a backpack and filled it with ammunition, and then a duffle bag with a couple more handguns, some smoke grenades, and a disassembled sniper rifle.

It wasn't until he turned and looked into a full-length mirror he realized how insane he appeared. Strands of hair stuck to his face, sweating profusely, his face red with deep creases near his mouth. He was a man on the edge. Fear crept up his spine to his skull, worry for Tessa and even fucking Digger. He needed to pull himself together and take care of business. Whoever took the people he loved would pay tenfold.

CHAPTER 29

essa wrapped a torn piece of the sheet around Digger's waist. Tightening the cloth, she hoped it would slow the bleeding. The deep knife wound on his side looked ugly, and maybe life-threatening. When they had tried to escape the locked bedroom they were being held in, one of the guards had jumped Digger and stabbed him during their struggle.

Digger was now chained to the bed frame while she was left untied. They believed her to be harmless. It was nice, at times, to be ignored. With her hands free, she could take care of Digger and plan another escape. In the beginning, they'd mistakenly believed only two men guarded them. But she and Digger had discovered, in the worst way, it was at least three.

The bedroom door banged open. A huge man dressed in black stood in the opening, holding a sack and two bottles of water.

"Here. Eat. Drink." The man tossed the sack and bottles onto the bed, then promptly turned and slammed the door shut behind him.

Inside the bag, she found a couple of burgers wrapped in wax paper and fries to match. Someone had even thrown in a few packs of ketchup and a stack of paper napkins. How thoughtful. Whoever had run the errand had been brought up right, despite being a kidnapper.

She unwrapped a sandwich and held it up for Digger to take a bite. His hands were fastened by handcuffs to chains around his waist. His hands couldn't reach his mouth. No matter how hard he pulled on the chains, they remained away from his mouth.

With one blue eye swollen shut and a jaw puffy and red, he grimaced as he chewed. She probably could take the torn sheet and soak it in the sink. Their kidnappers had given them what appeared to be a master bedroom with *en suite*, though it didn't have a door between the bath and bedroom, no mirrors or drawers, nothing to use as a weapon. She'd checked.

A sharp sting on her finger brought her attention back to Digger. He opened his mouth wide like a baby chick. He'd bitten her.

"Behave," she said, hopefully softly. She rotated the burger and he took another large bite.

When Digger finished chewing, he said, *"We'll find a way out of here. If not, Sen will find us."*

She'd caught his meaning.

For the last two days, she'd watched the sun set through the metal grille over the window. The assholes had taken their phones to keep Sen from tracking their whereabouts. Though she prayed for Sen to find them somehow, she had no other choice but to save herself and Digger. Life had taught her that as a small child. She must depend foremost on herself.

She turned to Digger and looked pointedly at his jeans.

He smirked.

"I need your belt," she said.

"Not sure if we have time for that."

Her eyes partially closed in frustration. She signed, *Stupid,* as she rolled her eyes.

From the expression on his face, he remembered that sign.

She flipped the big, silver Western-style buckle over and jerked his belt out of the loops. It would come in handy.

He tapped her leg with his foot. She looked down. Not seeing anything, she looked into his face.

"Babe, wait, look on the other side of the buckle." He nodded toward the belt.

She flipped the belt over and underneath the buckle was a thin, L-shaped steel rod nestled in the leather. She held up the small rod. Her eyebrows rose in question.

"Perfect for picking locks," he said. *"Watch my lips. I'll tell you how to unlock the cuffs."* He lifted his hands.

<<<>>>

They had a new plan.

Afraid the men in the other room would hear her if she spoke, Tessa signed, *Are you ready?*

They'd been locked up for four days total at this point. Sen obviously couldn't find them. So it was time to save themselves. With Digger's guidance she now knew how to pick handcuffs. But hopefully, she'd never need to use that skill again.

Digger nodded. His hands were finally free of the cuffs. Whenever the men came in to feed them, he rested his wrists in the cuffs without locking them in place.

His wound still seeped blood, but they were running out of time. He'd told her he overheard two of the guards discuss moving soon. They planned to kill him as she'd be the one to draw Sen out of his hiding place. That she would be easy to deal with. Stupid bastards would find out differently.

Though there were grids over the window, whoever had installed them hadn't thought about the regular hinges on the door. While the guards ate breakfast, the noise from the kitchen covered their progress. She followed Digger's lead when they had worked on loosening the pins. They carefully pushed them up, but not out. She wasn't exactly sure what they'd planned would work, but she couldn't wait around any longer for her shining knight. She was no ordinary damsel, anyway.

At that moment, the door swung slowly open.

Tessa stood and backed up to the wall, thumbing the design on the belt buckle without touching the newly sharpened edge. The old-fashioned iron rails beneath the bed had helped with that as she rubbed one side slowly during the early morning hours.

Her gaze glued to the door, she watched as the top edge tilted a little. They had already brought supper. So why were they coming in? Were they going to kill Digger now and take her out of the house under cover of darkness?

Who was that in the doorway? He was shorter than the others they'd seen. With bushy black hair, little, beady dark eyes, and a pointed nose, he only missed wiry whiskers to be a rat. Such a creepy, creepy man.

He looked over his shoulder and nodded his head, saying something before turning back to look them over.

She couldn't make out the words the stranger had said to the others, but when she glanced over to Digger, she caught a flash of anger in his eyes. Then her gaze went from one man to the other, trying to follow their conversation.

"Are these your boys, Rat Boy?" Digger lifted his chin.

She'd heard of Rat Boy and his brother, Teddy Bear. Cousins to the Whitfields. People said, despite having such a cuddly sounding name, Teddy Bear was the more dangerous of the two physically. Yet, Rat Boy was the leader and schemer.

"Yeah. I picked a good lot," he said, giving an ugly smirk. *"They tracked down that Whitfield bastard and then followed the wrong fucking car."* The man strutted in, leaving the door wide open. *"Where's the bastard?"* His question was directed at her. *"Don't give me that dumb look. I've been told you read lips."*

She grimaced and shrugged.

His eyes narrowed before his gaze travelled down her body.

What a really creepy man. Her stomach roiled in disgust.

Digger shook his chains, grabbing the man's attention. Giving Digger some room in case he needed to attack, she edged around a chair and stood off to the side as the two men began a stare down.

"...not my worries," Rat Boy finished.

What worries? She didn't catch that. Was he talking about Sen? If so, he should be more than worried.

Digger slowly stood, letting the chains fall to the floor as he held his wounded side. He was bigger than the asshole. Why hadn't he jumped him?

"How did you get out of those chains?" Startled, Rat Boy reached behind his back and pulled out a gun.

"Whoa," Digger said, palms out to stop him. *"Sen said he had things to do and went his own way. We're not his keeper. Let us go. I don't have a beef with you and your brother."*

"We know you and Sen are fuck buddies." Rat Boy's nasty grin made her want to hit him.

"Jealous?" Digger crossed his arms and smirked.

"Which one takes it in the ass?" Rat Boy moved a little closer to Digger, waving his gun like an idiot.

"Oh, you meant fucking each other." Digger rubbed his chin as if in concentration and looked down at the smaller man. *"I*

enjoy a tight masculine ass on occasion, but Sen's single-minded and prefers pussies and tits only."

Movement in Tessa's peripheral vision caught her attention. Her eyebrows rose as two men walked out the front door. What was happening? Why weren't they guarding their boss?

She carefully shifted to one side, hoping Rat Boy wouldn't notice. Where was the other one?

From what she could tell, the kitchen-and-living-room combination was empty. Had Rat Boy told his men to leave? Not to be witnesses to a murder?

A vibration in the air jarred her whole body. Rat Boy had fired the gun.

She snapped her head around and found the two men fighting for control of the weapon. Before she could react, one of Rat Boy's men returned and entered the bedroom. He stopped next to the open tottering door, pointing his gun at the fighting men. Without a thought, she pushed on the other side of the door with all her might. Luckily, it was heavy enough to knock the surprised man onto the floor. She lunged on top of the door, putting all of her weight across the surface. The man struggled with the weight of her and the door. Thank goodness, it was of solid wood. He was going to escape and kill them both if she didn't act quickly. The sharpened belt buckle was still in her hand. Before she knew what she'd done, the man screamed and clasped a hand over the cut she'd made at the side of his neck. Blood sprayed her face from between his fingers. In seconds, all of the tension in the man's body left him.

Her stomach roiled and she scrambled to the side and threw up. What had she done? Had she lost her mind? No. She mustn't think that way. If she'd done nothing, Digger and possibly herself would be dead.

Refusing to think further about her rash action, she

dropped the slippery belt buckle and scrambled off the door, ignoring the spreading blood on the carpet. Digger was weakening and barely holding his own.

She jerked the dead man's gun out of his hand and aimed it at Rat Boy. The men twisted and turned, not giving her a clear shot. At such close range, the bullet might go through one body and hit the other. She couldn't squeeze the trigger with the possibility of killing Digger.

She needed something to stop Rat Boy without endangering Digger. There wasn't another door to hold him down. What good was a gun? Then her only option came to her. In a few quick steps, she swung and smashed the gun's handle against the side of Rat Boy's head. He crumpled to the floor. Whew! It worked.

Digger slumped to the floor next to the man. His chest heaving, he reached over and checked Rat Boy's pulse.

"He's alive," Digger said, looking at her with clear relief on his face.

CHAPTER 30

Good thing Sen had men watching Rat Boy and Teddy Bear. After he'd scratched off Savalas having a contract on the Whitfields' heads, he'd moved his cousins to the top of the list with some of Angel Tally's people. During his interrogation of the Savalas associate, he'd described a large man with a southern accent as being involved in the FBI agent's plans. Problem was, there were several men in Marystown, especially part of the Tally's, with the same description. Even some that drove a white pickup.

He opened and closed his fist. The soreness from his bloody knuckles reminded him of how he'd lost his temper on learning Rat Boy had gone to the poor side of Sand City recently. Even with a fucked up name, the freak was an elitist. He'd never step foot in anyone's home worth less than a half mil. That was the clue they had been hunting for, and it pissed him off that it took so long to track him down.

As Sen parked a block away, three SUVs pulled in behind him. He wasn't taking a chance with Tessa's life or his best friend's. The last few days searching for them, he'd been ready to pull out his hair until Rat Boy finally made a move.

His men spilled out and quietly ran through the tree-filled lot adjacent to the property, spread out over the front yard, and waited for his orders. He directed some of them to surround the house and a few to follow him inside. The front door was ajar. Was he about to find their bodies? A chill slid across skin with that thought.

Pointing his Sig ahead, he toed open the door and stepped inside. He heard someone talking. With a flick of his fingers he sent men to silently search the other rooms as he walked toward the voices.

"He's alive." The voice was Digger's.

That was when Sen noticed a fallen door with a body sprawled on the floor beneath it. The man's head was surrounded by a large puddle of dark liquid that was probably blood. Stepping into the bedroom, he was taken aback by the sight of Tessa and Digger leaning over what appeared to be Rat Boy.

"What the hell happened here?" Sen crossed his arms and glared at the blood-splattered people.

He'd been going crazy, worried he'd be too late. Desperate to know where they'd been taken while tracking down who had them and if they were still alive and unharmed. Digger looked in bad shape with no shirt and a bloody bandage wrapped around his ribs, two black eyes, and blood covering one cheek with a cut on his forehead. Thankfully, Tessa appeared to be in slightly better shape. Hair mussed, bags under her eyes, blood dotting her face like red freckles covering her real ones while some streamed down her neck and soaked her blouse. He hoped none of the blood was hers.

After taking a long step over the fallen door, he squatted down and looked at the body underneath. No one he knew. The man's artery on one side had been cut.

"Move this." Sen waved over two of his men.

They picked up the door and leaned it against the bedroom wall.

"What the hell? Someone sliced his throat," one of the men said in disgust.

"No shit, Sherlock," Sen snapped as he picked up Tessa and turned to leave. "If you can't find some garbage bags, go and buy them. We need this body out of here."

Tessa grabbed the front of his shirt and tugged. Sen looked down into her crinkled, worried face. She then pointed to where his best friend sat, his back resting against the bed's footboard and Rat Boy's body.

"Digger, you okay?" Sen said over his shoulder as he walked toward the front door, stepping around the blood.

"Yeah. Just taking my time standing. The knife wound keeps bleeding like a son of a bitch." Digger groaned.

"Come along. Tessa's worried about you." He grinned down at Tessa when she huffed and narrowed her eyes at him. Sighing, Sen lifted his chin toward the guard watching from the living room. "You." The man jumped to attention. "Help Digger to his feet and drive him over to Quinn's." He took a couple of steps and stopped. "And don't tell Quinn that Tessa was here. Not a word," he warned.

"Rat Boy's alive. He's just knocked out," Digger piped up and then groaned.

Sen stopped and looked down at Tessa. With a second thought, he gave her a quick kiss and then hugged her to him, pressing her face to his chest. It was cheating, but he didn't want her to know what he said next.

With a jerk of his head, he ordered one of his men, "Get the two outside to take Rat Boy to the pawnshop's basement. I'll meet everyone there after Digger's stitched up."

"Yes, sir." The man hurried past.

After exiting the house, carrying her to his SUV, he settled Tessa in the passenger seat. After he slid in behind the steering wheel, he shifted the gear into reverse and checked on her before pressing the gas.

She tilted her head and signed, *What did you say that you didn't want me to know? And where are you taking me?*

Home.

I'm not ready to go home, and what about the other?

Mine.

You're working hard not to tell me, and the Whitfield Estate is the other way.

Not there. My home.

Her eyes widened.

He wasn't sure if it was good or bad that he'd surprised her, but he kind of liked it. Always good to keep his woman on her toes. And maybe it would keep her mind off Rat Boy and what he had planned for him.

By the time Sen parked his Land Rover in the garage attached to his condominium, Tessa had fallen asleep in the passenger seat. He gently closed the door and walked around to her door, skirting his motorcycle. It stood in the corner of the garage where one of his men had delivered the bike from where it had been stashed near Quinn's Funeral Home. His newly acquired Camaro was being repaired at a local shop. If he kept the sports car, he'd either need another place to live with a larger garage or sell his SUV.

Without waking her, he unbuckled and lifted Tessa out of the seat and carried her to his private elevator. In no time he'd entered his foyer and used his elbow to press the button for the lights. He continued up the steps, two at a time, leading to the second floor of his home. At the end of a long hallway was his master bedroom.

She would probably want a shower, but she needed rest more.

He placed her in the middle of his bed and pulled the duvet over her legs and shoulders. She stretched and turned onto her side, not even waking.

Unable to help himself, he grabbed a chair and scooted over to the bed where he could watch her sleep. There was so much to do, but seeing her in his bed brought a higher degree of protectiveness than he'd ever felt before. There had been other women who had slept in his bed. But they hadn't been Tessa.

How could he explain it to himself? Her dark lashes rested on her pale skin, and the circles beneath were beginning to fade as she slept. He hated seeing the blood on her skin, but didn't want to chance waking her yet.

He'd almost gone insane trying to find her. It helped knowing Digger had been by her side. Most of his life, he'd never depended on anyone for anything. His mom had died of cancer when he was a teenager. His brothers had their own problems, especially after their old man had given them the option of joining the military or going to prison. Jake had taken the U.S. Army route and Ethan chose prison, thinking he could get out in six months but ended up there for eighteen.

She was safe. In his bed. Where she belonged.

The cool dark room was comfortable after the maniac days…hell, weeks behind him. His gaze on the outline of Tessa's body beneath the covers blanked out for a second. He snapped open his eyes, but they gradually closed again. His body loosened and he slumped into the cushioned chair as he drifted off.

CHAPTER 31

Sen was having a great dream. Tessa was sucking hard on his dick, her mouth wet and hot. Cool hair brushed against his belly and legs. Preferring to stay asleep in the best fucking dream of his life, he subconsciously knew he needed to wake up. He had things to do.

Cracking open his eyes, he quickly squinted from the soft light on the nightstand at the far side of the bed. That side of the mattress was mussed, but no Tessa.

His gaze dropped to his lap. Tessa worked his dick like a pro. Oh fuuuck!

He threw his head back. She was good. Somehow she'd wiggled his open pants down his hips enough to fondle his balls as she swallowed him until her nose met his pubic hair.

With a grasp of her beautiful curls, he sped up her process. He was about to blow and wanted her to take it all. Just the thought of her doing something so sinfully dirty for him pushed him over the edge.

Even after days of fucking and playing as a trio, nothing compared to waking up with her mouth on him.

She hummed. Damn, that felt incredible.

Unable to hold back any longer, he pulled her away, lifted her before dropping her onto the bed. She landed knees spread. She grinned up at him. He wanted to hammer into her, but first a little payback was due.

His pants fell to the floor. Kicking them to the side, he tucked her legs over his shoulders and covered her pussy with his mouth. Licking the taut little clit, he inserted his thumb in her tighter hole. Drawing it out, he slowly thrust.

She squealed with surprise and then moaned with pleasure.

He grinned against her flesh as he sucked, licking her pussy while his thumb fucked her ass until she came on his face. The tremors felt great against his tongue.

Pleased with the result, he smirked as he looked up her body to her happy expression.

The blowjob she'd provided had been perfect, but it never satisfied like a good fuck could. Now his dick was ready for what he really wanted.

Releasing her legs, he plunged in and his hips began to pump into her, hard and fast. Her breasts jiggled. Fuck, that was sexy as hell. She was beautiful. He lowered his head and sucked in a nipple as her fingers dug into his scalp.

Going from one nipple to another, tugging and drawing hard, he released it with a pop and pushed her knees almost to her shoulders as he drilled her harder. She panted with each thrust. The woman and her enjoyment in sex was going to kill him one day.

"Sen!" she screamed.

That was the first time she'd spoken his name, and screaming it was music to his ears.

Damn. He loved her.

CHAPTER 32

What do you mean I have to go home? Tessa itched to include a few vulgar gestures as she signed, but held back. Frustrating man.

Earlier that morning, she'd showered and taken stock of all the bruises on her body. Goodness, she looked as if someone had used her as a punching bag. Every time she moved, she ached. The water had been pink going down the drain as she washed the blood off her.

Sen had blow-dried her hair and then carried her back to bed. They'd made love again before falling asleep.

He'd surprised her later with breakfast in bed and another round of good old-fashioned fucking. Oh yes, the man was good at it. Such stamina and imagination. And now he wanted to send her home.

Scooting up to rest her back against the headboard, she glared at him as he jerked on his navy blue boxer briefs. Oh yes, they cupped his ass just right. With a shake of her head, she returned to the subject. Sen had told her she needed to leave. One of her friends had tattled to her dad and reported she wasn't on vacation with friends, but with Digger and Sen.

Your father tracked down your city friends. He's causing a ruckus and refused to sew up Digger. We had to send him to a Birmingham contact. Sen crossed his arms and glowered back at her.

Had he expected her to argue? Well, yes, but she wasn't ready to leave. She wanted to help Sen track down Teddy Bear. She wasn't a quitter. Besides, she loved being around him despite the danger. Or maybe because of the danger. Her life had been boring, only school and work, work and school, with an occasional date to break up the monotony. Except the summer she had *fun* with Digger, she'd never felt so alive as she did being around Sen.

With his tall, lean body and soul-searing gaze, she needed Sen like air and water. Why couldn't he feel the same way?

Fine. Take me back home. I won't stop looking for Leslie. She slid off the bed and stood, planting her hands on her hips.

Leslie?

"Yes. Leslie Ashley Higginbotham. That's Teddy Bear's real name," she vocally said. She didn't feel like spelling out such a long name.

Sen burst out laughing.

No wonder he uses a nickname. He shook his head and wiped his eyes.

Had his family never told him his cousin's name? She couldn't believe he didn't know. Then again as dysfunctional as the family appeared to be, she shouldn't be surprised. From what she was told by her dad, Teddy Bear and Rat Boy were the sons of Dick Whitfield's younger sister. His aunt had never visited. There was a good reason his father was referred to as the meanest son of bitch in Sand County.

Quit being an ass. She slapped his shoulder and returned to the bed.

He grinned. *Now you've hurt my feelings.*

Yeah, right. Tears are about to run down your face—she paused, eyebrows raised—*from laughing too hard.*

His wicked grin had her surely returning it with her own evil smile.

You can't hold it back, you've got to tell me what Rat Boy's real name is.

"Tracy Carol," she said and then burst out in a chuckle. She hoped she didn't sound horrible.

"Oh, hell! Tracy Carol Higginbotham! Did my aunt hate men?" He'd forgotten to sign the words. Maybe like her, who wanted to bother signing such a long name?

She covered her mouth and shrugged, trying to hold in her laughter. It wasn't really funny, knowing how boys picked on each other. It must've been horrible for them growing up.

I have no idea, but who gave them their nicknames? That's what I want to know. She couldn't help pointing out.

Sen held his sides as he shook with laughter. She'd never seen him so taken by such hardy amusement.

Once he regained control, with a flick of his wrist, he tossed his jeans onto a nearby chair. He dove onto the bed, landing over her, caging her in with his muscled arms and legs.

She caught part of the words that crossed his lips. *"You make me forget. Rat Boy waiting...his brother on loose."*

His grin melted away as he continued to stare down into her face.

Then his mouth covered hers. Everything faded away. His tongue slid along hers. His kisses always took her breath away.

She threaded her fingers into his hair and pulled, wanting him closer. His bare chest against hers. He pulled away and bent down, pulled on and licked her nipple, but then he released her and flung the covers over her.

Before she could recover, the door slammed open.
Oh my God! How did he get in Sen's home?

CHAPTER 33

"**W**here is my brother, you ugly bastard?" Teddy Bear stood in the bedroom doorway with at least six other thugs standing behind him. They all pointed guns in Sen's direction.

Sen crossed his arms, maintaining an unworried stance as he blocked their view of Tessa. Where in the hell were his men?

"We're holding him for questioning," he answered, keeping his tone as dispassionate as possible in the dangerous situation.

"Questioning? Stupid motherfucker. You're not the cops." The redheaded, freckled man stepped into the room and edged a little to one side.

Sen calculated the distance between him and his cousin's gun. If he came a little nearer, he might be able to wrestle the gun away before the others shot at him.

Teddy Bear leaned to one side. His eyes widened when he spotted Tessa, obviously naked, beneath the sheet. He stepped closer, his attention no longer on Sen. "Hot damn! Her daddy's going to love this. Quinn has never been known for being a broad-minded man. Having his little girl fucking the slant—"

"Shut up, asshole." Sen interrupted Teddy Bear's racist remark as he kicked the gun out of his cousin's hand. The weapon flipped through the air and safely landed on the plush rug on the other side of the bed. Before Teddy Bear could dive for it, Sen threw a right. Blood gushed across the man's face, and he dropped to the floor, cussing and holding his nose.

Expecting a spray of bullets any second, Sen was surprised to see several of his men and others he didn't recognize had surrounded Teddy Bear's. Better late than never.

Just as he was about to ask what the holdup was, Digger walked through. For a person who looked like shit—black rings around both eyes, a purple jaw, a huge Band-Aid on his forehead, shirtless with bruises scattered across his torso, and a bloodied swatch of white gauze taped to his side—his friend made his day. Fuck, his timing could be a sight better, but he wouldn't complain.

"I would hug you, but I'm not sure of where without hurting you." Sen kicked the gun over to one of his men to secure it.

"Fuck, man. I'm so high on painkillers at this point, nothing can hurt me." Digger grinned and then his gaze shifted over to Tessa. "Hi, darling, how are you? You look a little pissed."

Hands flying, she signed something about stupid men and how she wanted to shoot them all. Damn, she looked so sexy doing that, but he had other matters to attend to. Sen looked away. One of the few drawbacks for her, he could shut her out by turning his head.

"Don't you ignore me. Look at me!"

He stopped walking and stood stock-still.

Shit, he'd forgotten for a moment that she could speak. He was tempted to cover his ears. How stupid was that? Just because he wanted to keep her out of this side of his business didn't give him the right to ignore her. With a sigh, he turned back to face her.

Why are you so mad? He held his hands out in question.

She glared at him and shook her head in disgust.

Raising his eyebrows at her, he added, *Were you cursing me or Teddy Bear?*

Her face flushed. *I'm not sure. Every man here, and maybe the situation. I hate feeling so helpless.*

The mattress dipped as he sat next to her. She leaned into him. Her warmth soaked into him. She felt good. His minty smelling soap drifted off her. Damn, he loved how she smelled like him. His. Only his from this moment on.

He wrapped his arms around her and held her tight. Later, once he cleared everyone out of his place, he'd be ready to freak out about the danger he kept placing Tessa in. For now, he wanted to feel her soft body against his, making sure she was safe once again. After a couple of moments, she relaxed and rested her head on his shoulder, and he pressed a cheek to the top of her head.

Digger cleared his throat. Sen didn't lift his head.

"I'll take Teddy Bear to see his brother," Digger said. "I'm guessing we can question them both and see what they are responsible for in all of this clusterfuck."

Sen nodded without a word. So many concerns clouded his mind, but number one was the woman in his arms. Once he was sure of her safety, he'd deal with all of the other crap.

Small hands pushed at him, trying to make him move. When he let her, she signed, *What are you going to do with him?* She pointed at Teddy Bear as Digger grasped the man's arm and helped him off the floor.

I'm not sure. We shouldn't kill them. No matter what, they are family. I'll have to think about it.

She grabbed his hand and pressed it to her cheek for a second. *But you can't let them go. They'll try to kill you and your brothers.*

Don't worry. I'll think of a solution. In the meanwhile, I have to take you back to your dad's home. Don't look at me like that. You know it's only right. Your dad is worried.

You promise not to forget me?

He clasped her upper arms and jerked her up against him, kissing her as if he wanted to inhale her, showing her how she was his. They were panting by the time he pulled away and dropped his hold.

Do you really think I would ever forget you? You belong to me.

And you're mine. She smiled.

He grinned back. Cupping her face, he made sure she could read his lips. "We have a lot to talk about, okay?"

She nodded, her eyes all shiny with unshed tears. Fuck, he hoped it was with happiness.

<<<>>>

After growing up with his old man, Sen was rarely afraid of anyone. When it came to people calling him names, as Teddy Bear had started to earlier, he was rarely bothered by it. His old man had called him names as long as the motherfucker had been alive. Such an appropriate profanity for the old man. He hadn't allowed Sen to call him "dad" or "father" though Sen had lived in the mansion all his life. His mom had been the old man's housekeeper's assistant. At a young age, he'd been ordered to call the old man Mr. Whitfield.

When he reached his teen years, he refused to call him "mister." The old man didn't deserve any respect, but he was required to respond with "yes, sir" and "no, sir" as in most southern households. So "sir" was the only word he would use within his hearing. His brothers had been allowed to call him "father." Heaven forbid, never the informal and affectionate "dad" or "daddy." He really wasn't the type. But as his brothers became older, they followed his lead and used sir and nothing else within the old man's hearing.

No. Sen wasn't afraid of anyone, but he did worry about how he'd ever win over her father. He would work at it. Whatever would make her happy, would make him happy.

Sen looked down to where Tessa stood next to him. She stared straight ahead at her father's front door, biting her bottom lip, hesitating in worry over her dad's animosity to his presence. Each second amped up her nervous anticipation of coming face-to-face with her father for the first time in around two weeks. How would she explain?

Lucius Quinn's prejudice had been ingrained from years of mourning his father's death during the U.S.–Vietnam war. He could only show Quinn he would treat his daughter with the highest esteem. The words *while I fuck her brains out* slid through his brain. Best not add that. It would defeat his attempt at cordiality.

"Won't help, asshole," he muttered to himself.

She'd told him she'd moved out of her dad's house when she was nineteen. The trust fund her mom had left her helped to pay the rent, leaving her paycheck for other necessities. They had stopped at her apartment to change into clean clothes which she insisted would boost her confidence in dealing with her dad. Whatever it took. His restraint had barely held him back from following her swaying ass into her bedroom. Instead, he had stood in the living room checking out her every feminine movement. Damn, she was all woman. Brought up as a good girl, she hadn't wasted time and soon they had headed to her father's house a few blocks away.

When she fumbled with the door key to her dad's house for the tenth time, Sen took it from her hand—did she really need all the gewgaws on the chain?—and inserted it into the lock. As soon as the door opened, a red-faced Quinn stood in front of him. Yeah. Things weren't looking good.

A fist slammed into his right eye. For a fifty-something-year-old, he had a pretty good left hook. The hit had knocked him back a couple of steps, but he proudly kept standing.

Tessa pushed her way between them.

"Stop it, Dad! You can't act that way. I'm an adult. Every lie I told you was my decision. I should've told you, but I knew you'd act this way."

"You're not even twenty-two yet," he said, hurt.

"You've always been horrible at remembering my age. In less than a month, I'll be twenty-four. That's why I rented the apartment, remember? I continue to hope you will finally see me as an adult." Though she was speaking, she signed the words too. Maybe she hoped the two communications would help him understand.

"But why that Whitfield?" Quinn waved his hand toward Sen.

She shrugged her shoulders. She kept her back to Sen and lowered her hands in close to her breasts. Why was she hiding what she was signing? Her father's eyebrows shot up as he shook his balding head.

Nodding, she moved her hands again, but this time Sen edged around to see.

Because the heart wants what the heart wants. She tilted her head and gave a lopsided grin. *Isn't that what you told your parents about Mom?*

Quinn shook his head. The old man's thick fingers signed, *You don't play fair.*

I learned from the best. Then she walked into her father's arms and hugged him tight.

Her father glared at Sen over her head. The look said, "Eat shit and die."

Then the old man's eyes blazed hatred. When Sen grinned widely, Quinn understood: you'll never be that lucky.

essa looked from one man to the other. Enough already. Sen's grin faded when he noticed her own angry glare. How could he bait her dad? Time to make peace, but her dad refused to talk to Sen and the same in return. Instead, they stood swapping glares.

Time for Sen to leave. She wanted to go with him, but she needed to calm her father down first. Besides, Sen had people waiting on him.

Stepping away from her dad, she made a shooing motion with her hands and signed, *Go ahead and take care of your business. I'll deal with my dad.*

I'll be back, Sen signed. *You and I have more to discuss. Don't leave this house. You're safer here.*

He took a step in the direction of the front door and hesitated, looking over his shoulder at her.

She waved her hands to the door again. *For goodness' sakes, go. I'll be fine.* She gave him a mock scowl this time.

He was so cute. Loose strands of hair hung over one eye. He looked as if he popped out of an anime. Yes. She was a goner for him.

After hesitating a second longer, he nodded and strode away.

When she turned her attention to her dad, he looked as if he wanted to tackle Sen and beat him to a bloody pulp. It appeared not to be the usual bigoted reason, but more of a "You messed with my little girl."

Oh, Dad.

With a tap on his shoulder, she grabbed his attention.

"You know what happened to your dad had nothing to do with Sen or his mom." In her childhood home, her father never teased her about her voice and she understood he never felt comfortable only signing. She hoped he could hear the love she had for him. She worked at keeping her voice soft. "From what you've told me, Sen's mom would've been a toddler when he died. Sen is special to me. As I told you earlier, I love him and I want you two to get along. You don't have to love him like a son, but you must understand he'd protect me with his life. And if you two got along, it would make me happy and you want me to be happy, right, Dad?"

He studied her face. Then his shoulders sagged.

His lips moved as he signed some of the words. *"Baby, you know you mean the world to me. I won't say it will be easy, but I'll try. You've always been a smart young lady."* Hands on his hips, he stared at the ceiling for moment. Then he continued, *"You know you have shitty taste in boyfriends. Don't think I didn't know about Digger."*

"You always acted as if you liked Digger," she said as she tilted her head.

"Yeah. I like the boy, but he's still a criminal. I had hoped you would find someone out of that business."

She understood her father, even though he got a couple of signs wrong. No one was perfect at ASL. She loved him for trying to do better.

"In Marystown? They are few and rarely around my age."

"Did I grasp what Whitfield signed? He's coming back for you?"

She squeezed her lips together because she didn't want to upset her dad, but she refused to lie to him anymore. "Yes. Later this evening."

"I should lock you up in your old bedroom."

He may say that, but he wouldn't. All her life he'd said that and never did. Except for the occasional craziness, he was a good dad.

She hugged him.

Tessa was bored. Bored with a capital B. Reclining on the squishy, well-worn couch in her father's den, she sleepily stared out the windows into the wet backyard. There had been blue skies when she'd arrived, but the clouds and rain had streamed in, matching her mood.

Through the cracked open door leading to her dad's study, she could see he was talking on the phone. If she were to guess, it was with his assistant at the funeral home. Since she was on *vacation* and her dad at home for the day, the man was loaded down with work. She bet there was a problem with a piece of equipment. She'd been telling her dad for months it was time to update the hardware in the embalming room. He'd replaced the coolers last year, and it had cost a fortune, but there were so many more items needing replacement.

The last thing she wanted to think about was work. She missed Sen. Sure, he said he'd return for her later today, but she wanted to be with the tall, lanky handsome man now. What if someone who didn't know the Whitfield cousins' contract was canceled decided to fulfill it?

Out of the corner of her eye, she caught sight of a red light blinking on the wall. Years ago, her dad had wired a light to a wall in nearly every room. They came on whenever someone rang the doorbell.

Outside beneath the button, a pocket-sized sign read, "Don't knock it. Ring my bell." Her dad thought it was hilarious.

She opened the door and smiled big.

"Hey, Tessa. Is Sen here with you?" Walter Finny said slowly as he leaned against the railing. Over the years, he'd visited her family home. He was always polite and jolly and from the pleasant expression on his face, he was in the same mood. The big fellow was okay, but this might be the first time he had ever spoken directly to her. How did he know she and Sen had become close? Or that he could be at her father's house? Especially considering how her father felt about Sen. Strange.

Before she motioned for him to come inside, a black truck with lifts and large mud tires pulled in.

Digger? What was he doing here?

"How's it going, Finny?" Digger's glance arrowed toward the burly man.

She didn't catch what Finny said, but from Digger's angry expression, he took offense.

A hand came down on Tessa's shoulder and she jumped. Her dad stood behind her and waved in Mr. Finny. Then he frowned at Digger.

"What are you doing here?" Her dad waited for Digger's reply instead of following Mr. Finny.

Turning to Digger, she frowned and shook her head. What was up with all these angry men?

"I promised Sen I would take Tessa out to eat this evening while he's busy. We're going to check out the new restaurant in Sand City."

They were? Why was he lying to her dad. What was he up to?

She signed to Digger, *Give me a minute.*

Ignoring the hostile men, she returned to her old room and stepped into the closet. Pulling down a shoebox from the top shelf, she lifted out the matching pink gun, just like the one taken by Savalas' goons and never returned. Grabbing a bag stuffed between some boxes, she put it inside. Last thing she needed was for her dad to ask about the gun and her need for one.

When she returned downstairs, Mr. Finny and her dad still stood in the middle of the living room, talking. She picked up her purse and stuck the bag and gun inside.

She drew her dad's attention and signed, *Going out with Digger. Have a nice night. I'll be safe with him.*

Her dad didn't respond, but his grim expression said he wasn't happy.

Geez. Men.

CHAPTER 35

One of the drawbacks of living in a small town and smaller than average-sized county was the hiring pool. The choices were minuscule at best and nonexistent at worst. If Sen brought in people from outside of the county, that opened the opportunity for a mole to be planted in his family's organization. That was one worry he didn't want added to all of the others.

He inhaled the musty air in the basement of the pawnshop. The same one he'd been shot in not long ago. It sat in the middle of a strip mall owned by the Whitfield Property organization. Sen used it whenever he needed privacy and a soundproof room. His brother, Jake, used the basement in the old house and the youngest, Ethan…well, Sen had no idea what he used. Probably one of his nightclubs had a basement or back room that served the same purpose.

He returned his attention to the three men with slumped shoulders and chins on chests as they shuffled their feet, afraid to look his way. They waited for his pronouncement on their fate.

"You're alive only because I'm short-handed. So count

yourself lucky. Next time you assholes let someone come into my home uninvited, I'll put an extra hole in your head. Get it?"

Relief was palpable in the dim room. The men nodded and mumbled, "Yes, sir."

"You." Sen pointed at the broadest of the bunch.

"Yes, sir?" The man looked as if he was about to pee in his pants.

"Come with me." Sen headed to the doorway leading to the other side of the basement.

The shorter of the two men being left behind piped up, "What about us, Mr. Whitfield?"

Sen said over his shoulder, "Make sure no one comes through this door."

He had four more men stationed upstairs, in and outside the pawn shop, but two more wouldn't hurt. He doubted they would fail him again, they knew the fatal consequences.

Once he closed the metal door, he pointed to the ground just inside.

"Stand right there. If it isn't my brothers trying to come in, shoot to kill. Understood?"

The big guy stared at him with wide eyes and nodded.

Sen turned his attention to the two men gagged and hanging from the ceiling by chains. No shirts or shoes, their pants hung from their hips, their skin coated in sweat and blood.

Beating men until they talked was part of the job he hated. It was a good thing the majority of the men he brought in there were quick to confess, especially when he wrapped their wrists with chains and started pulling them up to the beam running across the ceiling. But it appeared his cousins possessed steel spines. They cussed him the whole time, therefore the gags.

He walked around them, jerking off the tie holding the cloths in their mouths.

"You're going to regret doing this to us. You've gone too far. Cousin Dick never treated us this way," Teddy Bear complained.

With hair sleek with sweat and freckles disappearing into a bright red face, he looked like a petulant child despite being ten years older.

"Considering Dick Whitfield is dead, you shouldn't have come shooting at me and my brothers. There's no one to protect you, including your brother as he's in the same sinking boat." Sen nodded toward Rat Boy hanging beside him.

"Wait until I get my hands on you." Rat Boy grunted and began to cough when Sen slammed a fist into his stomach.

"I guess I'll wait for an eternity. You either tell me who really put the contract out or you can keep hanging there while I do some bag work. I can always use the exercise." Sen opened and closed his fist. Damn, he hadn't expected Rat Boy's abs to be so firm. The man apparently worked out.

Teddy Bear spit.

Moving quickly, Sen narrowly avoided the wad.

Sen swung. Blood and a tooth shot out of Teddy Bear's mouth.

Fuck. At this rate, his knuckles would be a mess. Then he would have to explain it to Tessa. Turning his back on the two men, he strode over to a long shelf on the cinderblock wall. An array of instruments used for torture were laid out. He picked up brass knuckles and slipped them on.

For the next two hours, he worked on the men. They were stubborn assholes.

Oddly, one finally broke. He'd expected it to be Rat Boy, but Teddy Bear started crying profusely.

"Stop, stop, please, God, stop." Most of the words were

slurred as he was missing more teeth and possibly had a broken jaw.

Taking one step to the side, Sen tossed the crowbar he'd used for the last fifteen minutes onto the shelf, picked up his Sig P365 and pointed it at Teddy Bear.

"Give me a name or I'll start shooting each limb," Sen warned.

"You motherfucker. Don't tell him," Rat Boy shouted at his brother.

"I don't give a damn. It-it-it was your brother. Fucking Ethan," Teddy Bear whined.

Without a second thought, he shot Teddy Bear in the thigh. What a stupid, fucking liar.

Teddy Bear screamed and began crying. Again.

"You're full of shit. I want the real asshole who put out the contract and I want the name now. I've fooled with you two jerk-offs long enough."

He seldom let go of his temper, but he couldn't control it any longer. They'd endangered Tessa too many times over the past couple of weeks. Now they accused Ethan, his own fucking brother, of wanting to kill him and Jake. Total bullshit.

The cousins continued to curse, stalling on giving the name he needed.

With a sigh, he shot Rat Boy in his thigh, matching his brother.

"What the fuck? Man, it was Teddy! He did it. He made the deal."

"You fucking liar!" Teddy Bear struggled with the chains. He began to swing and kicked out at Rat Boy. "Walter Finny went to Rat Boy and offered him a hundred thousand each to put you and your brothers into the ground."

What the fuck? Walter Finny? He never imagined the big guy had the guts to make a move on the Whitfield territory, no less put a contract out against him and his brothers. The few people who cared whether he lived or died when he was a kid.

His forehead wrinkled. Could Walter have been involved in the death of the old men too? The motherfucker!

"You traitor! You—" Rat Boy's tirade stopped as a small hole appeared between the cousin's eyes. Brains and skull fragments sprayed on the wall behind him.

Sen lowered his gun.

Teddy Bear's high-pitched scream had Sen rethinking his decision to spare the man. The hatred shining in the crazy man's eyes warned him that he'd come back and kill Sen and anyone he loved another time.

Tessa. No one would ever hurt her as long as he lived.

The echo of the gunshot ended his worry about her. Teddy Bear dangled from the chains beside his brother with a matching hole in the forehead.

Damn. He shut his eyes for a few seconds, breathing deeply. Despite the sharp copper and pungent nitroglycerin odors, it helped to regain control of his stomach.

Sen looked over to the husky guard at the door. The man straightened after throwing up in the corner.

"You got a truck?" Sen asked. Using the end of his T-shirt, he wiped away the perspiration and whatever else from his face.

"Yes, sir," the guard answered, his face pale as his body shook.

"Go and get your buddies upstairs. You can use the black plastic over in the corner to wrap up the bodies. You know where to take them?"

"Yes, sir. The swamp." The man's voice wobbled.

"When you return, wash down the floor with bleach. Be sure to wear the gas masks." Sen pointed to them above the shelf.

The man looked as if he was about to throw up again, but he held it in and nodded.

"Be sure it's all done before sunrise."

Sen walked out. He needed fresh air and a shower before he went to Tessa. He'd better warn her about Finny.

The bastard was dangerous. His former boss, Mac Tally, had used his own granddaughter to handle most of the deadbeats he came across. But Finny managed the worst of the worst. The man acted gregarious, but he was a snake in the grass. One that would bite an unsuspecting person without a thought or care.

Yeah, Sen needed Tessa to stay away from the man until he could be handled.

CHAPTER 36

essa stared out the passenger window at the trees blurring past the truck. Why was Digger in such a hurry? She'd never gone to Sand City this way. They'd been driving for about thirty minutes when Digger turned onto a dirt road and she realized where they were going. The barn where the illegal fights were held.

The big barn looked different in the midday light and without all of the cars and trucks parked in the dirt. During the ride, she'd kept telling herself everything was okay and Digger would never hurt her. But one thing she'd learned during the short time she'd spent with Sen, nothing was as it appeared.

Once they parked and Digger helped her out of the hundred-foot-tall monster truck—geez!—she started asking questions.

"Why did you bring me here?"

Palms flat, he motioned to lower her voice.

Crap! How embarrassing. She'd rather sign, but from the times he responded in kind, he obviously hadn't been practicing in the years she hadn't seen him.

He raised a finger for her to wait a minute, then clasped her hand, leading her to the so-called skybox she and Sen had enjoyed last time they were there. No food this time, of course, and the door to the office was open. They walked straight through the office to a door in the back she had missed before.

On the other side, was a little efficient apartment. Living-room-kitchen-bedroom combination in one area with another opened door leading into a massive bathroom. Nicely decorated in beige, brown, and spots of navy blue. Perfect for a single man.

She slapped his arm and then signed, *Answer me. Why are we here?*

To keep you safe, he signed in answer as his lips moved.

From what? she signed. She pushed his hands down. "Sen said the contract was for him and his brothers, not me." He irritated her with the secretive attitude.

When Digger started to sign again, she tilted her head in frustration. He sheepishly lowered his hands and said, *"Whenever you're around Sen, you're endangered."*

"I'm not helpless." She grimaced. "You don't have to say it. I know Sen would let himself be harmed before someone could hurt me."

"I feel the same." Digger made sure she read his lips before pulling her into his arms.

She squeezed him for a second and then pushed him away.

"Why here?" she asked.

"No one will think to look for you here. Take a nap. Watch TV. Whatever you want. I have the makings for spaghetti. You'll love my sauce." His lips lifted at the end.

The look he gave her said he wanted more, but she knew Digger well. He wouldn't try anything she didn't want. Their time together had been great fun, but she felt Sen wanted a monogamous relationship. The threesome had been on her bucket list and was wonderful. But it would be difficult to maintain, considering how she felt about Sen compared to Digger. She was okay with that, but how to explain that to Digger without hurting his feelings?

I love spaghetti. Meat? Chicken? she signed slowly so he could catch the words.

"Only for you will I make it with chicken," Digger said and then grinned. His blue eyes twinkled between the strands of blond hair. Even being slightly younger than Sen, he appeared to be a kid. Was it because his life had been easier than Sen's?

He was such a sweetheart, but she didn't love him like she did Sen. She didn't quite understand the difference, but just knew Townsend Whitfield was the one.

The next few hours flew by. While eating their meal and watching a football game with closed captions on the extra-wide-screen TV, she messaged her dad and then Sen. No answer from either one. Strange. She usually heard from her dad, not sure if Sen bothered with responding to texts. The sun had gone down completely hours ago. It was nearing midnight. The crazy days with Sen and Digger hit her all at once and her eyes became too heavy.

Suddenly she woke with a start to find her head resting on Digger's shoulder.

Digger had his phone pressed to his ear. His lips were moving but she only caught every other word.

She sat up and he glanced her way and kept talking.

"Where did he say he was going?" He listened and then said, *"I know where that's at. No. I'm not talking about the house, but the lake, dumbass."* Rolling his eyes, he grimaced. Then he said a few more words she missed. She wiggled on the couch to improve her view of his lips. *"Text me the address and tell the*

boys to meet me there." If it was possible, fire would be shooting out of his eyes, considering how angry he looked. *"Fuck, no. We can't wait until morning. The man might be dead by then."*

That last part she hoped she'd misunderstood. She scooted away and sat up on the couch.

"Sen?" She tugged at his sleeve.

Digger nodded and then put his phone away, turning for her to easily see his lips.

"For some ungodly reason, Walter Finny and some of his men jumped Sen. Someone overheard Finny say they were taking him to Smith Lake to dump his body after they had some fun with him." Digger shook his head. He picked up his boots from where he'd kicked them off earlier and slipped them on.

The lake he was talking about was known for bodies becoming tangled in flooded trees. Trees that were never cut down over sixty years ago when the dam had been built. Drowning victims were known to not ever surface again. So if a person tied big blocks onto a body and dumped it in the middle, it would never be seen again.

Digger walked over to a tall cabinet, unlocked it, and opened the front. It held half a dozen rifles while the same number of handguns lined the door.

He lifted a rifle and turned to her. *"Want a rifle or handgun?"*

She shook her head. Leaning over, she picked up her purse from where she'd left it earlier and pulled out her pink gun. Eyebrows raised, she waved it at him with the muzzle pointed up before jabbing it back into her purse.

"Cute, real cute." He nodded and grinned big. *"So you want to go with me to save Sen?"*

That was one of the things she loved about him. He knew she could handle firearms and never would leave her behind.

Once they took care of the problem, she would have a long talk with Sen.

She nodded and followed him out the door.

CHAPTER 37

*Y*eah, he was fucking up big time.

Digger flicked his gaze over at Tessa.

Sen was going to kill him for allowing her to tag along on the rescue mission.

Finny had a hard-on for the Whitfield territory from day one after Mac Tally had died. He'd acted all tame, going along with Angel Tally's authority when she had taken over her deceased grandfather's territory. But deep inside his guts Digger had known the old asshole would eventually find a way to worm his way into taking everything over. With the death of the two old men, a leash had dropped from Finny's neck.

The Whitfield boys had dropped the ball by not watching their backs.

Tessa's fidgeting in the passenger seat brought his attention back to her. She smoothed her T-shirt and crossed her hands over the purse on her lap. The ugly brown bag held the girlish pink gun. Despite the stupid color, he remembered what a crack shot she was even as a teenager. Her daddy had made sure she could protect herself in almost every situation. Hell, she'd killed a man to protect him just the day before. He owed her his life. She was a woman any man would be proud of.

"Keep your eyes on the road." She narrowed her eyes and asked, "What are you staring at?"

He shook his head. No way could he tell her what he was thinking. He stared at the road ahead. Despite what she thought, he loved her voice. Unique and all her. He had always felt proud he was only one of two people she would talk to. Until Sen.

Yeah. He'd seen it. Those two were in love with each other. Sen and Tessa. Tessa and Sen. He wanted to be part of that. He loved them both, but Sen was too straight. It was time for him to move on and let Sen and Tessa be together without him. Why was he rehashing something he realized a couple of days ago? He had no place in their life, only as a friend.

A buddy of his had been asking him to come up to Tennessee to visit for a while. Maybe he would.

First things first. He needed to save Sen and keep Tessa safe.

CHAPTER 38

"Tie him down tight to the chair."

Walter Finny stood in front of Sen, arms folded over his barrel chest and legs braced apart as if he were a captain on a pirate ship. Instead, they were in Tessa's house on Smith Lake.

Sen's gaze moved to Quinn. Sure, the man hated him, but he had no idea it was so much as to help Finny.

"So why have you fine gentlemen brought me here?" Sen kept his tone even and nonchalant, despite being tied to a chair. His cheek throbbed from another hit on the bruise left by Quinn earlier that day. He barely could see out of that eye. The swelling would probably get worse before sunset.

"Where are your brothers?" Finny began to pace back and forth.

"I'm not my brothers' keeper." Sen didn't bother to keep the sarcasm out of his voice.

Finny's ham-sized fist slammed into Sen's face once again. What was up with these left-handed men?

Yep, his eye would be closed soon. Blood trickled from his nose. Dammit, now he couldn't breathe out of his nose.

"Keep it up, asshole. I'll find your brothers eventually and they'll be buried with you deep in the waters of Smith Lake." Finny's beady eyes brightened in pure malice.

"Quinn, I never took you to be a greedy bastard. I thought you and Jake respected each other."

The older man's head lifted as he stared at Sen. His lost look helped to ease the worry in the back of Sen's mind. Maybe he was regretting this.

"I never would've involved myself in this shit if you hadn't come sniffing around my daughter. I'd told your old man to keep you boys away, but after he died, you decided she was free for the taking. So there must be sacrifices."

Bingo. In spite of his words, Quinn's look changed to full on regretful. He was worried how his daughter would take his *sacrifice*.

"You do know you won't take all three of us out, Finny? What do you hope to gain from this? If it is territory, there are other people who want it who are stronger and more connected than you. The Brothers of Mayhem for one. It's only been my agreement with them that held them back from taking over." Sen had never told a soul of the arms agreement he had with the motorcycle gang.

Finny's pissed look said his announcement had done its job. He wanted the man to be nervous and mad. Those emotions often caused people to make mistakes. Everyone knew that, besides the Whitfield boys, the other danger in the area was the Brothers.

"I can handle them. Don't you worry. Oh, wait. You'll be dead." Finny laughed, but it wasn't an easy laugh. "Tell me—"

Just then a racket at the front door interrupted his demand.

Two of Finny's men walked in, one holding a gun on Digger and the other pointed at one of Sen's men, the guy who was assigned to dispose of his cousins' bodies. Where was the man's buddy? Had Finny's men already killed him? Fuck. Hopefully, they had done what was needed before being captured.

Digger glanced his way and dipped his head. With his friend's confident entry into the cabin, Sen suspected he had a plan to get them out of this bad spot.

"Ambrose, I should've known you would be nearby." Finny turned back to Sen. "I didn't know you played both sides. Don't be mad. Everyone knows Ambrose here fucks everyone. Man, woman, probably animals too. Considering how wild he was as a kid and how crazy his old man was, no one is surprised by his deviant lifestyle."

Sen wanted to shut-the-fuck-up the man's mouth. Finny obviously loved the sound of it.

Ambrose? All these years, he never knew. Hell, he needed to talk to people more. Second time he'd been surprised by a person's true name.

Before Finny could say anything more, Sen asked, "You never did say why you decided to take over? From what I've heard, you've never been the 'idea guy,' and certainly not the 'detail person.' No more than the head thug for Mac."

"Yeah, I would love to know too," Digger added. "By the way, it's Mr. Ambrose Jasper Turner to you." One of Finny's men took a menacing step toward Digger. His friend merely smiled bigger. "Hey, I just wanted to make it clear who was speaking and I'm curious as to who came up with the plan."

"I didn't need her help in coming up with the idea," Finny said, anger seeping into every word.

"Her?" Sen couldn't imagine Angel would have a hand in the chaos. Certainly not part of the plan to kill her grandfather.

"Let's say, it's always good to have the government in the palm of your hand." Finny's smirk got Sen to thinking.

There was only one government female who had been

hanging around in the past couple of weeks. Special Agent Alex Carleton. It wouldn't be the first time someone with authority took another person's life for the greater good.

"What did Carleton promise you?" Sen needed the details before Digger put in play whatever he planned.

CHAPTER 39

essa reread the text from her father. *Hurry. I have news about Sen. Meet me at your lake house.*

She'd known something was off. Her dad never called him Sen. In front of her, the nicest way he referred to him was "that middle Whitfield boy." She didn't like thinking of the imprecations he normally used.

At the time, she'd been sitting in Digger's truck while he talked with a couple of Sen's men in a large parking lot next to a marina. Smith Lake was stretched out in front of her and Big Bridge down the road. Before she decided to get out of the truck and find out what they were talking about, he'd returned and jumped in.

"Who's dead?" She'd only caught a few words from their rapid-fire lip movements but knew something was wrong and wanted answers despite his you-know-better-than-to-ask look. "I'm guessing Sen had something to do with it."

He cranked the truck and turned his head toward her before backing out of the parking spot. *"Woman, you know I won't talk with you about stuff like that."*

"Fine. But Dad will. He sent me a text saying he has news about Sen." She put her phone in front of his face.

He slammed on the brakes. *"Don't put it so close to my face."* Covering her hand, he pulled it away and read the text and said, *"Quinn never calls him Sen."*

"I know, right? Something is weird. And why is Dad at my lake house?"

With the smell of tar assaulting her nose, she knew Digger had spun his tires as he turned toward her address. During the twists and turns on the narrow country roads, he called someone on the phone, probably the men he'd just left. When he hung up, she caught sight of a black SUV in the side mirror coming up fast. The two men Digger had spoken to were following them. Fifteen minutes later, they reached the top of a hill near the house and he slowed to a crawl.

There were several cars in the driveway. One of them was Sen's motorcycle with the brand "Indian" painted on the tank.

She stiffened. What was going on?

Digger clutched her arm as she reached for the latch. Eyes wide, she looked at him with concern.

He shook his head. *"Stay here."*

"You're crazy if you think I'll stay behind." The Caddie parked next to Sen's was her dad's. He wouldn't let anything happen to her. Same for Sen.

"Please stay here for me. Keep your gun handy. The doors locked. Please don't make me worry about you too."

The pleading showed in his eyes along with the words she read on his lips.

She nodded and sat back.

He pulled the truck to the side and stepped out as the following two men pulled to the side too. They'd split up and walked toward the house, one walking toward the far side while Digger and the other man went directly to the front door. They'd knocked, someone opened the door, and they entered, and nothing.

She grabbed her gun from her purse, sitting it beside her on the console as she checked her phone. She would give him thirty minutes and then she planned to go in.

Time ticked by as she continued to look at the weird text from her dad, still wondering what the hell was going on.

Tick, tock, tick, tock.

He had another twenty-five minutes. For the tenth time, she checked her phone. What? Had she expected Sen or Digger would text or call her immediately?

Tick, tock, tick, tock.

Maybe she could walk around the back and see what was happening. She hated not knowing. The steepness on one side of her property prevented people from noticing a small path to the back deck. It was used mainly for maintenance and a door that led to the basement hidden behind the flowering vegetation. Most people mistook the basement door in the kitchen as a pantry door.

She fingered the keys from her purse's side pocket. Time to see what was going on.

She looked at her phone one more time. Twenty-four more minutes.

Tick, tock, tick, tock.

Screw it.

Carefully, she slipped out of the truck, holding the gun down on one side, and eased the door closed. Darting across and down the road to her house, she found the path. A burly man stepped outside and stood on the side porch, watching a boatload of bikini-clad women float by. Without slowing down to see if he would turn toward her, she shot down the little trail, and in seconds was at the basement's entrance. Between the planks above her head, she spotted someone pacing from one end of the deck to the other. The pacing continued. Luck was on her side. No one appeared to notice her yet.

After slowly turning the key, she eased the door open. Hopefully, it hadn't squeaked. She closed it and reached out to flip on a light switch. If there was someone in the basement, they would have caught her by now.

Next, she gambled the steps wouldn't creak. All scary stories mentioned wooden steps giving someone or something away.

Reaching the landing, she took a deep breath. Her heart was beating a mile a minute. She turned off the light switch near the kitchen and then slowly turned the door knob with one hand. Her gun remained pointed to the floor in her other hand. Like she thought, no one had thought to lock it.

The open design of the kitchen-dining-living-room combination allowed her to see straight into the large area where several men stood. Sen, seated in one of her sturdy dining room chairs with his arms and legs tied down, had bruises on his face and blood streaming from his nose. Digger and only one of the men had their hands up, standing off to the side, backs against a wall. Where was the other guy?

The door knob was jerked out of her hands and she stumbled into the kitchen. Walter Finny grabbed her wrist. His body jerked.

Oh God, she had pulled the trigger in reflex. The gun shot wound in the middle of his chest had been small but quickly blossomed.

She was going to be sick. No. She couldn't. She wasn't safe. Remember, she'd sliced a man's throat open and was able to function afterwards. Stay in control. A gunshot wound should be easy-peasy. Anyway, Sen and Digger were still in danger. She swallowed, hoping everything stayed down. The guys depended on her. Though they didn't know it.

It was so weird. No one moved for several seconds.

Then Walter tottered back. The surprised look on his face was almost comical. At once, everyone began to move. It was surreal. The uncomfortable popping pressures on her ears told her the story before her eyes relayed the information to her brain. The action in front of her was like seeing a scene from an old gangster film. People pulling guns and firing. Sen somehow pushed out with his feet and knocked the chair over. Digger was firing at a man she'd never seen before, probably belonging to Walter. Then she caught sight of her dad grabbing a skillet and slamming it against a man's head. Another man she didn't know.

What about the two men outside? Would the fighting swing to Walter's side, no matter if he was alive or not?

In that instant, a man busted through the front door and promptly fell to the ground with a knife sticking out of his back.

Without realizing it, she had ducked as glass shattered from the French doors at the back deck. Walter's man in the back had tumbled through the glass. Had he been pushed or shot?

She glanced around and saw Digger with his gun pointed in that direction.

The room had a smoky look from all of the shooting. She covered her nose, not liking the acrid smell.

In seconds, Digger had Sen out of his bindings. As Sen stood, he slapped Digger on the back before hurrying to Tessa.

His hands moved, *Are you all right? Are you hurt?*

Before she could answer, he had wrapped his arms around her, squeezing her tight.

"Other than I can't breathe, I'm okay," she squeaked out.

He released her and then grabbed her shoulders, leaning back and looking her over. Then he fisted a hand and rotated it over his chest. *Sorry.* He clasped her shoulders again and shoved her to a kitchen chair to sit. He took her gun and placed it next to her on the table. Slowly stepping back, step by step, he ordered, *Stay here. Don't move. I'll be back in a few minutes.*

She wanted to argue, but truthfully, she was in a state of shock. No, not quite. But her body was telling her how close she'd come to dying. Tremors ran up and down her body. Her hands shook uncontrollably.

Yeah. She would stay put and let Sen handle the rest of this debacle.

CHAPTER 40

Sen hoped she'd stay put at the kitchen table. Time to check on his men and Digger.

The last few hours had been hell. During the chaos after Tessa shot Finny, he'd yelled to his people not to kill Quinn. He didn't give a fuck if the man was hurt, but Tessa would never forgive him if her dad lost his life in the fight. But as the skirmish had continued, he noticed Quinn helping to protect Tessa. His daughter meant more to him than any deal he'd made with Finny. The son of a bitch had that going for him.

Sen understood Tessa hadn't meant to shoot Finny. The appalled look on her face had given it away.

On cleaning up Tessa's lake house, he had given orders to dump the bodies in the swamp on the Whitfield property. Smith Lake had enough bodies dumped in it recently. Besides, Walter Finny would be missed and the last thing he needed was the authorities to search the waters and find him somehow.

"Tessa, you still good? I wish I had killed the motherfucker for you." He cupped her face as he leaned over her. "Are you okay?"

Damn, he had to fight back the tears. He hadn't cried since his old man had beat him with a belt when he was ten. But Tessa meant so much to him. If something had happened to…

He had to quit thinking about that.

She merely stared into his eyes. Was she going into shock?

Her beautiful pupils weren't dilated. He clasped her hands. They were warm. He released his hold when her eyes appeared to focus as she watched him. A strong need to tell her what he should've done days earlier came over him.

After pointing to himself, he closed his fists and crossed his arms against his chest and then pointed at her.

I love you, he signed. Her forehead wrinkled as if she didn't understand. Had he done it right? He continued to sign, *I love you, I love you, I love you.*

She hopped out of her seat and jumped into his arms and hugged him tight. His big hands covered her butt cheeks and lifted her until her legs came around his waist. Then she shouted, "I love you too."

He jerked his head back, his ears ringing from her words. He laughed. Crushing her to him, he wanted the house emptied so he could show her how much he loved her.

"Digger, can you handle the clean up here?"

His friend lifted his head from what one of the men was telling him.

"Yeah, Quinn said he has a bag in his car for this type of occasion and will patch everyone up." He scratched the scruff on his jaw. "Should I guess what you two love birds are going to do?"

"If you need me, call. I'll be at my place." Sen grinned. "We have a future to plan."

The older man stood up and said, "I know it doesn't matter to you, but you have my blessing. I see how much she means to you. That is all a father can ask, that a man love his daughter with all his heart as you do." Quinn looked as if the last few days had been years. There were dark half moons below his eyes, and etched-in creases near his mouth. "I know she loves you." Quinn turned to his daughter and signed, *He's a good man, sweetheart. If he's what you want, let me know. Otherwise, come home and we'll talk.*

Her grin spread across her face. She managed to sign while Sen held her, *He's all I wanted.*

Impatient for privacy, Sen carried her out the front door.

After a couple of days in bed showing Tessa how much she meant to him, Sen finally convinced her to marry him. She insisted on Christmastime. He would've done it the next day, but she wanted a wedding.

He stared up at the ceiling with Tessa in his arms. How could he be so lucky?

Yesterday, he'd called Jake. They agreed not to talk about everything over the airwaves until they met up with Ethan in a few days. They needed to make sure all of the loose ends were tied up. Sen couldn't wait to hear what they had to say. He would know if Finny had been telling the truth, but there still seemed to be something missing. A true connection to all of the death and mayhem.

Sen flinched. He looked down at the woman in his arms. Tessa grinned at him as if she hadn't pinched him and said, "What do you think about getting a butterfly tattoo? I know a wonderful tattoo artist who could do it for you."

He grimaced and shook his head. But deep inside he

knew he probably would be sporting his first tattoo before long. Anything Tessa wanted, he'd get for her.

CHAPTER 41

*L*ater that week, he and Tessa were in the repaired black Camaro heading to the monstrous house he'd grown up in. Sitting on the porch was Jake with Angel on his lap.

"They look happy," Tessa said out loud.

Sen nodded. It was good to see Jake smiling.

The roar of a motorcycle had passed them on the drive. Ethan laughing his ass off with the woman on the back holding on for dear life. By the time he parked near where the garage once stood—only charred wood and brick remained—Ethan and the woman were waiting. Sen recognized her then.

That's the new manager of Scene 69, Sen signed to Tessa. *Her name is Karma.*

What a cool name. Tessa clasped Sen's hand as he helped her out of the car.

Come on. Time to introduce you properly to my family. They will be your family too.

I always wanted brothers, she signed. *Looks like I will have sisters too.*

He looked at Jake and Ethan. It was unusual to see them beaming. During the last few weeks, they'd been mostly out of touch, but it appeared they all had found happiness while trying to survive. They deserved it as much as he did.

He knew so far who had killed the old men and set up the contract to murder them all. Now to find out the final details and who was the mastermind of it all.

He placed his arm around Tessa's shoulders. She was safe. He knew he was smiling like a fool, but he didn't give a damn. He loved the woman beside him and thank goodness she loved him.

ABOUT THE AUTHOR

CARLA SWAFFORD loves romance novels, action/adventure movies, and men, and her books reflect that. And on top of all that, she's crazy about hockey.

So, it's no surprise she writes spicy romantic suspense filled with mercenaries, motorcycle one-percenters, and southern criminals. And in the last few years, she's included sexy hockey players in books without suspense, except for the kind that asks, how will they ever find their happily ever after?

Married to her high school sweetheart, she lives in the Southeast U.S.

To find out more about Carla, be sure to follow her on Instagram and TikTok, and subscribe to her newsletter on her website. www.carlaswafford.com.

ALSO BY CARLA SWAFFORD

Trilogy: Brothers of Mayhem

Hidden Heat

Full Heat

Above currently published by Loveswept,

an imprint of Penguin/Random House in ebook only

Naked Heat

Series: The Circle Mercenaries

Circle of Desire

Circle of Danger

Circle of Deception

Above previously published by Avon,

an imprint of HarperCollins.

Circle of Dishonor (novella)

Circle of Defiance (novella

Kidnapped For A Day (short story)

Above novellas and short story available

together in one paperback

Series: An Atlanta Edge Hockey Romance

Crossing The Line

Fake Play

(more to come)

Trilogy: Southern Crime Family

Jake

Sen

Ethan (coming soon!)

Duo: Small-Town Romance

Loving The Small-Town Preacher's Son

Loving The Small-Town Hero